GIRL

AT THE

EDGE

GIRL

AT THE

EDGE

KAREN DIETRICH

GRAND CENTRAL
PUBLISHING

NEW YORK   BOSTON

Copyright © 2020 by Karen Dietrich
Reading group guide copyright © 2020 by Karen Dietrich and Hachette Book Group, Inc.

Cover design by Elizabeth Connor. Cover photo © Magdalena Russocka/Trevillon Images. Cover copyright © 2020 by Hachette Book Group, Inc.

Grand Central Publishing
Hachette Book Group
1290 Avenue of the Americas, New York, NY 10104
grandcentralpublishing.com
twitter.com/grandcentralpub

First Edition: March 2020

Grand Central Publishing is a division of Hachette Book Group, Inc. The Grand Central Publishing name and logo is a trademark of Hachette Book Group, Inc.

The publisher is not responsible for websites (or their content) that are not owned by the publisher.

The Hachette Speakers Bureau provides a wide range of authors for speaking events. To find out more, go to www.hachettespeakersbureau.com or call (866) 376-6591.

Library of Congress Cataloging-in-Publication Data

Names: Dietrich, Karen, author.
Title: Girl at the edge / Karen Dietrich.
Description: First edition. | New York : Grand Central Publishing, 2020. |
Identifiers: LCCN 2019041839 | ISBN 9781538732939 (trade paperback) |
ISBN 9781538732946 (ebook)
Subjects: GSAFD: Suspense fiction.
Classification: LCC PS3604.I3725 G57 2020 | DDC 813/.6–dc23
LC record available at https://lccn.loc.gov/2019041839

ISBNs: 978-1-5387-3293-9 (Trade paperback); 978-1-5387-3294-6 (ebook)

Printed in the United States of America

LSC-C

10 9 8 7 6 5 4 3 2 1

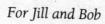

For Jill and Bob

My father went to sea, sea, sea
To see what he could see, see, see
But all that he could see, see, see
Was the bottom of the deep blue sea, sea, sea

—Nursery rhyme

GIRL

AT THE

EDGE

chapter one

My father is a murderer. When I say it out loud, it sounds like a set of dishes thrown on the kitchen floor—all that porcelain clattering, all those shards and slivers arranging themselves against the cool tile, an exploded mosaic. If you look long enough and hard enough, you can put them back together in your mind's eye. If you look long enough and hard enough, you can see where all the pieces fit.

Six months before I was born, my father walked into Ponce de Leon Mall in St. Augustine, Florida. When he walked out, eleven people were dead.

My father is a murderer.

When I say it out loud, something inside me gets bigger. I let it move around my insides until my entire body is swollen with it, my arms and legs inflated with the words. *My father is a murderer.* I feel my rib cage expand, as if I'm breathing in as deeply as I can, only it's not air that I'm full of—it's something else. Sometimes it feels cold, and I imagine mercury pooling inside me, liquid that makes me heavy and dense. Other times it feels hot like a grease fire, flames running through me until I'm bright as the Burning Man.

I don't know my father, so I don't know if murder fits him, the way a certain type of clothing fits a certain type of body. I do know that my father was married to someone else when he met my mother. When my mother became pregnant with me, his wife found out about us—my mother and unborn me—and she left him, and so he moved in with us.

When I was a kid, my imaginary friend was actually a father I'd invented. His name was Calvin, and I'd named him after a scented slip of paper I smelled at the perfume counter at Dillard's. I decided that Calvin sounds like the name of a father who isn't on death row at Raiford, the Florida State Prison, which is where my father is.

Old Sparky used to be kept there, but they don't use the electric chair anymore. It's all medical now, a shot in the arm, a syringe of sodium chloride that stops the heart. Inmates can still choose electrocution if they so desire, but no one has done that since Tiny Davis was put to death in the electric chair in 1999, blood appearing all over his white T-shirt, streaming from his death mask as he shook violently, his arms and legs trembling against the leather restraints as he moaned.

On death row in Florida, it's mostly men, and they're mostly murderers. I think of my father on a ship with many oars, and the men are lined up, shoulder to shoulder. My father is rowing, the muscles in his arms tensing and pulling with each stroke. My father is rowing toward death. He began rowing the morning he kidnapped his wife from the jewelry store in the mall where she was working, forced her into his car, and started driving south. At some point during the drive, he shot her in the head. Before he drove off with his wife, he killed eleven other people in the mall, but that, as my mother says, *is another story for another day.*

Where was my father going when he got into that car and began driving? Everyone knows you can't escape Florida by heading south. You'll drive through deep swamp, through the Keys, until eventually you'll hit water with nowhere else to go. When you reach the southern end of Key West, there's a large concrete buoy painted red and black and yellow. The buoy says *90 Miles to CUBA,* and it's considered the southernmost point in the continental U.S.A. Tourists have their pictures taken with it, handing cameras over to strangers so they can pose with the cement slab. But my father didn't make it that far, to the crystal-blue waters of the Florida Keys, those little islands dotting the ocean just beyond the tip of Florida on the map we studied in elementary school. The police apprehended him near Crescent Beach, a place named for a sliver of moon. They tracked him by helicopter and barricaded all the roads until he had no choice but to stop.

They had been talking to my father on his cell phone, trying to convince him to spare his wife's life, promising him that everything would be okay if he would just stop the car and let her go. Everyone makes mistakes, they told him. We can help you, the police told him. But my father didn't believe that. He knew they wouldn't help, couldn't help. He knew that no one could help him but himself—he just had to finish what he'd started. He couldn't ever turn back, would never turn back.

By my sixth birthday, my mother and I had moved west, to the other side of the state, to Pass-a-Grille, a small beach town on the southern end of St. Pete Beach, three and a half hours and two hundred miles from the yellow stucco apartment in St. Augustine, which is the oldest city in the United States and my first home on earth.

What I remember most about the yellow stucco apartment is the front door, which was painted dark green. My mother liked to take photos of me in front of the door, and my favorite is a picture that lives inside a photo album that lives inside my mother's closet—a candid shot of my mother holding baby-me in one hand as she unlocks the dark green door to the apartment with the other. Written on the back of the photograph are the words *Evelyn comes home* in my mother's small handwriting. In the photo, I could be anyone's daughter. You can't tell what my father did just by looking at me. I'm just a tiny figure swaddled in a hospital receiving blanket, white with the patented pink and blue stripes, just like all the other babies born in the year 2000, a leap year, and the start of a new millennium, the hysteria of the Y2K bug safely behind us.

What my father did is public knowledge so I'm sure that many people know more about it than I do. My father is famous in his own way, his name a part of the permanent record of the world. Anyone with an Internet connection can sift through the police reports describing the gun he used, the ammunition, the clothing he wore, all the way down to his socks and shoes. Anyone online can watch videos of survivors sharing their accounts of the deadly events of that day. Anyone online can read the names of the victims or listen to recordings of the multiple 911 calls made from inside the mall that afternoon. In the vast electronic archive, that invisible wireless cloud, lives a maze of articles and timelines, my father's name scattered to the digital wind like seed—in court transcripts, beneath mug shots, recorded on prison medical logs.

I'm sure there are people who maintain websites about my father, people who edit his Wikipedia page, people who write to him in prison, searching for his side of the story, desperate for his words. They catalog the evidence, replay the testimony, assemble the crime scene photos, the markers laid down by police to track where the shell casings fell, where the blood splattered to make abstract patterns on the floor.

I'm sure they are fascinated by his power—the power of the murderer. They paste hyperlinks at the bottom of the page, clickable pathways to the killings, the trial, the sentencing, the profiles of the victims, who were mothers and fathers and brothers and nieces and cousins, all people who were alive once, until my father decided they shouldn't be alive any longer.

These Internet groupies are just trying to make sense of the senseless, or maybe they admire the audacity it takes to simply walk into a space and claim twelve souls as your own. Maybe they envy him not asking for permission, not asking for forgiveness, but rather just going out and taking and taking and taking until there is nothing left, like Templeton, the greedy rat in *Charlotte's Web*, who will work only for the promise of reward, scavenging for food, his belly inflating as he eats his way through the fairgrounds after dark, feasting on anything sticky or savory or sweet.

They are using my father's full name when they refer to him—always first, middle, last, the way most murderers are known in America. Does it bring some sort of satisfaction, using all three names, like reprimanding a disobedient child? Does it make the victims' families feel better—to ignore the preference of a nickname, to take away a person's power over how they wish to be known? Do we feel safer when we execute Allen Lee Davis instead of Tiny Davis?

I can't pinpoint the exact moment I started to know about my father, the precise hour I learned what he did. There is no sit-down-and-have-a-serious-talk-with-my-mother memory in my mind, like the sex talk or the period talk.

How do you know how you know anything? It's difficult to trace the origins of knowledge, the beginning of learning. Do you remember learning the color blue or the number seven or the difference between hot and cold? Do you remember learning about pigs, pencils, butter, sneezes? Can you recall when you understood that rain was wet and cold?

Jean Piaget was a Swiss psychologist known for his pioneering work in child development. We learned about him in child development class in junior high, when I was still going to regular school. Child Development is a popular elective that many kids take for the famous end-of-term parenting project in which you carry a sack of flour around with you all day long, wrapped in a receiving blanket, a little knit cap on its flat head. Your task is to keep the "baby" safe and alive. So you bring it to class with you and tend to it regularly. You keep of log of how you care for it. You record all of your activities: when you pretend to feed it, when you change its diaper, when it lies inside its makeshift crib at night. You clean up after the pretend child, the thin coating of soft white flour it leaves behind, a trail of dust that appears everywhere the child has been, a kind of map to trace its movement around the house.

Piaget considered himself an epistemologist, meaning that he was interested in theories of knowledge—the ways in which justified belief is distinguished from opinion. He wanted to know all there is to know about knowledge. He wanted to learn about how we can really *know* things. Piaget understood that knowledge isn't something we're born with. He knew that the truth can't be seen all at once, even if we believe we've found it. Knowledge is slippery, a fish you try to hold in your hands in spite of its desperate wiggling, the slick scales that slip through your fingers.

We're lucky if we can ever truly know anything, lucky to glimpse, even if fleeting, that flash of smooth fin as the body breaks the water, like an older couple on the ship deck of a whale-watching expedition, a certain thickness of mist surrounding them.

We are born without knowledge—our brains just vessels open for programming, clean slates waiting to be muddied with the dirt of cognitive development, the nutrient-rich soil of knowing. I wasn't born knowing anything about who I was or where I came from. I was spared all of that, a trick of human nature, the ability to be born into blissful ignorance, for how awful would it be to come into this world with all of the knowledge of what came before you?

But then again, there are some things that we know without remembering how we arrived at that knowledge. Siblings separated at birth can still grow up to have similar interests, similar methods for making their way in the world. That's where genetics comes in, that complex system of what makes us who we are in the first place. And sometimes, in the dark of night, when I'm trying to fall asleep, my body remembers what it is I fear the most, what I won't allow myself to consider during the bright light of day—those inescapable molecules, the acids, the substances that remain a mystery to most of us, in spite of the fact that they are the building blocks of life.

This is what I've gathered so far: a collection of anecdotes, found receipts, a piece of an old photo, his name written inside an otherwise empty notebook under my mother's bed, a mix CD with my mother's name written on the mirrored surface in thin black Sharpie. A kid who sat next to me in reading group in first grade who whispered in my ear, *My dad says your dad killed people*, a kid in third grade who pinched my arm in the lunch line and got scared when I became angry and turned around to glare at her. *Don't kill me!* she said loudly, and some of the kids looked at me and laughed, and others pretended not to even notice. My mother drunk and crying in the bathroom, her girlfriend, Shea, begging her to open the door, and my mother screaming in a guttural voice I've only heard her use that night—*fuck him, fuck him!* She screamed until Shea finally picked the lock with a bobby pin and joined her inside the echoes off the bathroom tiles, and I ran into my room and played

The Lion King soundtrack, which was stuck inside my purple CD player at the time, the little tray frozen and refusing to open.

I've carried this information with me, this unraveling archive that has never reached an end, for my father is still alive and his story continues, even as he rows toward death. His actions are a rock thrown in the water, creating a wake, circles of motion emanating from the center out, ripples in the surface. His actions ended ancestral blood lines, tore lovers apart, left children without mothers and fathers, made orphans and widows with each squeeze of the trigger. And now his actions overshadow him. He's reduced to a mug shot, a name on a list—of mass murderers, mall murderers, death row inmates.

Over time, I moved beyond *what happened* at Ponce De Leon Mall on April 4, 2000, and I started moving toward *why it happened*. When my father was dressing himself in what would be the last items of clothing he'd wear as a free man, when he was preparing the gun and the ammunition, when he was doing all these mundane and awful things, did he feel some sort of trip wire activated, like a mouse stepping toward the cheese and triggering the mousetrap, that mechanism of death, the animal's skinny neck snapped in an instant?

The question resounds within my body. It lives and breathes and moves inside me. It always has. Sometimes the question is fluid and travels down my throat to my stomach and then down to my legs, pulsing toward my feet, all the way down to my toes. Sometimes the question is released from my body, but it inevitably returns, usually in the cooler air of dusk, approaching sunset.

The question remains and remains, tumbling like sea glass in salt water. I'll ask myself, and I'll ask myself, even though there is no answer. But every now and then, I hear a response in the distance of my mind, an answer that is really just another question, another voice from another room. *Why don't you ask him?*

chapter two

My mother stands in the ER waiting room at St. Pete General, shivering under a fleece blanket, her fever having spiked on the way over. It's late January, but the reception area and waiting room are still decorated for Christmas. Green paper wreaths hang from the ceiling, dangling by invisible threads. They sway ever so slightly from the current of the air-conditioning. They dance to music only they can hear.

A child's coloring book page is taped to the glass of the receptionist's window. It's a full-length image of Santa Claus, smiling gently in his red suit. He has a sack slung over his shoulder with cliché toys peeking out of the top: a baby doll, a stuffed lion, a jack-in-the-box. I can see the spots on the picture where the artist applied more pressure, all the gradient of shading, dark red and light.

The receptionist slides her little window to the side

and asks how she can help my mother. As Shea explains, the receptionist's fingernails tap the information into her keyboard. My mother tries not to talk above a whisper, her throat on fire from suspected strep, her second bout with the infection this month. My mother is more prone to strep than others, and being a preschool teacher doesn't help since the close quarters and exposure to children blend to create the ideal conditions for the contagious disease to spread.

I like the way everything echoes in here, all the hard surfaces receiving our sounds and then sending them back to us. Shea's voice is familiar, but slightly strange, amplified by the echoes.

My mother signs her name when instructed on the electronic pad. She presses gently at first and then harder and harder until her digital signature appears, an extra curl in the M in Mira for good measure.

Just last week, my mother finished the course of antibiotics from the first infection, but this morning, the pain returned, and by the time we'd finished dinner, her sentences were punctuated with sobs, as if she were swallowing glass with each breath, and then we all went into the bathroom and I watched in the mirror as Shea inspected my mother's throat. My mother stretched her mouth wide while Shea pointed a mini Maglite flashlight inside to illuminate the situation.

My mother said *ahhhh*, holding the note clear and steady until Shea was done, a musician waiting for the conductor to signal the song is over.

"Yep. They're back," Shea had said, referring to the little white spots on my mother's swollen tonsils.

"No, they can't be!" My mother looked at her own reflection in the mirror for a long time, wiping tears from her cheeks with her palms. "I'll be fine until to-morrow. I'll go to the walk-in clinic before school, or I'll just call out..." Her voice got softer and softer as Shea grabbed her hand.

"No, Mira. Let's go to the ER tonight and just get you checked. If it's strep, let's get the meds started. Get you fixed up." I saw the sadness in my mother's eyes as she faced the inevitability of another throat culture, another round of antibiotics, another round of fear that overusing antibiotics will create super-bugs, strains of bacteria that are resistant to treatment. While my mother doesn't allow hand sanitizer in her classroom, most people who work with children stock up on extra-large tubs of the stuff, walking up and down the aisles, doling it out like communion, the children's hands cupped and waiting for the clear gel to anoint them and make them holy and clean. I can't help but feel bad for the bacteria. They are only try-ing to survive, after all, only changing themselves into something strong enough to resist what surely feels like the threat of mass extinction.

After checking in with the receptionist, we sit on hard chairs and watch cable news on a small, bubble-screen TV mounted behind Plexiglas so you can't change the channel. Hospital waiting rooms can knock you over with their sadness, and this one is certainly no exception. An elderly woman naps in her wheelchair as her possible grandson looks down at his phone. He glides one thumb on the surface of the glass in an upward motion again and again, sweeping through information that glows from the bright white screen. A twenty-something father paces in a small circle, holding his possible daughter. She sucks on a green pacifier, pressing her blond head against his shoulder.

I like to invent backstories for strangers, but then it makes me imagine the backstories strangers might invent for me and my mother and Shea. I consider the clues they might notice about us, ponder the relationships they may conceive for us. I'm comforted by the fact that they would likely never guess my actual backstory in a million years. I'm comforted by the fact that, although it feels so burning and obvious to me on the inside, there are no signs or signals on the outside of me detailing my origins, no keys to decode where I come from.

A metal rack of brochures and pamphlets lives on one wall of the waiting room, a rotating display with tiny compartments for each stack. After we've waited for a while, my mother starts to feel restless, her nerves kicking in. She walks over to the display, the fleece blanket wrapped around her shoulders now. My mother reaches for the rack and sets it spinning like a wheel of fortune. When it stops, she pauses and then picks up a brochure and folds it into her pocket.

Eventually, a voice calls my mother's name, and we are ushered into triage—a sea of mostly empty beds draped in disinfected cotton, everything washed in shades of blue and green. After her vital signs are measured and submitted for the record—blood pressure, temperature, heart rate—my mother breathes deeply, inhaling and exhaling while the nurse listens to her lungs. After the throat culture is procured—my mother's tongue tamed with the wooden tongue depressor, the long swab rubbed on the back of her throat and around her tonsils, the sample of possible bacteria collected—my mother reclines in the mechanical bed, and the nurse opens and then closes the pale green privacy curtain. The small metal bearings along their small metal track make a bright pinging sound as the nurse leaves us alone to wait for the doctor, who will eventually swish the curtain open again, removing the thin barrier between us and the rest of the room. But for now, we have the illusion of being alone, just the three of us.

"It's probably me," Shea says, her palm on the top of my mother's head, smoothing her hair gently. "I'm probably a strep carrier. I've read about it. Some people are carriers. Why else haven't I caught it yet?" The room feels subfreezing and smells antiseptic, an aggressively sanitized igloo.

"Evelyn hasn't caught it yet either," my mother says, motioning toward me with one hand and then closing her eyes. "You're probably both carriers. I would be so lucky." My mother forces a blind smile and then settles herself into the flat pillow. "Kids have been dropping like flies for weeks now. It's making the rounds."

Her cheeks are bright pink, her eyes damp at the corners, tears catching the light. I want to take her picture because this is when my mother looks the most beautiful to me—these moments when she's not thinking about herself, when she's not even aware of her looks. We had left the house abruptly, not enough time for my mother to assess her appearance. She slipped sandals on over white gym socks, her feet freezing from the fever chills. She wrapped herself in an oversized cable knit cardigan that's missing two buttons. I can still see the remnants of this morning's mascara, faint black smudges along the bottom rims of her eyes.

A young doctor appears with the results of the throat culture. Her footsteps echo on the hard floor as she approaches my mother's bed. It is strep, yes, of course it's strep; it's just as we suspected. The young doctor tells my mother not to worry because strep is just very contagious, and they are seeing lots of cases right now. It's the season, she says, and it's not uncommon to have back-to-back infections, especially with such high rates of exposure. The young doctor says she'll send a prescription to the Walgreens down the street, and we can be on our way.

When we return home, Shea puts my mother to bed, covering her with an extra blanket. I stand in the threshold of their bedroom and watch as my mother burrows herself into the pillows and closes her eyes. She disappears into a sea of softness, only the top of her head visible. Shea leans over my mother and kisses her earlobe. Maybe I should feel uncomfortable around these displays of affection, but it's never bothered me. I've always been aware of their feelings for each other. They've never kept that from me.

After tucking my mother into bed, Shea puts her arms around me. "She's going to be just fine," she tells me. She squeezes me tight and then lets me go, pulls her phone from her back pocket, and types an e-mail with her thumbs while she talks. "I'm going to cancel my morning class tomorrow and help take care of her," she says. "My students will be thrilled to get the notification, even though they love discussing modernist poetry at eight a.m. I'm e-mailing them right now." When Shea's finished, she slips the phone back into her pocket and looks up at me. "What's on your schedule for tomorrow?"

"In English, a virtual class on *The Great Gatsby*. I still need to finish the prereading questions. Must be ready to dazzle them with my thoughts on the decline of the American dream in the 1920s. Then a trig quiz, then a voice chat with my history teacher to review the unit exam we took last week."

"Too much focus on testing," Shea says. She furrows her brow a bit to display her disapproval. Shea teaches literature at a liberal arts college in St. Petersburg. She eschews tests of any kind, preferring to evaluate her students on their contributions to discussions and their reactions to the text, in spite of department guidelines. The beauty of having tenure, Shea often says.

"No worries, the trig unit is cake. And I got an A on the history exam," I tell her. "So we'll just be reviewing my brilliance." I flash my best good-girl smile and then bat my eyes to make Shea laugh, but also to illustrate just how easy it has become for me to handle all of my online assignments. I'm halfway through my third year in cyberschool, and I've settled into a rhythm—wake up, log on, complete reading assignments, prepare for quizzes, schedule teacher chats, sign on to the message boards, post two paragraphs of meaningful interactions with peers (teachers are obsessed with all things *meaningful* these days), complete activity log, sign off. Most weeks, I've completed all the necessary work by Thursday morning, but I don't advertise that to my mother and Shea.

"Well, I hope we don't get in your way," Shea says. She slides her jeans off, throws them on top of the hamper, and then climbs into her side of the bed, under the covers with my mother, who is already asleep now, breathing with her mouth open, each inhale and exhale flickering like the beat of a moth's wings inside the house, when they become trapped, attracted to the light that eventually leads to their demise.

"Nah, never," I assure her. "Good night, Shea," I say, and she blows a small kiss my way as I turn off the lights and close the door and head down the darkened hall.

It's late now, after midnight, so I go to my own

room and close the door behind me. I flip the light switch, and everything is illuminated—my gold velour chair we found at the antique mall in Tarpon Springs, my purple plaid blanket thrown over the back, my map of the world pinned to the wall. I'd originally planned to use the map to document my travels, like I've seen in the movies, marking each city I've visited with silver thumbtacks, but I haven't left Florida yet.

I used to dream about moving to a place where nobody knows me, where I can reinvent myself, untether myself from death and blood and true crime specials on television. The idea stirs and stirs in me until it feels electric, a euphoric zap to the brain that reminds me that if all else fails, there's always the escape hatch, the rip cord, the possibility of floating down, down, down, to a new land that's a clean slate, far from the knowledge of who you are and what's come before you. Close your eyes and spin yourself around, lose your sense of direction for a moment. Then walk up to the map, your fingers outstretched, waiting for the feel of the paper on your hands, the signal that you've made it. Reach out and point to a place. Then open your eyes and see where you've landed, and remember that there are places on this blue and green earth where nobody knows your father's name, where nobody knows that you look like him, that you have his eyes, his hair color, his nose.

I grab my laptop from under the bed, wrap myself in the purple plaid blanket, and sit down on the velour chair. With one touch, the screen comes alive, and I enter my password. I open a web browser and click on the little blue star, the symbol that opens my list of saved bookmarks. I scroll down the list, the title of each one turning blue as the mouse hovers over it. I won't open any of the pages; I never do. I just want to make sure they are all still here—the television news clips, the articles, the reenactments, and the crime scene as diorama, actors standing in for my father, actors standing in for the dead.

Before I had this system, this way of organizing what my father did, every web search felt like pulling the silver arm of a slot machine. I'd look up something benign—the migratory patterns of birds or the number one song from the day I was born—and I'd hold my breath as I navigated the search results, paralyzed by the possibility of stumbling across something about him or what he did. Now I know that if I find him, I can just file him away with one click, putting him in this archive for safekeeping. Now I can let myself fall down the rabbit hole, getting lost in the vortex of the Web. I can click, click, click, sift through link after link, read until I'm high on information, until I lose track of time. When it's over, I won't remember it all, won't be able to find the trail of electronic breadcrumbs back to the beginning of the search, the opening through which I so quickly descended. I'll remember point A and point B, but not the in-between. Middles are just so ordinary, so forgettable. Give me a spectacular entrance, some dramatic music to stoke anticipation. Give me a tragic twist at the end of it all.

I click away from my bookmarks, and the list disappears, the links tucked back into their digital bed for now. Then I type the URL of Andy's blog, *Letters from the Death House*, into the address bar. I watch as the small picture of him loads at the top of the page. He is always smiling in his prison jumpsuit top, the collar of a bright white T-shirt peeking out from the orange. His name is Andrew Randolph Vail, but he signs his letters *Love, Andy*. He is on death row at Raiford, like my father. *Letters from the Death House* is maintained by his sister, Sherry. Each blog entry is a letter Andy sends Sherry from death row, scanned and uploaded, written on lined notebook paper in his own hand.

Andy is thirty-two years old, his face thin and clean shaven. He shares everything, his heart cracked open on the page, just waiting for me to enter. He writes about his daily life at Raiford, his interactions with other inmates, what he's reading, his exercise routine. He writes about the future, how he's making peace with his impending death. He tells his sister that he thinks of her on those nights when all he can hear are the cries of his fellow inmates bouncing off the cold walls.

There is no new entry to read tonight so I click on the Photos tab and scroll through the pictures I've already seen dozens of times—Andy as a kid at a birthday party, smiling without his two front teeth; Andy at the shoreline, building a sandcastle with a bright green pail; Andy as a teenager, posing with his prom date in front of a sparkly silver background.

I close my laptop and slide it under my bed. I turn off the lights and crawl under the covers, feeling the cool cotton on my bare legs. My eyes adjust, and within the darkness, I see Andy. I stare into his blue eyes as my fingers graze the skin of my inner thigh, search until they find the warm center. My fingers are cold at first, but they warm quickly from my own body heat. It always feels so good, this tingling that starts just below the surface, like tiny bubbles that form as water begins to boil. Eventually, the water spits and roils, and the bubbles swim to the top, and my back arcs as if I'm plugged into some invisible power source. My body rises, higher and higher, and I close my eyes. I feel like I'm climbing the steepest cliff, desperate to get to the top. When I reach the edge, I jump, and my body becomes a sail as I fly, every nerve inside me pulsing and raw. I press my face into the pillow to dampen my cries. When I open my eyes, Andy is gone.

When I wake in the morning, the apartment feels strange, too silent for a Wednesday. I'm used to the scurry of my mother as she gets ready for work, music streaming from the portable speaker that my mother takes with her from bedroom to kitchen to bathroom as she gets dressed, eats breakfast, and puts on the small amount of makeup that she wears to school—just powder, mascara, and lip gloss. I can track her location at any moment through the volume and clarity of the music, a kind of sonar I've been developing for as long as I can remember.

I walk out to the kitchen, and the coffeepot comes to life on its own, the timer still set as if it's just another work day, the machine simply doing what it's been programmed to do. I open a cupboard and assemble the ingredients for one of my favorite breakfasts, instant oatmeal topped with fruit cocktail in heavy syrup. I tear open the brown paper packet, mix the dehydrated oats with some water, and then pop them in the microwave and set it for one minute.

As the machine hums and the bowl spins inside on the glass turntable, I open the junk drawer and retrieve the can opener. I'm already thinking about how the instant oatmeal will absorb the sweetness of the thick syrup when I mix it all together, already anticipating delight when the microwave dings and I open it, reaching inside for the steamy bowl.

I crank the can open with the manual can opener, dump the fruit cocktail on top of the oatmeal, and then cross back to close the drawer. That's when I notice her—there inside the junk drawer—a girl's face smiling at the ceiling. It's one of the glossy brochures from the emergency room, the one my mother shoved into her pocket last night. It's rendered in all primary colors, the surefire way to signify that something is intended for children, as though kids aren't able to distinguish any other shades.

The top of the brochure says WAVELENGTHS in blue capital letters and under that in smaller print A SUPPORTIVE GROUP FOR YOUTH. A slanted crease runs just below the smiling girl's chin, the fold from my mother's hands still visible, although it appears that she attempted to smooth the brochure before she deposited it into the drawer, nestling it among the other odd items that amount to junk in our home, a few odd spools of thread, some pizza menus, an eyeglass repair kit, a few tealight candles.

I open the brochure, and inside, small black letters explain that Wavelengths is a free support group for children of incarcerated parents, run by licensed clinical social workers who specialize in working with adolescents and teens. There is a photo of two happy preteens on the inside—a boy with braces, a girl with braids. They are possibly thirteen or fourteen years old. It's not clear why the two of them are posing together, but they're both looking straight into the camera. The boy smiles wide, and the girl laughs politely. It's not a belly laugh, but the kind of natural-looking laugh that makes the subject look organically happy, not too forced. The small black letters go on to declare that one in twenty-eight children will have a parent become incarcerated before his or her eighteenth birthday.

I hear footsteps from the hall, and I quickly stuff the brochure back into the drawer and slam it shut. I'm mixing my oatmeal when my mother appears at the threshold of the room.

"Even when I'm sick, can't sleep in worth a damn," she says. Her voice is louder than last night, sounds more like her. She pats my elbow as she walks past me to the coffeemaker to pour herself a steaming cup.

She sits down at the small breakfast nook and takes a sip, eyeing me as I continue to stir. I think about letting it go, but that has never been my style when it comes to her.

"Wavelengths, Mom?" I sit down across from her at the table. "Really?" I swallow a spoonful of oatmeal waiting for her response.

"Okay, you saw the pamphlet," she says. "I was going to sit down and go over it with you sometime today." She takes another sip of coffee and straightens her spine a few degrees.

"What is there to go over, Mom?" I want to know. "This is the kind of shit I make fun of."

"Then go and make fun of it. Think of it as material. Fodder for jokes. Whatever. Just give it a chance, Evelyn."

"You think I need something like this? You think I need to talk to a bunch of strangers?"

"Hey, it's not something you have to commit your entire life to. Just something you could try on for size. See if it's helpful. You don't have anyone to talk to, Evelyn. At least not anyone else like you. Who knows what you're going through."

What I'm going through. A tidy euphemism, code for my father's condition, my condition, the current state of affairs.

"But I have you and Shea," I say. "I swear I'll start spilling my guts to you two as much as you want. We can talk all about what I'm going through."

"You know I worry," she says, and I can feel her staring at the top of my head so I finally look up, letting my eyes meet hers.

"Fine, I'll try it on for size," I say. "But if it doesn't fit, I'm taking it back."

"Way to extend that metaphor," she says. My mother smiles and stands, taking her mug with her back down the hall and to her bedroom, where Shea is likely still sleeping under the purple quilt. On the table, a thin streak of coffee has spilled, like evidence left behind.

chapter three

I know my mother worries. She doesn't have to remind me. Her worry covers the silences that arrive in those spaces when we've run out of things to say to each other. When we speak, my mother's worry appears to dissipate, the fog clearing, burned up by the sunlight of our words.

But fog is made up of tiny water droplets so when it disappears, it's not really gone. We believe the fog is gone because we believe what we see, but the water is still in the air. It has just transformed itself, shifting shape from liquid to gas. But my mother's worry is still there—even in those moments when all seems right with the world, when my mother smiles at me, when she rubs my shoulders or curls up next to me on my bed at night to gossip about her day. The worry is still there, but in another form, one that is easier for her to hide—worry stashed into a shoe box at the back of my mother's closet, hidden by the darkness the empty clothing casts, the limp sleeves of dresses and the empty pant legs that hang without bodies to fill them.

Shea works to manage my mother's worry. She relieves the pressure in my mother's worry, poking small holes in the shoe box, puncturing it slowly to allow some worry to escape. It makes a hissing sound, the worry slithering away for a bit only to return the next day and the next day and the next.

Some nights, I can't escape my mother's worry, and I wake in the small hours of morning, my heart pumping fast and loud with worry, like a hummingbird beating its wings against the cage of my chest. I'll lie very still, slow my breathing, and keep my eyes closed, attempting to clear the worry from my body, trying to send my thoughts to some far-off place. I'll imagine I'm on a small boat on the open sea, the sky clear blue and cloudless and the sun warming my skin.

Some nights it will work. The worry will drain slowly from my body, and I'll drift back to sleep. Other nights, the clear blue sky will turn dark, and thick clouds will roll in. I'll look up and see lightning above me, spider veins of bluish white flashing against the black. I'll hear thunder in the distance, moving closer and closer with each rumble.

On those nights, I can't sleep until I flip through that archive in my mind, *The Catalog of Everything I've Done Wrong*, pick an entry, any entry, and remember. I'm seven years old again, on the playground at the Montessori school. Kids run through the chain-linked area, weaving around the slides and climbing walls, kicking up bits of shredded tire with their heels. I sit on a swing and stare at the fence, trying to get my eyes to snap out of focus so I can look through one of the individual chain links. I close one eye like looking through a telescope, holding one eyelid down manually, my eye muscles refusing to operate independently. They come in a pair, after all, so they have to work together, blinking and crying in rhythm, sharing a secret language like twin sisters.

I start to swing, back and forth, back and forth, picking up momentum by pumping my legs to power my movements, propelling myself up and then back and up again, falling with gravity like a pendulum swinging through the air. I lean my head back and close my eyes because the sun can blind me if I'm not careful.

When I open my eyes, I notice something dark at the base of the fence, something that looks furry. I dig my heels into the dirt beneath the swing to slow down, a low cloud of dust rising around my feet until I come to a complete stop. I walk toward the fence, and when I reach it, I kneel down. I brush the leaves away with the back of my hand and find a dead mouse, its body curved into a C shape. I see the pointed snout and the whiskers, the black eyes that are open and shining like the tiniest black marbles I've ever seen.

I pull a paper clip from my pocket, and straighten the curves until it becomes a small, blunt needle. I jab the mouse's bloated belly with it, pushing harder each time, testing to see if it's sharp enough to pierce the skin. I just want to see what's inside. I slide the paper clip into the creature's mouth, parting its lips to see the teeth, which are long and yellow and slightly curved.

Then I push the paper clip into one glassy black eye. I push and push until the paper clip pokes clean through the back of the mouse's small head, and thick yellow liquid seeps from the corners of the eye socket.

I hear footsteps along the ground behind me and hear a teacher call out.

"What are you doing over here?" she asks.

"Nothing," I say. I dig into the ground with my fingernails, covering the dead mouse with dirt as fast as I can, but my hands aren't strong enough, and the dirt is too densely packed for me to penetrate.

"That doesn't look like nothing to me," she says.

"Show me what you have." Her voice gets louder, attracting the attention of other children until there is a small circle of them assembled and watching, waiting to see what I've found.

"It's nothing. It's nothing!" I keep repeating the words, but they sound muffled, like I'm screaming underwater. I pick up my left foot and stomp on the mouse as hard as I can. I pick up my right foot and stomp again. I stomp and jump and jump and stomp until my small weight has flattened the even smaller creature, his body now smashed into the ground, his fur soaked red and yellow with blood and pus. Then the teacher grabs me by the wrist and leads me back into the school.

My mother arrives to pick me up. I sit on the bright blue rug in the middle of the classroom, staring at my shoes as the teacher talks about me as if I'm not in the room. On the car ride home, I lean my head against the window, and I wait for my mother to raise her voice, wait for her to get angry with me. I wait and wait, but I only hear the sound of my own inhaling and exhaling. I watch my breath fog the glass. I wait and wait until I finally feel something—my mother's worry changing states, from solid to liquid to gas.

chapter four

Wavelengths meets in Tampa, on Monday nights. My mother and I don't talk much on the way there, the radio tuned to classic rock, my mother singing softly to Led Zeppelin under her breath to mask our silence. As we cross the Howard Frankland Bridge, the long concrete connection between St. Pete and Tampa, the sinking sun casts its colors on the canvas of the sky—pinks and reds and purples that last for a few minutes before they disappear until the next day. You can get used to sunsets in Florida, where the land is flat and the sky is wide. You can get spoiled being able to watch the sun's movements from anywhere.

It's dark when we arrive, and we get out of the car, my mother pausing to stretch for a moment. She stands, hands on hips. She tilts her head back, her face pointed toward the sky, while I reach inside the front pocket of my jeans for the red Jolly Rancher I've been hoarding all day. It looks like a small jewel in my palm, and will taste like wild strawberries, glossy and wet on my tongue.

The parking lot is not well lit; the dark reds of taillights and bright whites of headlights illuminate our way toward the entrance. The group meets in an empty office space in a strip mall near downtown Tampa. The space is nondescript inside, the only furniture two desks and a circle of institutional seating, those simple, neutral-colored chairs you usually find in waiting areas, those places people often find themselves in against their will.

Greg, the social worker and group leader, greets us. I learned his name from eavesdropping on my mother's phone call to enroll me in the group. Tall and thin, Greg leans over a bit while saying hello, an attempt to look me in the eye. "Hi, Evelyn. It's very nice to meet you, Evelyn," he says. I can already tell he's the type of person who will overuse your name in conversation, an obvious ploy to build rapport.

I take a seat in the circle while my mother chats with Greg for a moment, and then waves good-bye. She'll wander nearby WestShore Plaza for the next two hours, exploring the wide walkways of retail, perhaps reminiscing about her own adolescence, all that time she spent hanging out at shopping malls with her friends, her generation that wore ripped jeans and flannel shirts and called themselves mall rats.

There are twelve of us at the support group, all teenagers—five boys and seven girls, including me. I don't like sitting in a circle like this, feeling more comfortable in classrooms where I can lower my energy and sit in the back row. I can blend into the wall if I try hard enough, become something other than a murderer's daughter, something bright and full of air, something that feels lighter than my actual body.

I feel exposed here, like everyone is watching me, sizing me up from the bare toes sticking out of my sandals to the top of my head. This fiery feeling, which erupts in my stomach when I get nervous, spreads toward my mouth, giving me the sensation of hot, hot coals inside my throat. If I were to speak right now, only smoke and ash would come out.

"We have a few new faces tonight so let's begin by reviewing the ground rules," Greg says. He smiles, a flash of teeth appearing briefly between his lips. His voice is even and smooth, the kind of voice that can put me in a trance if I'm not careful. Once, in elementary school, we had a firefighter visit our class and talk to us about fire safety. His voice was pure buttery gold. I couldn't tell you the first thing about evacuation plans or fire extinguishers, but I remember the feeling of a thousand tingles on my neck and back and arms as he spoke. His voice was warm and inviting, a lullaby I could feel with my entire body, hushing me into a dream, a state of almost-sleep.

Greg takes a manila folder from his canvas messenger bag, one of those soft-sided cases with a shoulder strap. It's tan and worn and faded with use, or it might be secondhand. Any thrift store worth its salt has a healthy bag and purse section, those items people spend far too much money on, according to my mother. She'd never spend more than five dollars on a bag.

Greg pulls a small parcel of white paper from the folder, and hands it to the kid next to him, who takes one and passes the rest on to the next kid, and so on. The papers float along a conveyor belt of hands until they reach me. The handout looks like it was typed on a typewriter and photocopied badly. There are stray black streaks and smudges around the corners. Greg reads the ground rules out loud, and my eyes follow the words on my paper.

WAVELENGTHS GROUND RULES

1. What is said in the group is not to be discussed at any other place, at any other time.

2. We are here to share our own feelings and experiences, not to give advice.

3. We each share the responsibility for making this group work.

4. We try to accept people just as they are. Our goal is not to change people.

5. We try to give everyone an opportunity to share.

6. We have the right to speak and the right to remain silent.

7. We give supportive attention to the person speaking and avoid interrupting.

8. We have the right to ask questions and the right to refuse to answer.

9. We talk about what is present to us now, rather than the past.

10. We do not discuss group members who are not present.

"And remember, we really must strive to abide by these rules," Greg says. "They are the foundation on which we build a supportive environment. And within that environment, we can do the work. Together." Greg glances around the circle, nodding a little too vigorously. Some of the teens nod and smile along with Greg while others appear to look right through him. "You may choose to participate at any level you wish. You may ask questions, answer questions that are posed, or simply listen and observe. Sound good?" he asks the group but he's looking at me. I whisper the word *yes*, my throat still too hot to make audible sound.

"Excellent!" Greg says cheerfully, his voice taking on a higher note now, a few shades brighter than the voice that read through the ground rules. "Let's get started. Our topic tonight is acceptance. I'll begin by discussing a few things that will help us understand the topic, and then we can have an open share."

Greg is the sun, and we are fixed bodies around him. Like tiny planets without orbit, we are forced to remain in place while the sun sets off solar flares, sudden flashes of brightness ejecting clouds of electrons toward us. Greg wants to bathe us in sunbeams, a red-hot glare that dazzles and burns. He seems to know about the shadows within—the gloom and murk and muck that lives inside of every person—whether your parent is incarcerated or not—and his mission is to extinguish all of our shadows with the light of support and acceptance.

My mother has checked books out of the library on incarceration over the years. Some have been clinical and evidence-based, written by doctors and other experts in the field. Some have been more self-help or "new age" as the section usually reads in the bookstore. There's an entire business built around helping the friends and families of prisoners—helping us with our grief, our guilt, our anger. People see us as the ones left behind, the widows and widowers, the motherless daughters, the fatherless sons.

I understand the idea of getting help, of asking for support. I understand that it might help some people to realize that they aren't alone in all of this. But I've never understood why I have to accept it. Acceptance is heavy, an anchor that sinks to the bottom of the sea. When you accept something, it becomes real, permanent, and unmovable, a boulder you push and push up a mountain until you reach the top and you stay there, staring at the giant rock that will never get any smaller no matter how many times you try to chip away at it. Acceptance is Virginia Woolf walking into the river, her pockets weighed down with rocks. She walked into acceptance, one step at a time, acceptance up to her knees, her waist, her chest, and over her head, until she was submerged in it—acceptance finally filling up her lungs, stealing her breath.

I won't accept that chemicals will flow into my father's veins, a current of drugs that will feel like an anvil placed on his chest, heavy and unyielding, to make sure he stays submerged, to make sure he never comes up for air.

Greg is a confident leader, although at the beginning of the open share period he looks a bit nervous, beads of sweat appearing at his hairline like a message in Braille. The group members also seem to be experiencing various levels of uncertainty. Some are exhibiting the classic signs of avoidance, shrinking and sinking and hoping not to be seen, lowering their energies so they won't be called upon against their will. Others look restless and fidgety, twirling strands of hair around their fingers or bouncing their knees up and down rhythmically, a sign that they can't bear to be still. A boy who looks about my age raises his hand. His ears are stretched by wooden discs the size of nickels. Greg smiles and calls on him. "David, great. Thanks for sharing," Greg says.

"You're welcome," David begins. He sits up a little straighter in his chair, which causes a ripple effect throughout the circle, most of us correcting our posture too, like a choreographed dance, the mass movement of a hive mind. "So, when I think about acceptance, I think about all the stuff my mother has told me over the last two years, how she still loves me and how my father still loves me. She accepts the fact that I'll always love my dad, even though he hurt us." David pauses, his eyes shining through glassy tears that never spill out. They just remain, suspended like a liquid shield. "Sorry," David says, sniffling.

Greg tilts his head to one side, his face more serious than before. "It's okay. Take your time, David."

"And I also think about how my mother accepts me as a man separate from my father," David continues. "I mean, I'm sure she hates that I look almost exactly like him." David laughs gently, and the circle laughs, a small puff of air that lightens us. "I guess that's all. He's still my father, and I still love him, in spite of everything. And my mom understands."

Greg doesn't miss a beat. "Amazing, David. Thank you so much for your words. That's exactly why we're here, to share our experiences and to know that our words can help others. Sometimes it will help in big, monumental ways." Greg stretches his arms out as far as he can, attempting to measure the biggest breakthrough. "Sometimes it will help in smaller ways." He collapses the space between his hands so that his palms are almost touching. He squints one eye like he's looking through a microscope to see the tiniest of breakthroughs, epiphanies in miniature.

David looks younger to me now, his features softened, his hands small and folded on his lap. My vision blurs out of focus for a moment, and when I can see clearly again, there's someone standing right behind David. Is it his father?

They do look alike—they have the same bushy eyebrows, the same ears that stick out slightly, the same slanted nose. David's father puts his hands on David's shoulders, and then slides them around his throat. He starts to squeeze, crushing David's windpipe. David tries to pry his father's hands away, but his father is too strong. David opens his mouth but makes no sound. His face turns red; his eyes become bloodshot. His father's body tenses as he squeezes tighter and tighter, as he stops David's breath.

Do you still love me now, David? Do you still love me now?

I had more control over these visions when I was younger, could freeze the frame before it went too far. Now it's harder to make them stop. Closing my eyes doesn't help, for what I conjure in the darkness is worse than the visions that materialize before me, those ghosts only I can see. So I just have to watch. Then remind myself that it's not real.

I look down at my copy of the ground rules. We have the right to ask questions and the right to refuse to answer. We try to accept people just as they are. Our goal is not to change people. I fold the paper in half, then in fourths, then eighths, sixteenths, thirty-seconds, sixty-fourths. With each fold the paper becomes thicker, less defined, until it can no longer be folded anymore. When I finally open it up, it looks like failed origami—all those lines and creases come undone.

I look up again, and David's father is gone. There are no handprints around David's neck. His eyes are clear and blue. David wipes a tear from his cheek as Greg calls on the next person to share.

chapter five

The temperature is in the mid-seventies today, our version of winter. While the tourists from the North may not notice it, those of us who live here year-round can sense the change in the air. The humidity lessens, and the sun burns a few shades cooler. The sky is still clear and wide but a deeper, darker blue. Some prefer the Atlantic coast of Florida, but I like it here on the gulf side. I like my water a little murky, my waves a bit smaller, my own salty, makeshift ocean. I love to feel the warm gulf breeze on my arms and legs, love to hear the cries of seagulls in the air—those relentless high-pitched calls, *keeee-oh, keee-oh, keee-oh.*

I have a ritual on Saturdays. I like to wake up early, usually before my mother and Shea even begin to stir, and I walk down Gulf Way, as far south as I can go, down to the jetty. I don't take anything with me—not even my phone. If my mother wants to find me when she wakes up, she knows where I am. It's just a ten-minute walk from our apartment to my Saturday spot, a plot of sand next to the rock formation that juts out from the beach. The beach is rather quiet on Saturday mornings, mostly locals like me. Pass-a-Grille has a few small hotels in the historic district, but the pace is slower here, the area not as touristy as others on the Gulf Coast. Today, there are two beach joggers, a man and a woman in black spandex shorts. There is a middle-aged woman walking her gray poodle, and there are three twenty-something-looking women who are lounging under a blue-and-white-striped umbrella they've speared into the sand. Their sunglasses are mirrored, and I catch my own reflection in them for just a second as I walk by them, smelling coconut and straw-berry as I pass.

Since it's morning, the tide is still low, and the sand is wet and dense. I sit down near the edge of water, that line where two elements meet. The wind hits my skin, and the water licks the jetty rocks. The birds call out to each other, and there's all this movement out here, all this momentum I can feel, although I can't quite put my finger on where it comes from. All I know is that I feel like a small part of something big-ger than me when I'm out here. I'm the whole world when I'm out here.

My ritual continues as I sit and think and look straight ahead, examining the colors of the horizon, allowing my eyes to drift out of focus. I imagine what's happening on the other side of the Gulf of Mexico right at this moment. If I could swim 926 miles, cut a straight line through the water with my body, I'd reach Corpus Christi, Texas, another city on another beach, a place with a name that means *body of Christ*. I imagine someone sitting at the gulf's edge in Corpus Christi looking out into the vast nothingness of sky before them, not realizing that they are looking right at me, that we are looking at each other.

Something that Greg said at the end of group is sticking in my head, his voice repeating and repeating, no matter how hard I try to shake it from my brain. "Own your feelings. They belong to you, and only you." I've always felt the opposite, walking through life with a shield around me, a guard against feelings, especially about my father. In my dreams, I cast off all my feelings about him, shed them like an insect shedding its exoskeleton, a brittle replica that appears full but is actually hollow, crunching underfoot as you pass.

When you begin your life as the only child of a single mother, it can be difficult to distinguish between what is yours and what is hers. Our feelings are connected somehow, each one a small fishhook in a bowl full of fishhooks. Reach for one and you are bound to pull many, because they catch onto each other without even trying. Maybe it's inevitable that our feelings are all tangled up in each other, my mother and I having spent so much time together, the two of us against the world. My mother is an only child like me. Her father is dead, and she doesn't speak to her mother, hasn't since I was a toddler.

I shadowed my mother as a little girl, following her around the house most days when I was young. I was always just a few paces behind her, tailing her like a secret agent. I promise my intentions were purely observational. I simply wanted to commit to memory the changing inflections of my mother's voice, wanted to study her facial expressions, to find and catalog all the ways we are different and alike.

But my mother has grown accustomed to my behavior, however unsettling it may have been at first. Now it's taken on an endearing quality, and she'll call me Evelyn, the Spy, and we'll laugh about my voyeuristic tendencies. I can't help it. I just like to know what everyone else is up to. If I can peek through someone's window, or catch a glimpse of a family watching TV, then somehow it proves that I'm not alone. If I can read someone's blog or mine their Twitter feed for personal revelations, it's like reading someone's diary—so forbidden, but so human at the same time.

The first difference I remember recording is that my mother isn't afraid of insects and I have a mortal fear of anything with antennae or a segmented body or too many legs. To me, insects are the most terrifying creatures that exist, especially palmetto bugs, the large flying roaches that are everywhere down here in Florida.

I remember stumbling into the bathroom half asleep one night, only to find a palmetto bug that I later described as the size of a lobster, trying to get out of the bathtub, its legs so thin, so fine, I wondered how they could even hold up its body. I shrieked and ran into my mother's bedroom to tell her about the light tapping sound of the creature's legs on the blue porcelain.

She woke quickly, as mothers tend to do, always on the lookout for a child's cry for help. She went into the bathroom, scooped the bug into her palm, and took it outside, releasing it back into the wild. I followed her—into the bathroom, down the hallway, out the sliding glass door—until the palmetto bug was in the grass where it belonged, its black body looking shiny and wet in the moonlight. I pretended that the bug would never be able to find its way back to us. I pretended that it couldn't flatten itself, making its body thin enough to sneak back inside, through the tiniest crack or fissure.

I can do that—pretend that I don't see things, turn my energy down and turn my powers of perception off as I choose. If I pretend long enough and hard enough, sometimes things feel like they've disappeared and then they just don't matter anymore. In my elementary school days, I would sit at a Formica desk with my feet flat on the floor and pretend to be listening. I would even throw in a head nod or two, pretend I was there in the room with its faint smell of photocopy ink, with the other children, who mostly had geographic names like Dakota and Brooklyn. But the trick was, I wasn't really there at all.

After a few hours at the jetty, after I'm sure I've stared long enough into the colors of the sky, I stand up and find that my body has hardly made an impression in the dense sand. There's barely any proof I was here. I take Pass-a-Grille Way home, past Merry Pier, where a neon sign advertises sunset cruises for $25. I pass the historic Sea Horse Restaurant, serving breakfast and lunch and closed on Tuesdays. Outside, there's a small courtyard area where some locals wait on wooden benches that are painted dark green to match the stripes of the canvas awnings above the windows.

I reach our building, a concrete square with two units, one upstairs and one down. A woman lives alone upstairs, and sometimes I worry for her. In 1984, a woman was murdered in nearby Redington Shores, one of the few homicides recorded on the south Pinellas beaches. Her name was Kate Harvey, and although many neighbors in adjacent apartments heard her screams in the night, no one called the police. She was found dead days later, her throat cut, her body tortured. A man who lived across the street from her was eventually convicted of her murder. He'd broken into her apartment, waiting for her in the dark. He was sentenced to twenty years in prison, but cancer killed him after he'd served three.

I imagine police tape stretched across her door, bright yellow with black letters, an attempt to preserve the scene. Inside, they collect hairs and fibers, photograph the patterns of blood splatter on her bedroom wall. I conjure her body splayed across her bed, dark red soaking the bedspread, the sheets, all the way down to the mattress.

I walk through our front door and into the kitchen, and find my mother is at the table, shucking corn for lunch. Shea is standing at the sink, filling a large silver pot with water. My mother tears outer layers from the ears of sweet corn, depositing the bright green husks into a paper bag nestled between her legs. She takes extra care to remove the corn silk, which is fine as hair. Radiohead is playing from the portable speaker, their album *The Bends*, one of Shea's favorites from her high school days.

Shea glides from sink to refrigerator to stove like a dancer, her every movement appearing choreographed, a routine that springs from her body on its own. My father had his own choreography inside the jewelry store, his movements a careful sequence of steps. He sidestepped toward a customer and shot her point-blank in the back. He glided around the room and killed everyone in the store but his wife. He led her to his car, holding the gun against her ribs, holding her body close to him, his breath against her neck. In her ear, he whispered, *Don't you dare make a sound or you're dead.*

Shea sprinkles salt into the boiling water, rolls a lemon on the cutting board, and then slices it into wedges with a sharp knife. It's such a simple pleasure— the mortal pleasure of food, the taste and texture and aroma of it all. Perhaps that's why even the condemned are permitted a special request for their final meal, one last act of kindness before the final act of cruelty. I looked it up online once, wanting to know if the last meal was real or just an urban legend like Bloody Mary or Walt Disney's frozen head. But it's true.

I found that there are rituals and regulations for all the events leading up to execution. On the day of execution, the final meal will be served at approximately 4:00 p.m. The inmate may request a special meal, and accommodations will be made within reason. There's the primal joy of eating, the satisfaction of preferred taste and texture. Prior to 6:00 p.m., the inmate may shower and dress in clean clothes. There's also the primal joy of being clean, of water purifying the body, the symbolism of washing away sin.

The warden and certain individuals designated as operations personnel will assemble at approximately 5:55 p.m. in the lounge adjacent to the visiting room, along with witnesses to the execution. All necessary arrangements to carry out the execution shall be completed at the predetermined time. There are instructions to follow, an intricate plan in place. So many people and systems working to end one single life. So many people with access to my father's file.

Shortly after 6:00 p.m., the door will be unlocked, and the inmate will be removed from the holding cell. The inmate will be taken from the cell area into the execution chamber and secured to a gurney. A medically trained individual (not to be identified) shall insert an intravenous catheter into the condemned person's arm, and a saline solution will begin to flow.

At a predetermined time, the witnesses shall be escorted into the execution chamber.

Witnesses shall include the media: one Florida bureau representative designated by the Associated Press, one Florida Bureau representative designated by the United Press International, and one representative each from established print and broadcast media, provided those designated agree to meet with all media representatives present immediately after the execution. People love a good revenge story so the public will want to hear the details. And even though it's a secondhand account, their pulses will still flutter. They will still imagine my father's body sputtering and jolting as he dies under the glare of fluorescent light in a small room built like a glass theater.

No recording devices, audio or video, shall be permitted in the execution chamber. Reporters from the community where the crime was committed have first choice to witness the execution. Policy allows for up to five preapproved witnesses requested by the condemned. Policy allows for up to five immediate family members or close friends of the victim(s) to attend. Who will be there for my father? For his dead wife? Who will be there for the others, a dozen victims in all? Will the family members want to see him die? Or will it be enough for them to know that it happened, to see the death certificate in black and white?

Once the witnesses are in place, the warden shall allow the condemned person to make a last statement. There is a microphone secured above the gurney for this purpose, which will only be turned on briefly for the last words. Upon completion of the statement, if any, the warden shall signal for the execution to proceed. At this time, a designated individual shall induce, by syringe, substances necessary to cause death. This individual shall be visually separated from the execution chamber by a wall and a locked door and shall also not be identified.

First, an anesthetic is given to induce unconsciousness. Next, a muscle relaxant flows, causing paralysis and respiratory arrest. Finally a dose of sodium chloride is delivered, stopping the heart.

After the inmate is pronounced dead, the body shall be immediately removed from the execution chamber. The inmate may request their body be donated to the state anatomical board for medical research purposes.

The director of the Florida Department of Corrections shall return the death warrant and certificate to the clerk of the court with a statement showing what disposition was made of the body of the convict.

My father's death will be documented and pro-
cessed, his body removed according to a predetermined plan. Afterward, someone will disinfect the
room. Someone will wipe away what's left of my
father—the last molecules of him, the last traces of his
warm breath still clinging to the chamber walls. Someone will clean the window glass until it's so clear you'll
believe you can walk right through it.

Now Shea is putting a bright orange crab into the
silver pot. I pretend not to see how she handles it
so gently, how she lowers the body down carefully,
like a girl putting her favorite baby doll to bed. I
pretend the crab isn't struggling inside the pot, that
it isn't being boiled alive, drowned in the bubbling
waves, in salted water that spills from the pot and
splashes down, making a hissing sound on the electric burner that is coiled like a red-hot snake. And
when I finally take a bite of the sweet white meat
on my plate, I'll pretend that I'm eating air, that I'm
eating nothing at all.

chapter six

Greg has just asked a question, and we're all sitting in the circle in silence, looking at our shoes as if they'll save us from having to answer him, as if shoelaces can come up with something brilliant to say. "Open your hearts, open your minds," Greg says. "We are all here to listen." His voice is a soft pulse, the bass of a faint heartbeat, a patient on the table about to flatline. "Someone get us started. Break the ice," he says.

He lifts an imaginary hammer over his head, and then brings it down as if to shatter the invisible layer of ice over the group. "I'm sure you've all thought about the assignment from last group so you've done the hard part—you've fished those feelings out of the water. Now you just have to show us what you've caught."

But none of us seem willing to speak tonight. I

can feel the reluctance in the room. It hovers around our ankles like a low fog rolling in. *Throw me a bone!* Mrs. Sharp says during live chats in biology when our class grows silent like this. She begs like a hungry little puppy for our words, for someone to raise their virtual hand and discuss the functions of the various parts of the cell—the nucleus, cytoplasm, the mitochondria.

I'm not a teacher's pet, but I feel sorry for Greg. I wish someone would answer him because I certainly won't. It's not that I'm a bad student; it's just that I'm a bad follower. I'm not compelled to do what someone says just for the sake of obeying authority. Question authority! My mother has a magnet on the refrigerator that says that.

A girl finally raises her hand. It's her first night here, and Greg appears excited that she's already participating. She's looks about my age but shorter than me. She has dark hair and bangs that fall to her eyelashes. Sometimes she pushes her bangs to the side with her fingers, parting a thin curtain so she can see, and other times, she smooths them down, tries to pull the shade over her eyes.

Greg's eyes brighten—the whites of his eyes actually become whiter—and he turns to her. "Yes! Thank you, Clarisse! Welcome! And thank you for sharing!"

So much appreciation, and she only raised her hand. I half want her to be teasing him, half hope to hear her ask if she can go to the restroom, to watch Greg's eyes turn less white, less sparkling. Sclera. That's what you call the white part of the eye. If an eye were an egg, the sclera would be the egg white, the pupil the yolk, the unborn chicken baby.

"I feel pissed off," Clarisse says. Thwack. The sound of a bone being thrown against the wall.

"Okay," Greg says. "Now that's a start. Can you tell us more about that?"

Clarisse shifts her weight in her chair, uncrosses her legs, and crosses them again. She's wearing black jeans and green Chuck Taylors. If my mother saw her shoelaces, she might rip them out and soak them in bleach, and toss them over the shower curtain to dry. "I don't know," she says. "Like, I'm just pissed off that I have to deal with any of this."

"They are your feelings. So somewhere inside, there is a reason why you feel them," Greg says. "Take your time." He looks at her and then looks around the circle at the rest of us. "Can anyone here relate to what Clarisse is talking about?" he asks. The word *about* lingers in the air for what seems like a long time. We are silent again. So silent for so long that I'm beginning to wonder if I've imagined Greg's question.

I clear my throat, and the whole room turns to look at me. They think this is a signal that I have something to say. Is it? Does my body want me to say something, even though my mind wants me to keep quiet? And how much time has passed? It feels like forever, but that's impossible. There is no forever. I look around for a clock or a wristwatch on someone's arm but find no traces of time anywhere.

"What do you feel?" Greg asks. He's looking around the room, and I'm afraid every set of eyes in the room is boring into me. I feel naked and invisible all at once. I know this question too well. I ask myself all the time, but I never answer. It's not about the answer.

I look at Clarisse, and she's sweeping her bangs out of her eyes. She's wearing blue eye shadow, a pale shimmery shade of crystal blue, like Key West water. A wave of words tumbles around inside me, breaking and foaming, and I try to pretend that I'm not in this room, in this circle of children with missing parents, missing pieces of jigsaw puzzles that leave small patches of nothing where there should be sky, or a kitten's nose, or the center of a sunflower.

The waves of words crash fast and steady, an ocean rushing through the canals and trenches of my brain. *I feel like a rotten apple from a rotten tree. I feel like a little pebble of evil broken off from a big rock of evil. My father is evil. How can he not be? How can you just walk into a building and kill people, just walk right up to people and shoot them in the face without some evil in you? I feel like my insides are decayed. My insides are cavities full of bile and the thickest, darkest oil. I feel like I hate my father. He was evil before he went to jail, and now he's rotting even more. He's there right now, decomposing, rowing toward death. What do I feel? What do I feel? What do I feel? I feel they should just kill him already.*

"Okay, let's take a quick break," Greg says, interrupting my panic, the cold sensation filling my lungs. "Let's reconvene in ten minutes for wrap-up. Maybe some of you will want to share after a nice sugar rush." A lump is rising in my throat, that half-sick feeling of fear you get after watching a horror movie at night when you're all alone in the house and you're sure that every sound, each creak and settle of the house, each rap of a raindrop on the windowpanes, is a monster coming for you. I'm afraid that someone in the room has been reading my mind. I realize that I'm rocking forward and backward slightly in my chair so I stop as nonchalantly as possible and look around to see if anyone has noticed my movement in the first place, but the others are already standing and stretching, retrieving phones from their pockets, texting friends and boyfriends and girlfriends.

Everyone, that is, except Clarisse, who is still sitting in her chair across the circle from me, her green shoes flat on the floor. She's looking right at me, her blue-lidded eyes locked on mine for a few seconds before she bounces out of her chair and heads to the cookie table. I can't explain why, will never be able to explain why, but I follow her.

Tonight, Greg is serving an assorted cookie tray from Publix and off-brand lemon-lime soda. The soda is flat, no bubbles. Clarisse is standing over the cookies, holding a small plastic cup in her teeth as she surveys her choices, finally reaching for a thumbprint cookie, a dollop of thick icing in the middle radiating like a bright pink eye. She pours herself some soda, puts the entire cookie in her mouth, and then takes a long drink to wash it down.

"Hey," Clarisse says, and laughs, tilting her head back slightly. One high-pitched note rises in the air above us. Clarisse smiles, showing her top front teeth, which are small and pointy.

"Hey," I say back. I grab a chocolate chip cookie from the table and take a small bite, something to occupy my mouth and maybe prevent me from saying something stupid—something that makes me wish I hadn't opened my mouth and blurted out the first thing that came to mind.

"So why are you here?" Clarisse asks, and my face must register a peculiar reaction because she feels the need to clarify. "No offense," she says, "but you don't seem like the type." I grab a napkin from the table and use it to cover my mouth as I quickly chew the rest of the cookie, hoping to look natural, hoping that Clarisse can't sense how insecure I feel when people watch me eat.

"Why am I here?" I say out loud. When I don't know how to answer a question, I usually repeat it until either (a) I come up with an answer or (b) the person asking the question thinks I'm strange and finally gives up on talking to me. Clarisse doesn't give me a chance to say it again.

"Existential crisis?" Clarisse asks. She reaches for another cookie, oatmeal raisin this time. She chews the cookie deliberately, raises an eyebrow as she walks away.

After Wavelengths, Shea picks me up, and on the way home, we head south on Pinellas Bayway toward the beaches.

"So are you making any friends?" Shea asks.

"It's not that kind of group."

"Says who?

"Says me."

"Oh, teenagers!" Shea says in an exaggerated voice,

making me laugh. She smiles at the windshield, and then turns the music up—an album by Iron & Wine. The prickly sound of a banjo fills the car, and Sam Beam's hushed voice serenades us as Shea drives the rest of the way home.

chapter seven

My bedroom is quiet and dark. I turn on the lights and then go into my bathroom and close the door. I turn the shower on, twisting the hot water knob as far as it will go. The room begins to fill with steam as I get undressed, my clothes a pile on the floor. I sit naked on the sink, and take out a small piece of folded-up notebook paper—Clarisse's phone number on faint blue lines in green pen, her name above the ten digits. She dotted the *i* in *Clarisse* with a double star—two stars stacked on top of each other.

Toward the end of group, when Greg started talking about grounding techniques, when I couldn't bear to hear another word about coping skills, deep breathing, or emotional regulation, couldn't pretend to pay attention any longer, I went to the restroom. I didn't really have to go. I just stood at the sink washing my hands while singing "Happy Birthday" in my head the way they taught us in kindergarten, a measure to ensure you've washed away all of the invisible germs.

I was rubbing white foam into my palms and watching the iridescent soap bubbles circle the drain when Clarisse walked in. She smiled at me and then went into one of the stalls, starting to talk to me as she closed the door. "So what's your deal?" Clarisse asked.

I could hear the rustling of her clothing and the clink of her belt buckle as she moved inside the stall. I continued washing my hands. Looking at myself in the mirror, I watched my cheeks turn pink, blushing from the intimacy of this encounter, this girl I barely knew peeing while we talked.

"Are you one of those crazy hand washers?" Clarisse asked, her voice amplified by the hard tile inside the stall.

"Who, me?" I asked her in return, as if there were someone else in the room she could have been talking to. I turned off the water and waved one hand in front of the automatic towel dispenser. The red eye of the sensor acknowledged my presence, and a length of brown paper appeared. I tore it off and started drying my hands.

"Yes, you." Her voice was light, on the verge of laughter. "Are you a germophobe or something?" She flushed the toilet and then appeared at the sink next to me. "You know, like the OCD people on that show. They wash their hands until their skin is, like, rubbed raw and bleeding."

"Oh no. It's not that," I said, trying not to sound defensive. "I was just bored, you know? I felt like I was about to fall asleep if I didn't get up and walk around." I reached for the door handle to leave, but Clarisse put her hand on top of mine, stopping me.

"You know I actually like you," she said. And she took off the tiny drawstring backpack she wore, grabbing a pen and a little spiral notebook. "You seem like one of the only interesting people here." As she wrote her phone number on a piece of paper, she resembled a waitress taking my order, as if somehow she knew exactly what I wanted.

Now I hold the paper up to my face and breathe in the scent of the ink. I grab my phone and tap Clarisse's name and number into my contacts list. I catch my reflection in the mirror. These days, my body is an expanding territory—there is always something new to explore. I rub my breasts, pinching my nipples until they harden. I tilt my head to the side, wondering how Andy would like this pose. I open the camera on my phone and snap a picture, just to see what he would see if I could beam my body through the satellites to him, if I could reach him in the death house. If I could be his first taste of a girl in years.

I open *The Catalog of Everything I've Done Wrong* and add an entry: fallen in love with someone who doesn't love me back.

chapter eight

Clarisse's house is bigger than I'd imagined. I'd pictured her in a white Key West–style bungalow with two bedrooms and a tin roof. But really, her house is peach and has four bedrooms. It's built in what my mother and Shea call McMansion Style—a stucco house in a neighborhood with identical stucco houses in various shades of Florida neutral, which includes beige, tan, sandalwood, pink, and peach. Clarisse lives in Seffner, about twenty minutes northeast of Tampa, in a gated community called Darcy Lake. There are no sidewalks in Darcy Lake, only identical mailboxes lined up in rows, their little red flags in various positions based upon the status of their letters. Incoming or outgoing, I can never remember which means which.

My mother pulls up to the intercom at the gate, pushes the silver call button, and then enters the code that Clarisse has provided. The black wrought iron gate opens, and we are granted access. When we pull into Clarisse's driveway, my mother shuts the car off and turns to me. I'm sitting in the backseat with my red duffel bag and my pillow. Shea is in the passenger seat, her right hand dangling out the window, a swirl of smoke rising from the tip of her lit cigarette.

"You have everything, right?" my mother asks. I can only see the reflection of her eyes beaming back at me in the rearview mirror. "Your toothbrush, your phone, your deodorant?" She turns around to see me now. "Do you have your phone, Ev?" Her voice rises, and her eyes search my face for something—a sign that I will be okay. Shea reaches over and rubs the back of my mother's neck with her left hand.

"Yes, I have my phone," I answer. "I have everything." I unbuckle my seat belt and lean forward to give my mother a kiss on the cheek.

"And you'll text me tomorrow? Keep me posted on when I can come get you?" she says. She's been repeating this like a mantra the entire ride to Seffner. *Text me tomorrow, text me tomorrow.*

"I will text you tomorrow, Mom," I say.

"Okay, then. Have fun and mind your manners," she says.

"Aren't you coming in to meet Clarisse's mom?"

"Oh, right. You know what, I'll just meet her tomorrow when I pick you up. I love you."

"Love you too, Mom."

"Love you three," Shea says, and I give her a kiss on the cheek too.

After getting out of the car, I walk up to the front door of the house. It looks like solid wood, maybe dark cherry, with a small oval window made to imitate stained glass. I ring the doorbell and hear the muffled sound of chimes from inside the house. When Clarisse opens the front door, I turn around and wave at my mother and Shea in the car and Clarisse waves too. The car backs out of the driveway, my mother honking the horn good-bye. Shea's hand out the window offers a smoke signal farewell.

Inside the foyer, I meet Clarisse's mom, Jenny, and Uncle George. George must be Jenny's brother, as they both have the same small nose, and the same crooked teeth.

"It's nice to finally meet you, Evelyn," Jenny says. She is young, probably even younger than my mother and Shea. "We've heard so much about you." She looks self-conscious as soon as the words are spoken, shooting a nervous glance at George and then Clarisse.

"I hope you're hungry," George says. "Pizza will be here soon." He wears a Pink Floyd T-shirt and faded black jeans. He's definitely younger than Jenny, probably late twenties.

"Thank you for having me," I say, following my mother's instructions. "And pizza sounds great. I love pizza."

"It's from Cubby's, a great little mom-and-pop place down MLK Boulevard. New York style," he says. "As if there is any other, right?" Jenny smiles and nods in agreement.

"Well, just let us know when it's here," Clarisse says. "Come on, Evelyn. I'll give you the grand tour."

I slip off my sandals and follow her as she shows me around the various rooms of the cavernous house. The kitchen is sprawling with a marble center island, cherry cabinets, and a stainless steel refrigerator. There is a wooden rack hanging over the island, with wineglasses and goblets and flutes hanging upside down from their feet. Above the stove, knives are lined up in a neat row on a magnetic strip, their sharp ends pointed toward the ceiling. There is one knife missing, and I see a bloody handprint in its place for just a moment, until I blink it away. The blades catch the light, shining like diamonds in jewelry store cases. My father shattered those cases with bullets. Crushed glass rained onto the hard floor, sounding like hail in a summer storm.

The family room has a TV and a sectional couch of black leather. Three black dogs (one big, two small) are nestled on the couch, each occupying their own little territory. The big dog lifts his head for a moment and sniffs the air before settling back into position. One of the small dogs chews on something raw and bloody. He holds it between his front paws. It is dark red like a liver. The small dog devours it, his teeth stained pink until I close my eyes for a moment, reminding myself it isn't real.

The hallway leading toward the bedrooms has pastel blue walls and a white ceramic tile floor, cool on my bare feet. Clarisse points out the doors to the four bedrooms—one for her mother, one for George, one for George's exercise equipment, and one for Clarisse. Each closed door looks identical, as if they could all lead to the same place.

Clarisse's bedroom is big and mostly white, with one intensely dark red wall, the color of blood in a vial after it's been drawn from your body. It's not the bright primary red of fresh blood that seeps slowly from small scrapes and cuts, but the darker crimson that flows deep under your skin, inside your veins, that mysterious network of canals and rivers, invisible pathways of life. Clarisse has a queen-size bed outfitted in heather gray sheets and a neon pink comforter.

I sit on it, and it's so puffy I sink, feel the air releasing itself from invisible holes.

"It's goose down," Clarisse says. "My mom and George turn the house into the North Pole at night. I used to hate it, but now I can't stand sleeping in a warm room. I have to be freezing when I sleep. It's just so cozy." The room is indeed a freezer. It even smells cold, which I love, like the scent of the frosted glasses my mother and Shea use for margaritas sometimes, when they remember to chill them ahead of time. Sometimes I'll sneak a lick, my wet tongue on the dry frost of the glass, and it sticks for a moment until I gently tug myself away.

I know there are places where the air is truly cold— naturally cold, not air-conditioned cold—although I've never been to those places. There are places where frost appears on the ground and in the trees and even in your hair if you go outside while it's still wet from the shower. In those places, you can lick a frozen flag- pole or frozen mailbox, anything metal, and get your tongue stuck for real.

Clarisse's room has vaulted ceilings and a floor-to- ceiling window covered with vertical blinds. Their plastic edges make a tiny sound as they move together and apart, set in motion by the hissing AC vent. Clarisse doesn't have any stuffed animals or dolls, no bottles of perfume or nail polish cluttering a vanity. Everything is out of sight.

"Wow, your room is really clean," I say.

"Oh yeah? Well, let me show you something." Clarisse walks over to the double doors that take up half of an entire wall. The doors are white with silver-toned handles curved like question marks on the ends. Clarisse twists the question marks with both hands and swings the doors open with a *ta-da* motion.

It's a large walk-in closet, and inside, there is a fuzzy orange folding chair in a corner. There's a bookshelf littered with makeup instead of books—uncapped tubes of lipstick, half-empty blush compacts, and cylinders of mascara standing on end, arranged in an orderly line. On the bottom shelf are four cans of compressed air, the kind you find at an office supply store, used for cleaning computers and other electronics. Each can has a thin red straw taped to it, which can be placed over the nozzle to make it easy to reach tiny spaces—the intricate circuitry of a laptop or the charging port of a cell phone. There is crumpled clothing pushed to the edges of the small room. Inside-out jeans and T-shirts and socks peek out from the rubble, which includes a few empty plastic water bottles and Pixie Stix candy wrappers, those pastel-swirled straws that hold flavored sugar.

"My mom never comes in here," Clarisse says. "And just in case she ever tries, I keep it locked." She pulls a small silver key from inside her shirt, her bra I'm guessing, although she moves so smoothly it seems as though she just plucked it from a secret compartment inside her rib cage.

Clarisse sits down cross-legged on the floor of the closet, and I join her, matching my shape to hers. I eye the makeup on the shelf, wondering if we'll paint each other's faces, turning ourselves into giant doll heads. All week, I've been imagining the classic sleepover activities we might engage in tonight, the ones you see girls doing in the movies—maybe we'll conjure the dead with a séance or sneak vodka from an unlocked liquor cabinet. I pick up a bottle of nail polish and read the name of the color on the label. *Mint Condition*. It's a chalky pastel green color, and through the frosted glass of the bottle, it looks like green milk.

"You should put that color on your toes," Clarisse says in a voice so casual it makes me smile. This is what a friend sounds like when talking to another friend. The sound of pure ease of conversation, like unconscious speech. I'm out of my mind on Clarisse's friendship right now, her voice cool and comforting as white noise, a box fan whirring in the bedroom corner to lull you to sleep. I shake the nail polish bottle, and the small silver-mixing bead inside makes a lovely little sound, a tiny bell ringing.

I twist open the top of the nail polish bottle, and with the small brush, I sweep *Mint Condition* on my baby toe, concentrating deeply and trying to avoid painting all the skin around my toenail, which is inevitable in spite of my efforts. Clarisse grabs one of the cans of computer duster from the shelf, and pulls the trigger gently to let out just a small whistle of air.

"So have you tried it before?" she asks.

"Yeah, I'm not too bad at it," I say. "See?" I flash my finished baby toe at Clarisse. I go back to biting my tongue gently in concentration as I paint the next-to-baby-toe.

Clarisse laughs. "No, not nail polish. This stuff." She wiggles the can of air close to my face for a moment. Then she puts the nozzle in her mouth, and *sssssssss*—a sharp inhale, like she's breathing in a long ribbon of clouds.

Clarisse rests the can in the triangle of carpet she's created with her thin legs. She waits a few seconds, and then places the nozzle in her mouth again. Another pull of the plastic trigger, another hiss, another inhale, and she smiles without teeth, the biggest grin I've ever seen on a girl in person, as close to an ear-to-ear smile as you can get. I twist the nail polish bottle closed and place it back on the makeup shelf. Clarisse reaches her slender arm toward me, offering the can to me. And I take it.

The small closet becomes smaller, and the walls thin themselves out, transforming into papery palm fronds almost ready to fall from their trees. I think I feel something shift inside the bowl of my skull, but on second thought, no, it's subtler than that, more like a vibration, a small swarm of bees buzzing in the distance. Clarisse is moving her lips, but I only hear the sea—the waves swelling with air, getting fuller and fuller with each inhale.

The doorbell rings in the distance, an entire ocean away from me. I raise my arms toward Clarisse, and she grabs my hands, pulling me to my feet. We walk out of the closet, and position ourselves on Clarisse's bed in typical girl poses—on our stomachs with elbows on the comforter, our heads in our palms. If only we had the slick pages of a teen magazine open nearby.

Uncle George knocks twice before opening Clarisse's bedroom door with one hand, cardboard pizza box balanced on the palm of the other like a waiter's tray. "One New York style with sausage and mushrooms," he says, and his white teeth shine a smile in my direction. He glides over to Clarisse's desk, placing the pizza box down along with paper plates and napkins.

Then he pulls two cold cans of Wild Cherry Pepsi from his jeans pockets—Clarisse's favorite soda.

"Thank you," we say in unison, our girl voices blending like harmony, my voice a little higher than the low lilt of Clarisse's. Everything about her seems dense, filled with heavy air. George smiles and throws us a thumbs-up in our direction with his right hand.

"Enjoy," he says. "Let me know if you need anything."

"We will," Clarisse says. We watch our reflections eat pizza in the mirror above her dresser.

We're each on our second slice of pizza when Clarisse ends the silence.

"So what did your dad do?" she asks. She grabs a napkin and wipes grease from the corner of her mouth.

"Um, he owned a tree service business," I say with my mouth full of cheese. I take a second to chew and swallow. "Mostly palm trees. Planting and removing. Landscaping stuff. What did your dad do?"

"First-degree murder, kidnapping, and capital sexual battery," Clarisse says matter-of-factly. She reaches for another piece of pizza. "Those are the official convictions, but I can give you all the gory details too, if you want."

I laugh nervously, realizing what she meant by her

original question. "Oh, you want to know what my dad *did*."

Clarisse is looking at me through the mirror, her eyes square on mine. "Come on, Evelyn," she says. "I showed you mine. Now you show me yours. Haven't you ever played that game before?"

I look down and stare at my paper plate for a moment, searching for patterns in the grease spots as if they were clouds in the sky. "Mass shooting, I guess you'd call it. I mean, I don't know his actual convictions. He killed twelve people. The Ponce de Leon mall shooting in St. Augustine."

"Oh wow, then he's famous, right?" Clarisse asks and then licks her fingers.

"I guess so."

"My dad was Florida-famous for a while, but most people outside the state have probably forgotten about him by now."

"How long has it been?" I ask, hoping I don't sound overly interested in the answer. In the past, I've had a tendency to ask too many questions when I'm getting to know someone, appearing too invested in knowing every little detail about the person, acting more like an overzealous interviewer than a possible new friend.

"Ten years this year. Happy anniversary, right?" Clarisse says, laughing at her own joke. She gathers our used plates and napkins, stuffs them inside the pizza box, and throws the box on the floor. It lands without a sound. "Where is he?" she asks.

We're having this entire conversation through the mirror, speaking to each other, but also speaking to reflections of ourselves.

"He's on death row. At Raiford. Where is your dad?"

"Same," Clarisse says. She turns her head and smiles at me this time, not at the girl in the mirror. A feeling of relief rushes through me, like ripping off a Band-Aid and realizing that the wound beneath isn't nearly as bad as you had imagined. In fact, if you look closely, you swear you can already see a scab beginning to form, the skin working to rebuild itself, the body's own magic trick.

"Time for dessert now?" I ask, motioning toward the closet. I want to feel that fuzzy feeling again, go back to that gauzy world.

"Hell yeah," Clarisse says, and she grabs me by the wrist. She leads me back inside the small space, where we take turns, one inhale each, until once again there are no sharp lines, no thick boundaries. Everything is blurry. Shoes are piled up in the corner like severed feet. The walls are tinged pink, as if painted with the wisp of a paintbrush dipped in blood.

We both lie on our backs, looking up at the ceiling.

My left elbow touches Clarisse's right elbow, bare skin to bare skin. My brain tingles, the synapses on fire, an engine warming up for liftoff, as though my head could become a rocket ship, detach from my body, and climb up, up, up to the sky.

The sky is nothing like the ocean. It doesn't have an ending, does it? If you send yourself into the sky, will you fly and fly until you reach a boundary, smashing into a wall made of pure blue crystal? In the ocean, you will eventually reach bottom. You will reach the ocean floor, where the strange creatures live without light.

If you travel too far under the sea, your chest will implode—too much pressure exerted upon your body, too much to bear. If you travel too far in the sky, you will explode. Not enough pressure acting upon your body to keep your insides inside. I've always wondered which is a better way to die.

"I have another question for you," Clarisse says to the ceiling. "About your father."

"Okay, shoot," I say, and we both start laughing again. "Sorry," I say when we finally compose ourselves.

"Are you afraid of him?" Clarisse asks.

"No. I've never even met him. He's been locked up since before I was born."

"You've never been to Raiford to visit him?"

"No. Have you been there?"

"Just once. After he was sentenced. My mom wouldn't let me go to the trial, and she said she wanted me to see him one more time before, you know." Clarisse's voice lowers at the end of the sentence.

"What is Raiford like?" I ask. I've imagined visiting my father, sitting across from him in the visiting quarters, a pane of reinforced glass separating us. I've imagined my father's hand reaching for the black telephone receiver so I can hear him, although I've never allowed the daydream to go any further, never allowed myself to actually conjure a voice for him. Still, I imagine how his lips might curl into a smile as he realizes how much I look like him, a young girl version of himself, like a reflection in a magic mirror.

"Scary. And pretty depressing, actually. Which is why we never went back. I remember sitting there and looking at him and wondering if he ever thought about the little girl he killed. She was about my age, and we looked similar. I wondered if I reminded him of her."

"Were there any signs? Before he did it? Did he have a history?"

"No signs, no history. He was just an ordinary guy. It seemed to come out of nowhere. It makes me angry, what he did. But it also makes me afraid . . ."

"Of him? He's away for life. He'll never be able to hurt you or anyone else ever again."

"No, not afraid of him so much, although I guess that's a part of it. More like afraid of myself. Not all the time. But sometimes, when I think about what he did and how he just snapped."

I turn my head toward Clarisse, and she is still looking up at the ceiling. A tear frees itself from the corner of her eye, rolling down her temple. She wipes it away with her fingertip. "I don't know, maybe I'm being crazy, but if there was something in him that made him do it, then maybe that same something is in me. Do you ever think about stuff like that?" Clarisse breathes deeply and holds the air in her lungs for a few seconds, waiting for me to answer.

"We are individuals, just like Greg says. Remember?" My left hand reaches for her right hand, and I lace my fingers with hers. "We get to start from scratch."

Clarisse turns onto her side and exhales, her warm breath tickling my neck. She buries her head in my armpit and slings her other arm across my rib cage.

I feel a pulsing within me, as though I can feel my own heart pumping blood through my veins. My blood, but my father's blood too, and as soon as I think it, I try to stop the idea, the thought that will gather other thoughts and accelerate like a runaway truck if I don't hurry up and slam on the brakes.

To start from scratch didn't begin as a baking phrase. It had to do with a starting line for a race that was drawn or scratched in the dirt. If you started from scratch, it meant you started from the same place as everyone else. You started at zero.

Clarisse and I started at zero when we were born, in spite of what our fathers did. We were born from our mothers' bodies, a mercy that I cling to. Our mothers grew our tiny cells, forming our bodies inside their wombs. Yes, our fathers added ingredients to conjure us into being, but they aren't raising us, aren't doing any of the difficult stuff that comes afterward. And I'm hoping it's the afterward that will matter most for us— the kneading of dough, the waiting for us to rise.

chapter nine

When I open my eyes in the morning, it takes a moment to remember where I am. I've spent so few nights away from home, that my body needs time to adjust. I roll over, and Clarisse is already awake, staring at her phone in her hands.

"About time," she says. "You know you snore, right?"

"I do not!" I pull hardened bits of sleep from my eyelashes.

"Fine. I'll just have to record you next time," Clarisse says, and my heart quickens as I think of *next time*.

"What are you doing?" I ask. I grab my phone from the nightstand, sit up, and move closer to her.

"Lurking on Instagram," she says. "I have someone I need to check up on every now and then."

"Keep your enemies close, right?"

"And your ex-boyfriends closer. This is Jake," she says, tapping his image on her screen with her fingernail. "Just look at him. He's so fucking perfect I want to die." She scrolls through his Instagram feed, showing me a picture of him behind the wheel of a black convertible. "He's rich too. His parents are both doctors." She scrolls some more, and stops on a photo of Jake shirtless on the beach. "And he loved going down on me. *Loved* it."

"What happened?" I ask.

"He graduated and then went to FSU. He said he wanted to do the long-distance thing with me, but then he started dating this fake bitch." She clicks to a girl's profile. "Just look at her smile," she says. "Her teeth are so blinding white, it's obnoxious. She's like a brainless Barbie doll." She scrolls through the photo feed to show me—beach Barbie posing in a string bikini with her hands on her hips, drunk Barbie holding a red Solo cup, Jake hugging her from behind.

"I have someone I like to check up on too," I say. I unlock my phone and start swiping through my camera roll, looking for the right screen shot to show her.

"Oooh, an ex? Let me see." She cuddles up to me, resting her chin on my shoulder so she can see my screen.

"No, not an ex. Just this guy I know online. He's cute, right?" I look at Clarisse from the corner of my eye, watching for her reaction as she considers the photo.

"Yeah, he has that scruffy professor vibe going on. Have you met offline?"

"No, we've never met. He's not from around here. He lives close to Gainesville."

"Shit, then you should definitely go hook up with him sometime. I'll come with. I'm not really into older guys, but you can just drop me off at UF. I'm sure I'll find a party to stumble into." Clarisse smiles at the idea and then turns her attention back to Jake's feed, examining a photo of him riding a waverunner. "What's your guy's name?" she asks.

"Andy," I say. I lock my phone, making him disappear.

I open *The Catalog of Everything I've Done Wrong*, add an entry: lied to someone, even though they might be the only person who could understand the truth.

chapter ten

At Wavelengths tonight, Greg is talking about judgment. Specifically, he's telling us that we have a right not to be judged, blamed, or labeled because of a parent's incarceration.

"It's important to remember that, if someone is judging you, that's their action. They are making that judgment through their lens, their experience. And it has nothing to do with you." I'm looking down at my feet, not because judgment-and-blame-and-labeling talk makes me uncomfortable, but because I'm afraid I might burst into flames if I look at Clarisse. It's a special kind of fire—it feels so good it hurts. If I'm not careful with Clarisse, I'll burn and burn until I'm unrecognizable, nothing but charred remains.

"None of you are to blame for any of this." Greg has his overly serious face on now. His eyebrows lose their arches, forming straight lines above his eyes, and he purses his lips, as if he's just tasted something slightly sour and he's trying to camouflage his reaction. "It's a completely normal feeling—to feel *responsible*—but it's just not true. Feeling blame can lead to guilt. And guilt is not a useful emotion. It's not a part of the journey."

Greg reads a passage from his therapist book, a large white binder that he keeps in his messenger bag. "Guilt and shame often go hand in hand. The same action may give rise to feelings of both shame and guilt, where the former reflects how we feel about *ourselves* and the latter involves awareness that our actions have injured *someone else*." He reads to the group the way I remember elementary school teachers reading aloud to the class, looking up from the text every so often to make eye contact with the audience. "In other words, shame relates to self, guilt to others." Greg is wearing a black collared shirt tonight with tiny silver snaps instead of buttons. It's a long-sleeved shirt, but he has the sleeves rolled up to his elbows. I stare at the dark hair on his forearms, another focal point to distract me from Clarisse, who is pitching heat into the room like a girl-shaped furnace.

"Guilt is a feeling of responsibility or remorse for some offense, crime, or wrong. Shame is the painful feeling that arises from the consciousness of something dishonorable, improper, etc., done by oneself or another." The room appears generally unimpressed with these definitions, but Greg continues. "So guilt involves the awareness of having done something wrong; it arises from our actions. Shame is a painful feeling about how we appear to others (and to ourselves) and doesn't necessarily depend on our having done anything."

He pauses to take a sip from his water bottle. "Here's a hypothetical. If I say something hurtful to a friend, I might feel guilty because I hurt my friend. More painfully, I might also feel ashamed that I am the sort of person who would behave that way. Guilt arose as a result of inflicting pain on somebody else; I felt shame in relation to myself."

I think about my own offenses, flipping through *The Catalog of Everything I've Done Wrong*. Was it wrong to lie to Clarisse about Andy? Was it even a lie? Andy *is* someone I know online, after all. Andy *does* live near Gainesville, after all. The truth slips from my hands, a silvery fish that shimmers as it swims away.

Greg makes an *a-ha!* face, his physical cue that we should be nearing an epiphany. "It's really important to remember that none of you have done anything wrong. You aren't responsible for the actions of your parents. Not by the wildest stretch of the imagination did any of you have anything to do with why your parents are where they are."

Brandon raises his hand slightly, his fingertips just above the top of his head. Greg gives him a little glance and then makes a soft stop sign in the air with his hand, a signal to dismiss Brandon's question because we already know what it is.

Brandon often wonders if the things we discuss at Wavelengths apply to him because, as he says, his situation is "very unique." Every time he reminds us of his unique situation, I want to quote *Fight Club*: *You are not special. You are not a beautiful and unique snowflake.*

I could recite Brandon's story from memory, but he would probably enjoy that too much, would be smitten with the idea of me paying that much attention to him. Brandon harassed a girl at his school. He posted despicable things about her online and wrote *whore* sixty-nine times on her locker with a Sharpie. He told everyone at school that she had given him HIV, that she was a prostitute on the weekends, and that her family sacrificed animals in satanic rituals. He poured maple syrup in her hair during a pep rally. He threw rotten eggs against her bedroom window and tried to kidnap her dog.

The school counselors did "everything they could."

The local police did "everything they could." The girl's family was planning to move out of town. They had already withdrawn the girl from school.

Still, the harassment continued, and the girl's mother finally got fed up with it. So the girl's mother went to Brandon's house one day to confront Brandon's mother in the driveway as she was getting into her car. The two women started shouting at each other. Then the girl's mother pushed Brandon's mother. And that's when the little worm in Brandon's mother spoke up. You know that little worm . . . we all have one inside us, lying dormant, burrowing deeper and deeper inside until that moment when the tripwire is activated, the machinery engaged.

Brandon's mother beat the girl's mother so severely that she was in a medically induced coma for a week. Her brain was so traumatized that they had to take the top of her skull off to make room for the swelling.

I wish Greg would take Brandon's question. I would like to hear Greg try to explain how Brandon isn't even the least bit responsible for his mother serving a fifteen-year prison sentence for attempted murder. Events happen in a chain—a chain Brandon started when he typed that first message online. He kept adding links to the chain. When he uncapped the Sharpie. When he bought the eggs and let them sit in the backseat of his car in the blazing sun so they would rot. Brandon's mother was just another link caught up in Brandon's chain. She's in the women's prison now, and Brandon is here, sweating in a folding aluminum chair with the rest of us. I wish Greg would tell us all why Brandon shouldn't feel guilty. *People are the choices they make*, I can hear him say in response. *Your parents made their choices, and you make yours.*

Still looking at my feet, I begin to get that feeling of being stared at, and I know who's doing the staring. I feel weak, forget my resolve, and look up. Clarisse is smiling at me. I make the choice to smile back. *That's all we are—each and every one of us—choices.*

After the mouse incident, my mother transferred me to public school, deciding that a no-frills education would be better for me. I made a choice to turn down my energy. I practiced and practiced every chance I got. I twisted the dial at school, notch by notch, until I felt I could blend seamlessly into the atmosphere, making it easier to put on the brakes if needed. I realized I could make myself nearly invisible if I tried hard enough and concentrated long enough. For a long while, it seemed to work like a charm, a talisman to ward off my mother's worry.

I would make the smallest movements possible, as if I were balancing a heavy book on my head, learning how to be a pageant contestant. I would sit at my desk, my arms quietly resting at my sides. I would try not to stir up too many vibrations. It worked for years.

But then came junior high and Tina Bristol, and my energy started rising again. In *The Catalog of Everything I've Done Wrong*, it starts in eighth grade on a Friday afternoon, when Tina and I volunteered to clean the chalkboard erasers.

We had to go underneath the cafeteria stairwell, where there was a little alcove in which the eraser-cleaning machine lived. It was bizarre, actually, a relic from the past. The machine was very loud when you turned it on, and it sucked the chalk dust out of erasers, collecting it in a blue bag that inflated itself with air as it worked. There was a metal tray on the top of the machine upon which you placed the dusty eraser, moving it back and forth. Then you flipped a switch (like a light switch on the wall) and presto! The machine went to work, devouring the chalk dust and rendering the eraser almost good as new.

When it was just the two of us, the atmosphere changed. I felt a subtle shift, a sensation of pressure building, although I couldn't quite put my finger on it, couldn't give a name to the feeling.

Tina and I started spending lunch period in the library together. After eating our peanut butter and jelly sandwiches, we'd make fun of book titles or invent our own parodies of them, lampooning the dramatic-looking covers of old books from the seventies and eighties that often resembled paintings, depicting teenagers' faces looking serious or sad or elated.

Tina Bristol had a mother and a father and three older brothers. They owned an RV and loved the outdoors, making frequent trips to the RV park in Bartow and canoeing on the Peace River, the men of the family pulling bass and snook from the water to fix on the grill that evening. Tina had a toughness about her, a no-nonsense sort of approach to people and things. She wasn't easily upset and knew how to stand her ground around the boys in school who would try and snap our bras or trip us on the way to the pencil sharpener. And she didn't flinch at kids who hurled insults, the bullies who only wanted to hurt others with their words. *They are the broken ones*, Tina told me. *Not us.*

The last day of eighth grade, Tina and I stayed after to help our English teacher pack up her classroom. We removed the decorative edging from the two bulletin boards that flanked her desk. We squatted under chairs and scraped away dried chewing gum of various colors with small putty knives. We took inventory of novels and textbooks, counting and recording them on a clipboard, and then piled them on a cart with wheels. We rolled the cart to the elevator, which we rode to the third floor of the building to deposit them in the book room, a small closet that smelled like musty paper and ink.

The door to the book room was propped open with a small wooden wedge when we arrived. We moved our books from the cart to the shelves, tucking them into their beds for the summer among volumes of Scholastic Readers, hardback editions of *Holes*, and paperbacks copies of *Tiger Eyes* and *The Diary of Anne Frank*.

If I ever forget what happened next, I can open *The Catalog of Everything I've Done Wrong*, remember how I tried the doorknob, noticing it was locked. How I slid the wedge out from under the door, and it slammed shut. How Tina screamed from inside until her voice was raw. How she pounded her fists against the heavy door. How I listened from the other side.

chapter eleven

I'm working on homework, solving algebraic fractions on a worksheet I printed from my laptop. Fractions are important, Miss Apploff says in her video lectures, one mathematical concept we will actually use in real life. It's important to know how to divide things up, how to turn a whole into parts, how to make parts whole again.

I wish it were that simple with people. If you're missing something, you could just find your complement, your common denominator, become an equation, and make yourself solvable.

But I know that's not the way it works. The word *fraction* comes from fracture, which means to break. There are many words for breaking something. Destroy, smash, crack, cut, split, splinter. There aren't as many words for healing, for putting things back together again.

I always work in pencil for math problems because it's easier to erase mistakes. When I'm finished, I'll scan the worksheet and upload it online, beaming it over Wi-Fi signal for Miss Apploff to review. In algebra, you always have to show your work. The answer alone doesn't matter so much. What matters is how you got there.

I've worked halfway down the page when the doorbell rings, its high-pitched ding drawing attention to how quiet the apartment has been all morning. I look through the peephole and see the mail carrier smiling back at me, his facial features slightly enlarged, an effect of the curved lens. He's an older man with shaggy gray hair peeking out from under his navy blue sun hat. I reach for the brass door chain, slide it across, and open the door.

"Just need a signature for return receipt on this, miss." He hands me a large white envelope with a green card attached and points out the spot for me to sign by the X. He retrieves a pen from his shirt pocket, clicking the end before handing it to me. As I sign my name, I try to decipher the return address from the corner of my eye, wondering if it's something for my mother from the state, maybe a renewal notice for her Child Development Associate credential. The mail carrier removes the green card from the envelope, tearing it at the perforations. He places it inside his mailbag and then hands the envelope over to me, along with the rest of our mail.

"Thanks," he says with a smile. He raises his eyebrows as he turns and walks away.

I put the stack of mail on the kitchen table, flipping through a few bills and a copy of *The Paris Review* for Shea, until I reach the large white envelope. There are three stamps on the top-right corner and a large postmark of thick black ink stamped over them. It's addressed to *Mira Gibson and Evelyn Gibson*. The words are small, the letters very neat, running straight across the envelope. When I write without lines, my words inevitably slant upward, no matter how hard I try to keep them level. A teacher once told me that according to handwriting analysis, upward writing means the writer is an optimist.

I read the return address.

Michael Hayes
DC#353091
23916 NW 83rd Avenue
Raiford, FL 32026

When you read words, you hear them in your mind's voice, and when you haven't read certain words in a very long time, they sound strange, even inside your brain, even though you aren't saying them out loud. Of course I know my father's name is Michael— it was the most popular name for a boy born in 1975. Of course I know that he's in Raiford, a place that exists in the middle of the state, even though I've never been there, even though I've never even wanted to think about the word. Now I stare at it, imagining all the other ways it could be spelled. *Ray Ferd. Ray Ford. Rae Ford.* It could be a man's name or a woman's name.

The envelope is crinkled at the corner, as though it's traveled halfway across the world to reach me, instead of only two hundred miles from Raiford to Pass-a-Grille. I imagine my father's hands tucking paper into the envelope, my father with pen in hand. His right or left? It occurs to me that I don't even know— addressing the envelope so neatly, taking his time, for really that is all my father really has now—time.

The envelope feels light in my hands, a feather with words inside. I want to open it, but opening it will be an act of letting him into my life, allowing his words to reach me, and I'm not sure I can fathom that. Fathom is a unit of measure, a way to test the depths of the ocean. But to fathom something also means to understand. In the Old English, it meant *the outstretched arms*, as though you could reach your arms out wide and embrace the ocean—a way to comprehend, to make sense of something so vast, so senseless.

I run my hands along the edges of the envelope, wishing I could divine its contents without opening, like a fortune-teller or mystic who could predict the words within. I've always been fascinated by psychics and palm readers, all those mysterious people who promise to tell you the future. A long time ago, my mother would take me to a woman named Bianca, a psychic who worked out of a small bungalow behind the boardwalk on Madeira Beach, a neon sign in her living room window pulsing red and pink—$10 SPECIAL.

Inside, I would sit across from her at a small round table draped in purple linen. The window air conditioner would tick and hum, and Miss B, as she wanted to be called, would give me a piece of crystal. She would instruct me to hold on to it while she asked me four questions. Her voice was soft and low as she explained the process. "I'm going to ask you four questions and four questions only. Your answers to these four questions will tell me everything I need to know."

My mother would sit on the white wicker love seat in the corner, but I wouldn't look at her. I would pretend that she wasn't there. It was easier to answer the questions if I believed it was only me and Miss B in the room.

There are things you know in the very very dark core of yourself. You don't know how they got there, but you know they are real. Sometimes I dream that my brain is the sea, layered with strange creatures you can't see from the surface. You have to dive down, down, down, to get to the heart of yourself, to go beneath everything you think you know.

I slide my finger under the sealed flap of the envelope and free it from the adhesive. I reach inside, pull out the single sheet of paper inside, with cursive writing in blue ink.

Dear Mira & Evelyn,

I hope you are both doing well. I thought about calling but I wasn't sure if either of you would want to speak to me so I'm writing instead.

Unfortunately, I have some bad news. My mother died. Mira, you know how much Ella loved Evelyn. She had a Limoges butter dish from France that she wanted Evelyn to have. There is a lawyer in Treasure Island representing Ella's estate named Dana Apple. Her phone number is (727) 555-8989. You can contact her, and she'll make arrangements to get the dish to you.

If you want to write to me, that would be great. I would be really happy to hear from you. You can use the return address on this envelope to reach me. Make sure you include my DC number. And just so you know, all of my mail is monitored.

Sincerely,
Michael

I go back to my laptop, search "Limoges butter dish," and find that Limoges is a city in France, not a brand name. Any hard-paste porcelain made in that area from 1771 to the present can be classified as Limoges. The pieces are collectible, and valuable enough that there are counterfeits to look out for, articles that explain how to spot a fake.

We don't store our butter in a porcelain dish. We simply buy the spreadable stuff that comes in its own plastic tub. Perhaps my grandmother was an old-fashioned woman? According to her obituary, she was born in 1947, so maybe she grew up with a mother who taught her old-fashioned ways. Online it says that Limoges porcelain was a popular part of a young woman's hope chest, along with linens and other household items she would take to her new home after marriage.

I put the letter back in its envelope and take it to my room, sliding it into the space between my mattress and box spring. I open *The Catalog of Everything I've Done Wrong* and add an entry for today: hid something important from my mother.

I've had dreams about my father contacting me, but he calls instead of writing a letter. In these dreams, I get to the point of the phone ringing, my mother announcing that it's my father on the line, but the scene ends just as I put the receiver to my lips. Just like that, the dream world dissolves, and I say *hello, hello* in my mind until I realize I'm awake.

I go out to the patio, through the sliding glass door, and sit on one of the plastic Adirondack chairs. I stare straight out into the space in front of me, toward the inlet. I let my eyes slide out of focus, letting the edges blur until I have that feeling that my two eyes have merged to become one. I like looking at the world like this, through my one blurred eye. Everything softens and curves, all the sharp angles removed. The problem is that, once I become aware that this is happening, it usually stops so I've found that the trick is not to acknowledge what's happening at all. If I want to stay in this trance, it's better not to think about it.

chapter twelve

My mother found the letter when she was pulling the sheets off my bed for the laundry. She deals best with unpleasant conversations when we're in public, which is why she interrogates me about hiding the letter while we're at the self-checkout line at Winn-Dixie.

"It's an outrageous violation of my trust, Evelyn," she says in a steady, emotionless voice, the one she uses to convey seriousness.

We each have our roles. My mother scans. The glowing red eye of the self-service machine reads the hidden information in every barcode. The conveyor belt sends each item to the bagging area, where my waiting hands place them into plastic bags.

"He wrote, *Mira, you know how much Ella loved Evelyn*," I say as I bag cans of green beans. "What did he mean by that?"

"He meant exactly what he wrote," she says. She scans two loaves of bread—*beep, beep*—and they ride the belt to the end of the lane. I scoop them up gently for they are delicate bodies that must be handled with care. "But that's not what I want to discuss. I want to discuss you deliberately hiding the letter from me, when you know damn well that it's important. It was also addressed to me, Evelyn. You don't have the right to keep something like that from me. It's unacceptable."

"Okay, but why did he address that statement to you? Why didn't he just say, *Ella loved Evelyn*?"

"Well, I'm not in his head so I can't tell you why he wrote what he wrote." She's trying her best to remain nonchalant, but I can tell she's bothered by my question. "I still haven't heard an apology for hiding it from me."

"I'm sorry, Mom. I really am. I guess I thought the letter would upset you. Now what about the lawyer?" I ask.

"What about her?"

"When are you going to call her?"

"I'll get around to it."

"When?"

"When I get around to it, Evelyn." My mother scans the final item and follows the robotic voice prompts to complete the sale. When the little printer spits out the receipt, she grabs it, crumpling it into the front pocket of her shorts. "I didn't realize you were so excited to get a butter dish." I push the cart, and she walks next to me. We pass through the automatic sliding doors and step out onto the hot asphalt of the parking lot.

"Well, I wouldn't say *excited*, but I am curious. I've never inherited anything. Let alone something collectible from France."

"I'll call this week and get her to ship it to you, okay?"

I don't respond. My mother pops the trunk open, and we load the grocery bags inside.

"Okay?" she tries again. Then says, "Evelyn, isn't that what you want?" She closes the trunk, and we get in the car. She starts the engine and immediately rolls all the windows down so the stifling heat can begin to escape.

"Well, I was thinking. Treasure Island isn't that far," I say. "I thought maybe we could just go there and pick up the butter dish ourselves. In person. Maybe I could even see Ella's house?"

"Ev, I don't know if that's a good idea."

"But why? It's not like Ella will be there. She's dead." It's not a nice way to end a sentence, I know, but it gets my mother's attention in a way that most other words don't. She looks over at me, and I can feel her thinking about death—my soon-to-be-dead father at Raiford, my dead grandmother whose last dying wish was for me to have her French butter dish.

"You really want to go?" my mother asks.

"Yes, I really do."

She turns on the radio, and The Decemberists start singing a song about a joint suicide. If you don't listen to the words, if you just let the jaunty accordion carry you away, you can be fooled into thinking it's a song about something happy and uplifting, not a suicide pact made by two lovers from different parts of town.

"Fine, Evelyn. We'll go to Treasure Island. Give me some time to arrange it."

"Thanks, Mom."

"You're welcome," she says, and she reaches over and pats my knee with the soft palm of her hand, before putting the car in gear.

I feel bad asking my mother for things. She's already given me so much. She gave me life, and although it sounds cliché, it's true. There is something to be said for the person who nurtured you with their own body, keeping you safe inside them for nearly a year, and then endured incredible pain to birth you into existence.

How difficult it all must have been for her. Giving

birth to a baby, pushing and crying and panting in a hospital room while the baby's father lived in a prison cell, a room with only hard surfaces, nothing soft to comfort him. My mother pushed me into the world in spite of her circumstances. She brought me to life, and then she kept breathing in and out, waking up each morning and going to bed each night. She bought me baby clothes and bathed me. She sang to me, and she planned my meals. She took me to Sears for photos for my first Christmas. She dressed me in a red velvet jumper with white trim. My mother did all of these things because she wanted to, not because she had to. I know that. I know there were options, and I don't blame her if she ever considered them. She didn't have the answers, and the questions were difficult, but she kept asking them. She kept figuring it out. My mother went on living, went on loving me, even though there must have been voices, real or imaginary, telling her to do otherwise. And for that, I can't help but love her back.

chapter thirteen

The mall in Clearwater has an ice-skating rink in center court, a nice feature, since we are forced to perform all of our winter activities indoors. In real winter, most people can ice-skate outside, on a frozen lake under the dark blue of night, their bodies bundled in layers against the cold air.

On the second floor, Clarisse and I rest our bare elbows on the polished silver railing and lean over to watch a girl in a dark green velour bodysuit. She practices single axels across the center of the ice, her hair pulled into a tight bun, her skates the same nude color as her tights. It's hard to determine where her feet end and her legs begin. Her skates are sharp—they make a piercing sound as she carves the ice. I see her nick the surface with her toe pick, bringing her body to a hard stop. She pulls one skate from her foot and drags the blade across her throat. It's sharp

enough to slice tender flesh. Her mouth makes a gur-
gling sound. I see blood pouring from her carotid
artery, soaking the green velour. I remind myself it's
not real.

I feel uneasy inside enclosed malls like this and
prefer open-air shopping centers where you can walk
outside between stores. There are no windows here,
no natural light, no signs of the outside world. My
father knew what he was doing when he chose Ponce
de Leon Mall in St. Augustine for his crime scene. I
look around me and think of how easy it would be
to open fire on these unsuspecting people. The exit
doors are so far away. How many would make it out
alive?

Clarisse and I share ice cream from Marble Slab
Creamery, where they mix in toppings of your choice
right in front of you. The boy behind the counter
scooped chocolate ice cream onto a cold slab of marble and added rainbow sprinkles, white chocolate
chips, and miniature peanut butter cups, folding and
mixing with two small stainless steel spades until they
were evenly distributed, a colorful sprinkle in each
bite. He then scraped the entire concoction into the
waffle cone bowl that Clarisse now passes to me as
she licks a speck of ice cream from the corner of her
mouth.

My mother took me to Ponce de Leon Mall once, just before we moved away from St. Augustine. I was five and needed dress shoes for a children's chorus recital we were having at school. I remember my mother pulling me along by the hand because I wasn't walking fast enough. She was in a hurry, rushing me to try on black patent leather Mary Janes, rushing to pay the clerk and get back to the car. I didn't realize the importance of the place at the time but now I wish I could go back to Ponce de Leon, recording the sights and sounds and smells, taking in all the details of the last place my father existed as a free man.

I dig the spoon into the sweetness to create the perfect bite for myself just as three teenage girls approach us from behind. I can feel their presence, their energy hovering close, so warm and textured I swear I could reach out and touch it, as though angst were something tangible, something you could roll between your fingers, squeeze within your palm. One of the girls taps Clarisse on the shoulder, and Clarisse turns around with a laugh already on her lips.

"What are you assholes doing here?" Clarisse asks the group. "I didn't think they let Armwood rats mix with the rest of society." I swallow the ice cream in my mouth and feel the cold travel down my throat, a freezing sensation shocking my chest as though my stomach is on fire and the ice cream is putting out the blaze. I turn around, wiping my mouth with a napkin.

A girl with blond hair stained purple at the ends speaks first. "Trying on prom dresses, what else? The mall in Brandon is shit. Plus everyone is shopping there. We want to be unique." She's wearing tight black shorts and a flowing bohemian-style top—it's so sheer and white I can see her black bra underneath, her breasts pushed together by the padding and underwire. Her fingernails are long and pointy and painted pink with gold glittery stripes. She swings her hair over her shoulder, runs one nail along her temple, and then eyes me up and down. "I'm Samantha," she tells me. "And you're Evelyn, right?"

She looks me in the eyes, and for a moment, I fear that I'm turning five different shades of red from embarrassment that this girl knows my name and is looking at me while I stand here in cutoff jeans and a Care Bears T-shirt, holding a giant waffle cup full of ice cream.

"Yes, hi," I say. "I'm Evelyn." I force a weak smile.

"This is Ashley, and this is Emily," Samantha says, and each girl nods unenthusiastically as her name is mentioned. Samantha moves closer to Clarisse, putting one arm around her shoulder. "You are a goddamn sight for sore eyes," she tells her. "Where the hell have you been hiding?" She then whispers something into Clarisse's ear, and Clarisse covers her mouth to stifle a laugh.

"I've been around. You just weren't looking hard enough," Clarisse tells her. Ashley and Emily keep their distance, both looking down at their cell phones as Samantha and Clarisse talk quietly. I see Samantha hand something off quickly to Clarisse. Then I see Clarisse shove something into the waistband of her shorts. Samantha gives Clarisse a hug and then turns to her sidekicks, who put their phones away in unison and appear to stand up a little straighter, as though waiting for further instruction.

"It was nice to meet you, Evelyn," Samantha tells me, looking me right in the eyes. Samantha's lips are painted dark pink, her eyeliner black and perfectly winged at each corner, her eyes resembling a beautiful cat's.

"It was nice to meet you too, Samantha," I say back, an obedient bird who learns to mimic when necessary.

The girls walk away, and Clarisse and I turn back toward the ice. A birthday party is getting started, a dozen small children clinging to the edges of the rink as they attempt to carve the ice, their young bodies not heavy enough to leave traces on the surface.

"They sure seem nice," I tell Clarisse, although my voice doesn't sound like I'm sure of anything. I pass Clarisse the ice cream, and she scrapes the bottom of the bowl with her spoon, one last bite of ice cream and peanut butter cup. She nibbles on the edges of the waffle cone bowl.

"They do?" Clarisse asks, a question as answer.

"Well, they're your friends so they must be all right," I say.

"Yeah, Samantha is definitely all right," Clarisse says. She reaches into her waistband and pulls out something thin and white. I don't get a good look at it until she presses it into my palm and closes my fingers around it. It feels light and delicate, barely register-ing as weight in my hand. I open my fingers slightly to peek and quickly realize it's a joint. I try my best to camouflage the expression of surprise on my face, suddenly worried about the mall cop we saw on a Segway earlier, patrolling the polished halls, looking for would-be criminals.

"Relax," Clarisse says softly, "I'll carry it." She takes the joint back, tucking it back into her waistband, and we start walking.

"Where are we going?" I ask.

"Out to the parking garage. Just trust me," Clarisse requests, and of course I follow her. Of course I trust her.

"Is Samantha a drug dealer? Did she just sell you drugs? In the mall?" I ask as we walk, lowering my voice so the mothers pushing strollers don't hear me as they pass.

"No, of course not," Clarisse says. "She just gave it to me. She likes to share. Her boyfriend's brother has a connection so she's pretty much always holding."

We reach the parking garage and climb the stairs to the top level, where most people avoid parking because they don't want their cars becoming too hot in the unrelenting heat. The sky is completely cloudless today—so clear and blue you wonder if you could swim the sky like an ocean, paddling your body through invisible waves.

Once we're sure the coast is clear, we sit down on the hot concrete side by side. Clarisse lights the joint, takes one hit, and then passes it to me. "It's very mellow," she assures me.

I hold the joint between my thumb and index finger, copying Clarisse's technique. I inhale, feel the smoke in my lungs for a moment until I exhale, and pass it back to Clarisse. I start coughing, covering my mouth with both hands to muffle the sound.

"Easy now," Clarisse whispers. "Think about something distracting. Like Greg naked."

"Oh my God, what? No!" My coughing dissolves into hacking, and I elbow Clarisse in the ribs. My limbs feel lighter, my body more flexible from the weed. "He's like our older brother or something. I can't think of him like that."

"Well I *can*, and I do," Clarisse says, and then she makes her eyes roll back in her head a bit and puts on a theatrical moan. "Oh, Greg, oh, Greg, yeah, pull out that big binder, Greg." She takes one more hit from the joint and then stubs it out on the cement next to her. "Come on, Evelyn. You're telling me you've never thought about Greg while masturbating?"

"Clarisse! You're a bad girl!"

"Wait, are you saying you *don't* masturbate?" Clarisse stands up, tucking the remains of the joint into her front pocket. "Evelyn, this is an emergency. Let's just go get you a vibrator. They have them at Spencer's in the mall."

"This is not an emergency."

"Well, you don't know what you're missing. But hey, you can always go manual." She puts a hand up in the air, laughing as she wiggles her fingers. Then she grabs my hand and leads me toward the parking garage stairs. "Here's a tip for when you try it," she says softly in my ear. "Just think of Greg getting you from behind. I'm sure he likes doggy style." Clarisse barks as we float down the stairs and onto the street. I laugh until I can barely breathe. We walk about half a mile to a nearby playground.

We sit on the swings after kicking off our shoes. We pump our legs to make our bodies move. Boys play basketball on the cement court next to us, shirtless and glistening in sweat. I watch their bodies as they glide and jump, weaving around each other to move the ball toward the hoop, my stoned brain mesmerized by their beauty.

I see one boy grab another by the shoulders, slamming his head onto the hard concrete. He tries to get up, but before he can stand, another boy runs over, and kicks him in the face. Blood splatters on the court. I have to watch. Then remind myself it isn't real.

"You're right though, Evelyn," Clarisse says. She swings higher and higher, and with each descent, her hair floats as if underwater.

"About what?"

"I *am* a bad girl."

"Oh, I was just kidding." I pump my legs with more force, attempting to catch up with her, but I can't make her height no matter how hard I try.

"It's okay. It's true."

"Clarisse, you're not bad because you think about Greg that way. Thoughts don't make you bad."

"Oh really? Well, what if I think about other stuff too?"

"What other stuff?" I dig my heels into the dirt to slow down and eventually come to a complete stop, a small cloud of dust around my ankles. Deep inside, somewhere at the very bottom of me, a small voice hopes that Clarisse will never answer, that she will just allow the question to spin and swirl, a skater making endless figure eights on the surface of the ice.

"Sometimes I think about what it would be like to kill someone." Clarisse swings forward and then back, and just when she's at the highest point, she frees her hands from the chains she's been holding on to so tightly and allows her body to fly from the swing, her hair fanning out as she cuts through the muggy air.

I hear the boys on the basketball court, the noises they make as they move the ball down the court, defending themselves, trying to steal, using their bodies to win or lose. I feel the sweat pooled inside my bra, my damp T-shirt clinging to my back.

"That still doesn't make you bad, Clarisse. Thoughts are not the same as actions."

Clarisse turns around and walks toward me and then sits down at my feet, hugging her knees to her chest. She looks up at me, and I swear that her eyes are shimmering pink, reflecting that rose-gold glow of near dusk that is all around us now.

"Maybe that's true for other people. For normal people. Not me. What if that's how it started? With my father? What if it started as thoughts, and it grew and grew until it became more than that?" She pulls the collar of her T-shirt up to her face to wipe the shiny tears that are now running down her cheeks.

"Your father is sick, Clarisse. Mine is too. They are fucked-up."

"Yeah, they *are* fucked-up, so what does that make us? Second-generation fucked-up. Maybe you don't get it. Maybe you don't understand how it feels. It's like when Dr. Jekyll locked himself up in his study. He knew he was becoming Mr. Hyde, and he knew he couldn't stop it."

"You're not a monster, Clarisse. You're not roaming the streets at nights murdering innocent children."

"Did you know we lived in a trailer park when it happened?" Clarisse asks, but she doesn't give me time to respond or react; she just keeps talking. "There was a little girl who lived next to us with her mom. My father climbed in that little girl's bedroom through her unlocked window. He woke her up and said it was time to play a game. He led her out of the window and into the woods behind the trailer park, way out past the lake, and told her they were going to play hide and seek. He told her that her mother was already out there, hiding, and that he would help her find her. They walked and walked and eventually..." Clarisse's voice trails off, low and ragged. She hugs her knees tighter, making her body as small as possible.

I see Clarisse's father and the little girl in the distance. I can't freeze the frame. I have to watch. He is young and handsome. He holds the little girl's hand. She wears a purple nightgown, a thin ruffle at the hem. Her eyes search the dark, her body tunes itself, tries to locate her mother's vibrations. He whispers in her ear. *Keep going, keep going.* He pats her on the head.

"She was my age, Evelyn. We played together. We set up a tea party in my bedroom one day, and my father sat there with us smiling and laughing and drinking invisible tea from a pink cup, and the whole time he was thinking about strangling her and raping her. Slitting her throat and wrapping her body in a garbage bag."

He whispers again. *We're almost there, honey.* Something starts to pool inside of her—a fear that churns slowly, picking up speed as they walk. She wants to turn back now. He feels her fear, knows it's almost time. She calls for her mother, her voice warm and small in the night. He covers her mouth with one hand while wrapping the long fingers of the other around her neck. *Don't you dare make another sound.*

I feel an idea forming inside me. It begins in my feet and then moves to my legs, making them feel restless and warm. As the idea gains momentum, it continues to rise up through me. It follows my nerves, that spidery network of highways and byways that allow the body to feel. People look like maps on the inside, all these channels that usher fluids and proteins and oxygen—all those ingredients of being human that we don't even have to think about.

"Listen to me, Clarisse. Whatever fucked your father up, whatever made him kill that little girl, it isn't in you." I put my hand on her head, stroking her hair. She flinches at my touch at first, like an animal, wild and unsure, but I keep going, smoothing her hair gently with my fingertips until her breathing slows. "And I can prove it."

She looks up at me now and raises one eyebrow. "How?"

It's simple, so clear to me now. I'll test Clarisse, conducting an experiment of sorts. I'll put her in a situation where she has the opportunity to kill someone. I'll let her prove she isn't a murderer. Clarisse isn't a murderer because, you see, a murderer isn't made on the day she's born, the day she's pushed from a mother's womb, sent down the birth canal to land crying and gasping into waiting hands. A murderer is born on the day she kills.

I sit down on the ground next to Clarisse and whisper my idea in her ear. She listens, and eventually she whispers back. Sometimes, the imagery is too easy. Unraveling a tapestry begins by pulling a single thread. Rivers begin as wading pools you can walk across with just a few steps, before they rush wider and wider, curve into muscular currents. The test begins as a pinprick—a scratching at the surface of a scab, to see what it might feel like to rip it off completely. We'll start slowly and see what it's like to tear just a corner of the dried blood, rip the almost skin that is trying to heal itself. When that doesn't hurt, when that starts to feel good, we'll pick some more and we'll peel some more and we'll scratch some more until the wound is reopened, and even though blood is rising to the surface like a small red pond, we won't feel the pain.

By the time the sun has disappeared completely, by the time we've walked back to the mall, where my mother and Shea are waiting to pick us up, my feelings are set in stone, and I am sure of what we must do. The test will save Clarisse. The test will save both of us.

chapter fourteen

LETTERS FROM THE DEATH HOUSE

Dear Sis,

Last night I decided I should figure out what I believe in when it comes to the afterlife. So I thought about it, and I decided that I don't believe in heaven or hell. You know I never paid any mind in church when mom dragged us there every now and then. It seemed really fake to me, like something adults just made up to scare kids. I don't believe there's one place where everyone goes, where you meet up with other dead people. I believe you just go to your own place, like you can make your own heaven. It's a nice thing to think about, really it is. It's been on my mind all day now so I thought I'd pick up a pen and put my thoughts on paper and send them to you.

I want my heaven to be on the Loxahatchee River. I'm going to picture it every day in my mind. I will picture the Spanish moss that hangs from the live oaks. And I'll picture that spot where the river gets narrow and there are so many cypress knees, it's like an obstacle course and you have to steer the canoe carefully so as not to hit them.

I have a plan for that day now, when it comes, so you don't have to worry about me. When they take me down to the death chamber and strap me to the bed, I will close my eyes and picture myself on the Loxahatchee, and I'll just breathe until it's all over and then I'll just be there. I want you to know that you don't have to feel bad about it, Sis. You can just think of me on a grand trip along the river.

Give Kimmy a hug from me. Give yourself one, too.

Love,
Andy

I open a new tab and look up the Loxahatchee River. It's seven miles long. It starts near Jupiter, Florida, and empties into the Atlantic. You can rent a canoe at an outpost in Dickinson State Park and paddle until your arms get tired, until you reach the inlet, where the river spills into the ocean. Loxahatchee is Seminole for *river of turtles*. They stand on the banks, warm their cold blood. Manatee feed on mangrove leaves, shoal grass, and floating hyacinth. Bald cypress branches filter the sun, beams of light casting shadows on the water.

There is just enough room in the canoe for the two of us. We float along the river together. We paddle in rhythm, propelling ourselves toward the open water. That's my idea of heaven, and it *is* a nice thing to think about—that if you love something fiercely enough, it could be yours forever.

chapter fifteen

G reg begins making low, throat-clearing noises, our signal to settle in. I turn to survey the group and see the usual participants and one new girl. She is younger than most of us, and looks either terrified or completely bored—I can't tell which just yet. She's wearing a stonewashed denim jumper and green tights, perhaps something she found in a pile of clothes her mother meant to donate. Very 1985. The name tag sticker over her heart says SOPHIE.

"There's no theme tonight. It's a round robin night," Greg announces. "I want to know what everyone's been up to." There is a slight murmur from the group, a collective laboring of breath. Clarisse and I look at each other from across the circle, and we try not to smile at each other too widely, try not to break out into laughter, because Greg doesn't want to know what we've been up to.

We are all a bit tense now, except for the new girl, who doesn't know that by *round robin*, Greg means, "I'll go around the circle and force everyone to say something that's happening in his or her life, and I won't let anyone cop out and just share what they ate for dinner last night."

I could say something. It's not too late to come clean, to shine a light inside the dark center of me. It's not too late to swim out to the swell, to reach the rolling wave before it breaks and crashes.

Greg moves his focus around the room, and kids reluctantly talk out loud about the happenings in their lives. When it's the new girl's turn, she sits up a bit straighter in her chair in anticipation.

"Since it's your first visit, Sophie, perhaps you can just share a bit about yourself with us. You can talk about what brings you here tonight. You can talk about the past, the present, the future. There are no limitations. And we are all here to support you." Greg looks around the room. "Remember the ground rules, folks," he reminds us. Greg is using his best making-the-new-kid-comfortable voice, which is even softer and lighter than his usual voice.

"Well, I've never been to something like this before," Sophie begins. She has an elastic hair tie in her hands, stretching it as she talks. "I've never really wanted to talk about my mother. Still don't want to talk about her, if I'm being honest." She laughs that uncomfortable little laugh that our group is used to, a way to burn off nerves. The circle laughs along with Sophie to release some tension. I can feel the room relax. I've felt it before—the feeling of releasing a small amount of air out of an overinflated balloon so that it doesn't stretch too far and pop, making a loud sound that you're sure sounds like the pop of a gun. I see Sophie's shoulders lower just slightly, a sign that she's starting to let her guard down.

"Welcome, Sophie. I know I'm speaking for everyone when I say I'm glad you're here."

"Thanks," Sophie says, her brown eyes soft and slightly sad. "I'm starting to realize that something good can come out of talking about her and what she did."

"Exactly," Greg says. His face looks open and kind, his body throwing supportive energy toward Sophie as she tells us a bit about her story.

Sophie says she entered the foster care system at age two, when her mother was charged with triple homicide. She was eventually convicted of murdering Sophie's father, his girlfriend, and his girlfriend's sister at the home that they shared in Bradenton. Sophie was outside in her mother's blue Buick during the murders, strapped into her car seat and told to wait while Mommy went inside to see Daddy for a minute. Her mother was sentenced to life in prison without the possibility of parole.

"Sometimes I think I want to know why she did it, and other times I think it doesn't matter and I should just move on," Sophie says. "I guess I'm just a walking jumble of feelings. So my foster mom found the Wavelengths, and we decided that coming here might help me feel like less of a jumble."

"Thanks, Sophie," Greg says. "Thanks for sharing some of your experience. That's a great start."

Clarisse scoots her chair back and makes Greg notice her. He smiles at her but she doesn't smile back. Her defenses are engaged, an invisible barricade surrounding her, but it doesn't deter Greg.

"Clarisse!" Greg says in his cheery I'm-trying-to-make-sad-kids-talk voice. "It's your turn. Please share something with us."

Clarisse uncrosses her legs and crosses them the other way. I can see the bottom of one of her shoes—all the tread is gone, the rubber sole smooth from so many steps. She looks at Greg. His eyes are hopeful, like mine.

"Well, my father is finally getting a hearing for his appeal," she says. "His lawyers are asking for the death sentence to be commuted to life in prison."

The group reacts as we usually do when legal matters are discussed. We all know something about appeals and parole and retrials and reduced sentences and time off for good behavior.

"And how does that make you feel, Clarisse?" It's Greg's voice, but really it's mine too.

"Honestly, I really don't care about it. It doesn't affect me. Either way he's dead to me," Clarisse says, and then laughs through her nose. She leans back in her chair and tilts her face toward the ceiling as though she's bathing in sunlight. A few of us squirm in our seats a little.

"You don't have to talk about it at all if you aren't comfortable, Clarisse," Greg says, using his therapist voice to turn the conversation around. "It may take a while to process. You know you have an outlet for your feelings when you're ready to share." Clarisse looks at me and then down at her feet. She bites her lower lip.

When group ends, Clarisse goes right for the cookies and lemonade.

"Hey!" I say, tapping her on the shoulder. "Why didn't you tell me about the appeal?" I ask. I can feel Clarisse gathering her energy, her bright, bright light, just like the meaning of her name—bright and shining, like a flame. I look in her eyes and she looks in mine and we're just two girls with murderer fathers standing in silence.

"I don't know," Clarisse says. "I guess I just didn't want to talk about it. Like, what's the point? Does it really matter? Death sentence, life sentence, it's all the same, really. Anyway, it doesn't change what we have to do. It doesn't change the test."

She grabs a napkin and piles cookies on it like a tower, six or seven cookies balancing on top of each other. "I'm just a little sick of this Wavelengths shit," Clarisse says. "I wish I could just disappear for a while," she says. "Do you ever feel that way?"

"All the time," I say. I reach over and take a cookie from the top of her tower, starting to nibble at the sugary edge.

"All the time," Clarisse repeats. She reaches her hand up toward mine, and I move my hand down toward hers in a high-five. We connect, palm to palm, lifeline against lifeline and all the other lines like maps on our skin that can tell our fortunes, our fate.

chapter sixteen

As I walk home from the jetty, my nerves tingle with expectation. I get to sleep over at Clarisse's house tonight. I get to lie next to her in her big bed, feeling the cool sheets chilling my skin. I get to listen to Clarisse breathe after she falls asleep, watch her chest rise and fall. Sometimes her legs twitch, as if she's chasing something in her dreams.

I feel different when I'm with Clarisse. She makes the whole world thick with the most delicious beauty. I can't stand leaving her, for that is when I'm reminded that beautiful things are temporary after all. I'll be in the car with my mother or Shea on the way home from Clarisse's, and I'll look out the passenger side window and the scenery will become artificial before my eyes, all my surroundings suddenly unreal. The world will transform into a hideous diorama, everything crudely fashioned, every flaw magnified—each crack in the highway, every unopened bud on every tree, every dead animal swarmed with flies. It will be as if the veil has been pulled back on the atmosphere, and I can see the bones, the skeleton within.

I'll want more than anything to command my mother or Shea to turn the car around, to let me return to Clarisse forever, to let me never leave her ever again, but I know that's impossible, at least for now, and the nesting dolls inside my sternum will close up, one by one, and my smallest and smoothest heart will be trapped inside. Until Clarisse and I are together again.

I have some time to kill before Clarisse and George pick me up so I stop at the Gulf Beaches Historical Museum. Housed in a small building on 10th Street that was once a church, it's now a historic landmark full of photos, news clippings, and artifacts from the early days of the settlement of the Gulf Beaches. As I walk through the white gates of the property, a sign implores me to *Come take a walk into history*, a call I can seldom resist. I've spent a lot of time in this space over the years, and the old lady volunteer always greets me with a pleased expression on her face, so glad that a young local is interested in history. Inside there are photographs and legal documents under glass and scrapbooks you can flip through, full of newspaper pages preserved in plastic film. There are a few old telephones on display and a telegraph key that you can actually play with.

My favorite thing to do at the museum is to read the stories about Silas Dent, who was known as the "Happy Hermit of Cabbage Key." Silas was from Georgia and came here to the Gulf Beach barrier islands in 1900 with his family to farm. The Dents ran a dairy farm for a while, and for some time, you could hear moos in the distance along with the cries of the seagulls, until it became clear that the cows weren't suited for beach life. So the Dent family bought acreage inland, near the city of Largo, and moved the cows and themselves there. But Silas chose to stay on tiny Cabbage Key, living simply in a grass hut that he'd constructed himself.

In pictures, Silas has a long white beard, and his skin looks dark and leathery from the sun. He has beady, little eyes. He squints when he smiles in the sunshine. According to the stories about him in the museum, Silas loved three things best—nature, Christmas, and children. Although he had a reputation as a hermit, preferring his own company and adamantly living alone until he died in 1952, Silas would visit Pass-a-Grille every December, rowing his boat across the Boca Ciega Bay and docking at Merry

Pier. He dressed up as Santa Claus for the children, passing out gifts he made for them or purchased with money he saved throughout the year. It was the only time Silas traded in his usual attire of faded denim overalls.

Silas had a unique way of rowing. He sat in his rowboat facing forward, instead of backward, so he could see in the direction he was traveling. According to a story in the *St. Petersburg Times*, when Silas was asked why he did that, he replied, "Never much worried 'bout where I been, more 'bout where I'se going."

I make it home and get my overnight bag packed. When I hear George honk the horn outside, I kiss my mother and Shea good-bye. The drive to Clarisse's house takes longer than usual because, once we cross the Howard Frankland Bridge, George likes to take side roads and back roads from Tampa to Seffner, avoiding the Crosstown Expressway and the infamous I-4, that eternally congested highway that cuts east-west through the middle of the state, the main artery for tourists flocking to the theme parks and other Orlando attractions.

After dinner, Jenny and George start cleaning up, scraping leftover chicken stir-fry and rice into Pyrex bowls to store in the fridge.

I sit quietly, sipping my water, while Clarisse gets a

rag from the kitchen and wipes the table clean, leaving a faint trace of vinegar and lemon in the air. George makes all-natural cleaning solutions. He even makes his own laundry detergent with borax and baking soda and grated flakes of Ivory soap in a mason jar.

"You girls should go outside and catch some air," George says. "Sunset should be happening soon."

There's a rope hammock in Clarisse's backyard, slung between two orange trees. In kingdom Plantae, oranges belong to the genus *Citrus*. The early Spanish explorers, possibly even Ponce de León himself, planted the first orange trees near St. Augustine in the mid-1500s. They were happy to discover that the sandy soil in Florida was ideal for growing.

Clarisse throws herself into the hammock and stretches out, her hands behind her head like a pillow, her elbows pointing out. I sit on the patchy grass at the base of one tree and begin poking at a fallen orange, its skin dotted with dark spots that will soon become moldy and green.

"I don't care about sunsets anymore," Clarisse says. "So long and drawn out. Just bring on the nighttime already." There is a heaviness between us. Not just the humidity in the air but the weight of the test, and everything we have left to plan.

"Maybe you're just too used to them," I tell her. "If

you lived in one of those places where it's dark for months at a time, then maybe you'd care about sunsets again."

Clarisse rolls onto her side to face me. "I'd actually like to try that sometime. Living in total darkness."

"Me too," I say, and then we exist in silence for a few minutes until the sunset is complete and the katydids begin to sing, hidden in the trees all around us. Down at the bottom of the deep blue sea, there are creatures that live their entire lives in the dark. They are colorless, because color serves no purpose without light to see. They must survive extreme conditions, for the sea floor is a hostile environment, creatures mostly surviving on marine snow, a constant shower of organic leftovers that floats down from the upper layers of the ocean.

"Come here," Clarisse says, patting the empty space next to her in the hammock, an invitation to lie down, an invitation I accept with my entire body.

"I've found the perfect target for you," I say. We've taken to using this term when we talk about the test because it makes us forget that we're talking about an actual person, a living, breathing human being, but also because it's benign compared to *victim* and wouldn't alarm someone immediately if they overheard us.

"Who?"

"My grandmother."

"Wait, I thought your grandmother just died," Clarisse says. "Isn't that what the letter was all about?" The hammock sways, and I feel the rope give slightly under our collective weight.

"That was my father's mother. I'm talking about my other grandmother. My mother's mother. Emerald."

"I thought you didn't have anything to do with her."

"I don't. That's what makes her so perfect."

"I don't know, Evelyn." Clarisse is whispering, and I can feel her breath on my earlobe. "Wouldn't she recognize you if she saw you?"

"She hasn't seen me since I was a baby," I say. In the photo albums of my babyhood, there is one picture of Emerald holding me. I'm very small and swaddled in a blue receiving blanket, only the very top of my head peeking out and giving me away. Otherwise you might think that Emerald is just holding a wadded-up blanket. In the photo, Emerald looks like my mother, but her hair is styled differently, all swept up and pinned into a bun at the top of her head.

"How can you be so sure? Maybe she's seen you around town. Or maybe your mom posted pictures of you on Facebook. You know how parents have ruined Facebook."

I laugh because she's right—parents *have* ruined Facebook. No teenager wants to be anywhere near their parents in the digital world, which is why we've all migrated to newer platforms like Snapchat and Instagram. "This is the best part. She doesn't live around here, hasn't for years. I looked her up and get this—she lives in Celebration. You know that town right next to Disney World that Walt Disney invented?"

"She lives there? No way! George has been there before. He said it looks so perfect, it's creepy. It reminded him of the fake town from that movie *The Truman Show*. And I thought Darcy Lake was bad. I guess it could always be worse."

"I'm sure Emerald won't recognize me, but I could always change my appearance a bit when we go there, just in case. And my mother doesn't really use Facebook, so that's not an issue. She's not really into social media at all. Probably because of him."

Clarisse grabs a strand of my hair and twists it between her thumb and forefinger. "I still don't know. Shouldn't it be a stranger? It seems like that would be easier. I mean, even if she's not in your life, she's still your grandmother. Wouldn't you feel bad if I actually, you know, go through with it?"

This is the part of the test that we haven't really

talked about, and that's because I know that Clarisse will pass the test. So there's nothing to discuss.

"But she *is* a stranger to me, Clarisse. She doesn't mean anything to me. She abandoned my mother and me a long time ago. So she's perfect. Plus, she's old—seventy-seven. The average life expectancy in the United States is seventy-eight point seventy-four years. What are the odds that she'll live much longer anyway?"

"Why did Emerald abandon you and your mom?" Clarisse asks.

"She didn't approve of my mom being in a relationship with Shea. Isn't that awful? Can you ever imagine doing that to your own child? The only thing my mom has ever said about Emerald is that she's a hateful person."

I tell this lie because I know that Clarisse needs to hear it. If she believes Emerald is a bad person, she will be able to take the test. But the truth is, I've never been sure why Emerald is no longer in our lives. I know that she was around when I was born, but her presence disappeared after that one photograph when I was a baby. I don't know if she abandoned us or if my mother was the one who ended the relationship. I only know that we don't speak of her so there's never been a chance to find out.

"Okay then, target acquired," Clarisse says, and she rests her chin on my shoulder. "Now I need a weapon."

"Well, I'm thinking it has to be a knife. If you want to re-create the conditions of his crime."

"But I thought we gave up on that rule. I think it can work without being so specific. Plus stabbing is so messy. I was thinking a gun would be so much easier."

"No, guns are for cowards. Anyone can stand there and pull a trigger. That's not testing anything. My father was a coward; that's why he used a gun. He didn't have the nerve to walk up to a stranger, get close enough to stab them. Plus stabbing is more physical work. It proves you're serious." The hammock swings, making its own small wind. "Plus, do *you* have a gun?"

"True. And if I use a knife, I can just take one from the kitchen. George has a lot of knives. Really sharp ones too."

"You can't just use a kitchen knife, Clarisse. You need to get a new knife, specifically for this. Something that can't be traced back to either of us. Don't you ever watch crime shows?"

"Making a purchase is traceable too. It creates a record. Don't *you* ever watch crime shows?" I think for a minute, letting the drone of the katydids hypnotize me. "Hey, I'll just steal a knife from Walmart," Clarisse says. "Samantha and I stole a can of duster from the one in Valrico before. It's pretty easy. They don't have a store detective there, but you do have to be aware of the security cameras. They're on the ceiling."

"Detectives? Stores actually have those?" I ask.

"Yes, most stores do. Samantha says they're usually fat older guys, but they can look like anybody. It's their behavior you need to watch, not just their appearance. Samantha steals shit all the time. She never gets caught."

The katydids get louder and louder, a chorus multiplying in the night. I close my eyes and make a silent wish—that Clarisse will pass the test.

chapter seventeen

I open a private browsing tab on my laptop, find Emerald's address through White Pages. It really isn't difficult to find most people, especially if you know their full name and the city where they live. I type the address into Google Maps and click Enter. In street view, I use the arrows to spin myself around, getting my virtual bearings straight.

Emerald's house is a sky-blue bungalow on Teal Avenue in Celebration. Her front lawn is impeccably groomed, like all of the others on the street, with blades of grass sheared so short it looks like soft green carpet. Emerald's front porch is full of potted plants—hydrangeas and bromeliad and hibiscus and what looks like jasmine, although I can't be sure.

I click myself down the street, past the parked Mercedeses and BMWs, their license plates blurred out for privacy. The only people in the street view are landscaping workers and pool maintenance staff, men in jeans and dark T-shirts who tend to the tasks the homeowners have outsourced. It's a quiet-looking street. There shouldn't be too many people around to notice us.

Then I check *Letters from the Death House*, and find a new entry has been uploaded, a letter from Andy written on yellow legal paper. He begins on the first blue line, his handwriting small and neat.

Dear Sis,

A search team tore up my cell this morning, hunting for contraband and excess property. They were nice enough about it so it didn't bother me. And it only took me a few minutes to put everything back together. Having a cell that's only 6 x 9 makes it pretty easy, I guess. After I fixed everything up, I looked out the window and realized we got a light frost last night. The crows pecking around out on the yard looked like they didn't know what to do about it!

I've been keeping myself busy with reading and writing. I'm on the third Harry Potter book right now. I've liked them all so far, and I hope I can get my hands on all of the movies to watch once I've read the whole series. The books actually inspired me to start writing some fantasy stories of my own. I have one story that Kimmy might like, about unicorns and dragons. Maybe I'll send it to you when it's ready, and you can read it to her.

I might get one of the guys to make some artwork for it, too. There are quite a few guys in here who know how to draw. I'm sure my actual writing isn't very good at all, but it's nice to get lost in my imagination and make up stories. It gets my mind off things. It feels good to create. Turning a blank piece of paper into a story makes me feel like anything is possible.

Thanks for sticking with me all these years, sis. And thanks for putting my words online. It might sound silly, but it makes me feel less alone.

Love,
Andy

Maybe I should post a comment, telling him that he makes me feel less alone too. Maybe it would mean something to him just to know that I'm out here and reading his words.

My phone buzzes, and I look down. It's a text from Clarisse.

Call me. It's about the test.

Clarisse and I have agreed not to discuss the test over text or e-mail or instant messenger. Phone calls are okay as long as we don't speak in specific terms, just in case.

"Do you remember Clue? The board game?" Clarisse asks me as soon as she answers. We are beyond hellos and good-byes.

"Sure. I always had to be Miss Scarlett because my favorite color was red."

"There were six weapons in the game. Remember? You had to move the little pieces around to the different rooms. Candlestick, knife, lead pipe, revolver, rope, and wrench."

"Yeah, and they were all made of metal except the rope, which was made of plastic."

"Yeah, well, it just got me thinking, that's all. I think there's a better option. Something that doesn't leave so many clues behind. I thought maybe you'd want to think about it too."

"You're a genius," I say.

"I know, right?" I can tell she's smiling. I hear it in her voice. "Good night, Ev."

"Good night."

The weapon is the last decision we need to make. My first suggestion was a knife, but the more Clarisse thought about it, the more squeamish she became.

Too much blood, she decided. So I came up with the idea of bludgeoning Emerald to death. But with what?

This is where our collective imagination stalled. Many ordinary objects could be used to kill someone, but we want something tried and true. We didn't want to conduct a Google search for "good objects for bludgeoning," even in a private browser window, because computers can be seized and search histories scanned. Casey Anthony searched for *fool-proof suffocation methods* on the last day her daughter was seen alive, and although she was acquitted, the court of public opinion has rendered her eternally guilty.

I close my laptop and tiptoe out to the kitchen to find the toolkit my mother keeps in the cabinet under the sink. I unzip the red nylon bag, sorting through several screwdrivers of various sizes, a pair of pliers, and a roll of plumber's tape until I finally see an adjustable wrench lying at the bottom. It has a red handle and jagged silver teeth. I reach for it, and the small light above the stove hits its body, making it shine. I feel the weight of it in my hand. It's heavy and surely able to do harm if wielded with enough force.

I imagine Clarisse raising the wrench above her head, and my pulse quickens, my breath catching up to match. For a moment, a paralyzing fear washes over me, and I'm frozen, my feet planted firmly on the cool kitchen tile. My imagination halts because I know Clarisse will pass the test. She'll lower the wrench, sobbing and running from the darkness of it all. And just like that, the fear releases me, and I can move again, for this is just a game and Clarisse and I are just tokens making our way around the board. I'm just Evelyn, in the kitchen, with the wrench.

chapter eighteen

Florida heat is brutal. You don't need to live here long to know that. I've lived here all of my life so I've grown accustomed to a thin layer of sweat coating my skin at all times. My mother and Shea don't mind the heat. In fact, they seem to enjoy it. They love going to outdoor concerts even on the most swelter-ing days. Today we're at Vinoy Park, a waterfront park on Tampa Bay, for a folk music and food festival, the sweet and spicy smells of barbecued meats traveling through the warm air.

My mother and Shea are in line at the beer tent while Clarisse and I sit on a blanket in the field. There are families with toddlers waddling around. There are babies sleeping in strollers, canopies shading them from harsh ultraviolet rays. There are older couples holding hands, white shorts to match their white hair. There are rich people who have docked their boats at the nearby marina, their gold watches glinting in the sun as they walk by.

"So I'll come get you tomorrow morning around nine. Bright and early." Clarisse is going over the details of our trip to Celebration one more time. Onstage, a guitar player closes his eyes as he plucks the strings, fuzzy amplified tones emanating from two speakers stacked on either side of an elevated platform.

"That's fine with me," I answer. We're both sitting with our legs stretched out in front of us, leaning back on our palms. Concertgoers walk around us—women in sundresses with spaghetti straps, men in skinny jeans and fitted tees that look like magazine models. A girl in all black—black linen shorts, black tank top, and black gladiator sandals—walks in front of us. Her eyes are on Clarisse until I notice her staring. Then she looks away.

"It will be fun to see the mermaids again," Clarisse says. "I remember wanting to be one so bad when I was a kid, but I was sure I'd never be able to grow my hair long enough."

She's playing along with the story we've made up about the trip we're taking tomorrow. Of course our mothers don't know we're going to Celebration. They think we're going to Weeki Wachee Springs State

Park, a tourist attraction about an hour north. The park's most famous feature is an aquarium-like setting where you pay to watch women in mermaid tails swim in circles beneath the clear natural spring water. Clarisse and I both went to Weeki Wachee as kids so we'll have a frame of reference, believable stories to tell about our trip when we return. We're going to see a mermaid show and then ride the glass-bottom boat on Weeki Wachee River.

"Remember, Weeki Wachee closes at five thirty," I say. "So I told my mom we should be back in Pass-a-Grille around six thirty or seven. That gives us time to stop for something to eat on the way back. I'm sure you'll be hungry."

Clarisse shakes her head, trying not to laugh. She touches the top of my hand with hers and then takes a sip of the giant plastic cup of fresh lemonade that sits between us, sold from a stand at the edge of the park. You stand in line and watch as they load lemons into a stainless steel press and pull the lever to squeeze. They scoop ice into a silver tumbler, pour in water and sugar, and shake it up. Then they finally hand you a sticky cup of refreshment— so cold, so sweet.

There isn't a cloud in the sky today, nothing to block out the sun, that ball of white light beating the tops of our heads at high noon. Onstage, they are between bands, instrumental music playing while they tear down and then set up for the next act. The woman in all black walks past us again, this time smiling at Clarisse and then taking her phone from her pocket and tapping the screen as if she's sending a text.

"Do you know her?" I ask Clarisse.

Clarisse puts her hand to her forehead to form a visor to shield the sun from her eyes, squinting in the distance to consider the woman. She shakes her head no.

The next band takes the stage, and I can see my mother and Shea are right in front, where they usually are at concerts, if they can help it. Shea is standing behind my mother, her arms wrapped around my mother's waist as my mother holds their plastic cups of beer, one in each of her hands.

The woman in all black walks past us one more time. Maybe she's lost her friends. Maybe she's a little drunk or a little stoned. Or maybe she's just trying to sneak another look at Clarisse. Does this woman know who Clarisse is? Her identity isn't secret, and if you follow the stories of murderers, of their families and their victims, you might be able to recognize her. There is nothing to protect her, to protect me, and why should there be? We are both a part of history, another entry in the archive of facts about our fathers and what they did.

Sometimes things unravel quickly, as they did with my father. The lever is pulled, and sanity is broken, the madman gone mad in what seems like an instant. My father didn't seem to have planned his attacks so some refer to his murders as a crime of passion, which is usually defined as a violent act committed because of a strong sudden impulse rather than as a premeditated crime. Crimes of passion are common in cases of infidelity, but it was my father who was unfaithful to his wife, not the other way around. My mother was the other woman, although I'm not sure if she knew that at the time. My father told my mother he was recently divorced, and my mother believed him.

Other times, things unravel slowly, as they did in the case of Clarisse's father, whose name is Benjamin. Jenny found a few clues here and there, but nothing that couldn't be explained away—an odd sock in the dryer that didn't belong to anyone, a strange charge on a credit card statement. He could always make it work, could always clear the air of any suspicion, until one day he couldn't.

Benjamin was handsome and charming, a family

man who doted on his daughter. He was nothing to fear. Sweet and approachable with an easy smile, that is how one reporter described him when covering his trial and sentencing.

One morning, Jenny and Clarisse woke up to a sheriff's deputy knocking on their trailer door. The deputy told Jenny that the little girl next door was missing, and that's when Jenny rubbed the sleep from her eyes and realized that Benjamin was gone too. Jenny called friends and family, hoping to find him, surely not wanting to connect his disappearance to the little girl next door. Her name was Jocelyn, and by the end of the day, a search team had found her body buried in a shallow grave near the lake.

By the next morning, Benjamin had surrendered to police, confessing to everything. Jenny and Clarisse moved in with George. Clarisse was seven years old. She understood what was happening. When I read the details of her father's case online, I longed for a time machine, so I could go back in time and comfort little Clarisse, holding her hand and telling her that everything was going to be okay.

One night at Clarisse's, when I was sure she was asleep, I crept out of her bed and into the closet, where I had seen a clear plastic box on the shelf that appeared to be full of photos. I slid the lid off and ran my hands through its contents, and eventually I found what looked like Clarisse's baby book, one of those memory keepers with spaces to write important milestones—first word, first tooth, first haircut. I flipped through the book until a page caught my eye. Clarisse's third birthday. There's a photo taped to the page—little Clarisse sitting on her father's lap. She's wearing a blue dress with yellow stripes, her small toes peeking out from white sandals. She's holding up three chubby fingers on one chubby hand. Her father is laughing so hard that his face is wrinkled and you can barely see his eyes. There's a cake on the table next to them, a round layer cake with thick scallops of hard white icing. Clarisse is just a little girl, so happy to be with her father. Close the book there and you can pretend that's the end of the story. The happy little girl blows out the birthday candles. The happy little girl makes a wish.

"I'm ready," Clarisse says, and I know she's talking about tomorrow. She's ready to take the test, to rid her body of the question that gnaws at her, threatening to consume her. The question that haunts her most nights if she's not careful. She's been smoking her brain into mush before bed, getting so high she forgets who she is. Only then can she fall into a sleep

without nightmares, without dreams in which she re-
lives what her father did, over and over. If Clarisse
can prove she has her own fate, one different from his,
then she will be free. She's counting on it. And I'm
counting on her.

chapter nineteen

I can't believe you're missing a Saturday morning at the jetty." Shea cracks a brown egg into a cast iron skillet on the stove as I pour orange juice into my glass. "This could make the local news, Ev. This could be bigger than the famous beach parking kerfuffle of 2015." Sunny-side up, the egg sizzles, becoming a puddle of white against the black, the yolk suspended in the center like a blind eye. Shea pulls two slices of rye bread from a bag and drops them in the toaster.

"I think I'll survive *one* Saturday without the jetty." I drink my juice, savoring the sensation of pulp against the inside of my cheek for a moment before swallowing.

"Ah, but will the jetty survive one Saturday without you?" Shea pokes at the egg yolk with one finger, testing its consistency. The toaster dings as toast pops up.

"I'm sure no one will even notice I'm missing," I say, but I'm thinking of the old man gliding the wand of his metal detector over the surface of the sand and looking for me from the corner of his eye, the slow beeps of the machine speeding up as he uncovers a broken necklace or a silver dollar.

"I haven't been to Weeki Wachee in ages," Shea says. She plucks the toast from the toaster and scrapes butter on each slice with the blunt edge of the knife. "You know I hate to be a feminist killjoy, but..."

"But that's never stopped you before. Go on."

Shea laughs at me through her nose as she plates the egg, scooping it gently from the skillet with a purple-handled spatula. "But I just think the mermaid show is exploitative. You know, in a historical context, the mermaid myth was perpetuated so sailors could have a scapegoat for rough waters. They believed these hybrid fish women, who were depicted with bare breasts, of course, could calm or stir the sea at will. Not to mention the sexual fantasy of it all."

"Well, Professor Killjoy, they have Prince Eric in the show at Weeki Wachee now," I say. "So there."

"Oh, great!" Shea says sarcastically. "And I'm sure he's fully clothed, right? Not just wearing a seashell that barely covers his bits?"

"You must be a blast at dinner parties, Shea."

"Ha, well, the joke's on you, Ev. I never get invited to dinner parties."

I feign a shocked face before I finish my juice in one big gulp.

"You know I'm just reminding you of your power. Women don't exist to fulfill the needs of others. Society would like you to believe that."

"Says the woman who is currently making breakfast in bed for her girlfriend."

As I walk over and place the empty glass in the dishwasher, Shea swats my shoulder lightly with the back of her hand. "Not so loud," she says. "This breakfast in bed is supposed to be a surprise!"

"Well, you two crazy kids have fun," I say as I sling my backpack onto my back. The wrench is inside, wrapped up in a sweatshirt along with two pairs of rubber gloves and a roll of duct tape, just in case.

I peek out the front window and watch for Clarisse. Any minute now, she'll pull up in George's bright blue hatchback with tinted windows, and I'll kiss my mother and Shea good-bye. I'll get in the car, and Clarisse will drive north on I-275. We'll cross the Howard Frankland Bridge, and I'll see sunlight reflecting on the water on either side of us. I'll watch for dolphins like I always do, letting my eyes search the chop of the bay, desperate for the thrill of a smooth gray body breaking the water, that moment of magic when you see just a glimpse of its beauty before it dives under again, just below the surface yet out of sight forever. I like to think that it's always the same dolphin I see jumping from the bay, intoxicated by the idea that the dolphin is searching for me too, swimming alongside the bridge and waiting to catch a glimpse of me through the glass. For isn't that all we want in this life, human and animal alike? To see one another? To know we have been seen?

Before we get to I-4, the highway that will take us across the center of the state and toward Celebration, Clarisse announces that she needs to stop for gas. She signals and then merges onto the ramp, and eventually we're parked at a 7-Eleven, and I'm filling the tank while Clarisse goes inside for snacks. "It's not a road trip without snacks," she says over her shoulder as she walks away from me, pulls one of the glass doors, and disappears inside.

By the time Clarisse returns, I'm already back in the passenger seat. She gets in the driver's side and hands me a Wild Cherry Pepsi and puts another in the cup holder between us. I hold the cool of the bottle to my forehead, a relief after standing in the heat pumping gas.

Clarisse starts the car and then tears open a package

of Twizzlers. She rips one strand away from the others, holding it between her teeth as she drives. There's construction most of the way along I-4 with fat barrels striped orange and white. We play the license plate game for a while to see how many states we can spot. We rack them up quickly, because it seems most everyone here is from somewhere else.

We're using my phone to navigate, the address punched in, the electronic voice directing Clarisse to exit toward Celebration. We park on Teal Avenue, two houses down from Emerald's. I reach for the back-pack between my feet, unzip the main compartment, and put the rolled-up sweatshirt onto my lap. I slide the wrench from within the sweatshirt, offering it to Clarisse.

She reaches out to touch it, pulling away as soon as her skin makes contact as if testing a hot stove and miscalculating, burning herself.

"Hold it. Get used to the weight of it," I tell her, but she's looking down at my lap now, eyeing the rest of the supplies—duct tape, rubber gloves, Clorox disinfectant wipes. Then she looks straight ahead, sitting still as a stone.

"What's wrong?" I ask, but Clarisse doesn't respond. She rests her chin on the top of the steering wheel. "Reesey Cup, you okay?" I use the pet name I made up for her, the one she allows only when it's the two of us.

"I can't do it. I can't do it, Evelyn." She takes her sunglasses off, leans over, and presses her face against my shoulder. "I can't do it. I don't want to do it. I can't, I don't want to, I don't want to, I can't do it, I won't." The words tumble and fall, cascading like waterfalls from her lips.

"Shhh, shhh, shhh. It's okay, it's okay. Clarisse, it's okay." I put everything back in the backpack and zip it up.

Clarisse looks up at me, her face wet with tears. "I can't do it. I can't do it."

I run my fingers through her hair. "It's okay," I tell her. "It's all going to be okay." I say it over and over. I repeat it like a mantra until she stops crying, until her breath returns to normal.

I open *The Catalog of Everything I've Done Wrong* and add a new entry: made Clarisse cry.

Then I grab the backpack and get out of the car.

chapter twenty

I ring the doorbell, and a dog barks from inside the house. Emerald opens the door, holding a Chihuahua. I know it's her because she looks like my mother, but her hair is lighter, a silvery blond that touches her shoulders.

"Can I help you?" She smiles at me. The dog pants in her arms.

"Oh, I lost my cat. I was just going around the neighborhood to see if anyone's seen her."

"Oh no, I'm so sorry," she says. "Do you have a picture of the cat?"

"I do," I say. I grab my phone from my pocket and begin to scroll through my photos.

"Here, come on in for a minute," she says. She takes a step back to make way for me. "I'm hiding from the pollen today. Allergies." I walk inside the house, and she closes the door behind me. She puts the dog on the hardwood floor. It runs over to me, sniffing my shoes.

"You're the Wilcox girl. Abby, right?" she asks. "You live on Honeysuckle?" She walks over to an over-stuffed denim chair and sits down. The dog runs over and jumps onto her lap.

"Yes. I'm really sorry to bother you about this. I'm going to put up some flyers. I just thought I'd ask some people on Teal first. I thought maybe she cut through your yard."

"Oh, it's fine, really. We don't mind the company, do we, Lola?" The dog licks her chin in response.

The walls are painted a soft blue. A white ceiling fan whirs above us. "This is a good one," I say, looking down at my phone. "Here." I offer it to her, and she takes it, squinting to look at the picture of a long-haired calico on the screen.

"Oh, what a beauty," she says. "You know, I haven't seen her, but I'll definitely keep an eye out for her." She hands the phone back to me and then starts coughing. "Oh, this damn pollen. My car was com-pletely covered in it this morning. It's just awful this year." She stands up, coughs more, holds one finger in the air as if to say, *Just a minute*, and excuses herself to the kitchen. Lola follows. The metal tags on her collar jingle as she trots behind Emerald.

I can hear Emerald's movement in the next room, the sounds of her getting a glass, and filling it with ice and water. I slide my phone back into my pocket. "Yeah, my mom has allergies too," I say loud enough for her to hear. "She's been really miserable lately." I stand at the threshold of the living room, just out of her sight.

"Oh really? Your mother?" she calls back. "I thought it was just you and your dad over there." She walks back into the room, holding a frosted tumbler of water. She takes a long drink from it, keeping her eyes on me.

"Oh, I meant my stepmother. My dad just got remarried."

"Well, I'm sorry. I didn't realize. How nice for your father," Emerald says. "I guess Lola and I are out of the neighborhood loop," she says with a laugh. She sits down, and the dog jumps back onto her lap.

"That's okay. They didn't make a deal about it. Didn't have a big ceremony or anything. It was just the three of us at the courthouse."

"Now that was my style," she says. "I never had those dreams of being a bride and having a big extravagant wedding." She takes another sip of cold water and rests the glass on the coffee table in front of her. "But of course, this was during the Vietnam draft so we wanted to get married quick, in case his number was called. So it all worked out, I suppose."

"Then what happened? I mean, did he end up getting drafted?"

"Actually, they did call his number, but his asthma made him ineligible. We were lucky. It was a tense process, the whole thing. We were barely eighteen, just kids really. Not much older than you are now." She looks off in the distance, as if something has caught her eye—a memory of my grandfather, a vision of him in a shirt and tie, reciting his marriage vows in a small courthouse room, the threat of war looming over him like a dark cloud. "I'm sorry. I could bore you all day with stories if you'd like. Lola can attest to that." She strokes the dog's fur vigorously and then gives the animal a quick kiss on the nose.

"No, it's fine," I say. "I don't mind at all. Hey, could I use your bathroom real quick before I go?"

"Sure thing. Top of the stairs."

"Thanks." I climb the stairs slowly, holding on to the smooth curve of the railing until I reach the top. The bathroom door is open. I stand at the threshold and peer inside. It's all bright white subway tile with silvery accents. The shower curtain is pale peach. A fluffy white hand towel hangs on a shiny hook. Sunlight streams in through a skylight overhead, making the floor look slick with rain.

I walk down a short hallway to a bedroom that must be Emerald's. There's a mirrored vanity in dark cherry wood. There's a small brass tray full of makeup brushes. There are tubes of lipstick lined up in a row. I could tip one over with a finger, setting off a chain reaction if I wanted to, knocking them all down like dominoes. There's a hairbrush with traces of Emerald, a few strands of her silvery blond hair trapped in the bristles. There's a pair of small tortoiseshell hair combs with delicate pointed teeth. I place my hand over one of them, cupping it into my palm, and making it disappear into the front pocket of my shorts.

The telephone rings, a landline with an ancient analog sound. I hear Emerald's footsteps on the floor below me and hear the echo of her answering, saying hello.

I descend the stairs carefully, and now I'm standing behind Emerald as she dismisses what sounds like a telemarketer on the line.

"No, not interested," she says. "Sorry." Her voice is firm but sweet. "But thank you for calling."

I stand behind her as she places the slim receiver on

a cradle anchored to the wall. She turns around, and her eyes get wide when she realizes I'm here.

"Oh my goodness, you startled me, dear," she says, one hand on her chest. Her skin is thin, bluish veins visible beneath the surface.

"I'm sorry. I didn't mean to scare you."

The phone cord dangles on the wall behind her. I reach for it, stretch out the smooth curls, and make the cord straight and taut. I wrap it around her throat.

She flails her arms at me, punching me in the stomach with weak fists. I pull the cord tighter and tighter until she can't breathe. The dog barks. I kick the dog, and she whimpers, running away.

Emerald digs at the cord with her fingernails. She scratches her neck, making a small slice that draws blood. She opens and closes her mouth, a fish out of water.

I remind myself it isn't real, repeat it over and over in my head, my own voice singing to me—it's not real, it's not real. I can't freeze the frame, and I don't want to watch. Not this time.

I turn and run to the front door, flinging it open. I hear Emerald's voice, alive and calling after me, something about looking for the cat. She sounds like she's speaking through an underwater tunnel, her voice thick and wavy in my ears.

I don't turn back, don't say anything in response.

I walk through the door and into bright white sunlight that hurts my eyes. I squint as I walk back to the car. I'm barely able to see, my eyes slow to adjust, but I can feel Clarisse's presence. I know she's waiting for me.

chapter twenty-one

We consider going to Weeki Wachee after all but decide to spend the rest of the day in Ybor City, a historic section of Tampa that was once the center of the cigar-rolling industry. We park at the top of the parking garage, and Clarisse lights the joint she'd stashed in her bra at home, before handing it to me. We take turns, passing it from our lips to our fingers and back, getting higher and higher until it's gone.

We get out of the car and hold hands as we walk down the stairs and onto the street. I feel like I'm walking on air, my legs warm and flexible, my cheeks hurting from smiling so much.

We eat at the Columbia, which the menu states is the oldest restaurant in Florida, family owned since 1905. We're seated in the Patio Room, with high ceilings and a sky light above that bathes us in white.

There are colorful Spanish tiles on the walls and a marble fountain in the center of the room—it looks like a young man riding a fish, with the creature's tail and the man's legs intertwined. When I point it out to Clarisse, the waiter tells us the piece is called "Eros and Dolphin," and it's a replica of a statue found in the ruins of Pompeii, buried in volcanic ash.

"Who is Eros?" Clarisse asks, and I swear the waiter blushes as he explains that Eros is the god of love. We order two Cuban sandwiches, a slice of key lime pie, and a piece of mango mousse cake. I ask for lemonade, and Clarisse orders a beer with the confidence of a stoned seventeen-year-old. She winks at the waiter, and he nods and smiles and starts walking away, and for a minute, I think she may have actually charmed him into it. But seconds later he is back and asking for some ID, which Clarisse pretends to look for in her tiny bag until she finally looks up and tells him a café con leche would be just fabulous.

After we're finished eating, Clarisse pays for everything with cash her mother gave her for the day, which she will say she spent on the mermaid show and the glass-bottom boat ride. We step back into the brutal sunshine and walk down Seventh Avenue. It's the main drag of Ybor City, lined with bars and shops and restaurants. Two men walk past us smoking cigars, and I breathe in the woodsy scent that reminds me of hickory, of a bonfire burning on the beach at night. There's a tattoo parlor on the corner, and we turn our hands into makeshift binoculars, using them to cut the glare so we can peer through the glass to see inside, where a woman lies on her stomach while a tattooed man presses a contraption to the back of her thigh, purple and black ink smeared on her tanned skin.

When we make it back to the car, we're hot and sweaty from the sun. Clarisse starts the engine and turns the AC on full blast. She leans her face into the air vent and lets out a loud sigh. "I didn't know failing a test could feel this good," she says. "Although I have to admit, I was a little freaked out when you went and knocked on Grandma's front door. Why didn't you just tell me you were going to pretend you were a neighbor looking for a cat? I would have loved to play along. I'm pretty good at getting into character, actually."

"Oh, so you like role play?" I surprise myself by saying it out loud, still a little high on the weed and the excitement of the day.

"I've been known to put on a show," Clarisse says. "You, on the other hand, you seem like the voyeur type. I bet you like to watch." She turns to face me, her eyes narrowing as if she's trying to read my mind, unlock my secrets.

"I don't know," I say. "I mean, I guess I've never had the chance. What about you?"

"Well, why watch," she says, "when it's so much fun to join in?" She looks at me, raising her eyebrows, and we laugh together. The sounds of our voices blend until I can't tell where hers ends and mine begins. I want to kiss her, and I think she might want to kiss me too, but then she puts the car in gear and turns the radio on and we drive.

As we merge onto the highway, Clarisse reaches over, placing a cool palm on the back of my neck. "I don't think anyone else would go through this shit with me," she says. I look over and see her smiling, although tears are welled up in her eyes. "So thank you for that. I owe you one, Ev."

"Well, I've been keeping track," I say, tapping my finger to my temple. "So I'll let you know when I need to cash in."

After Clarisse delivers me home on time, after I satisfy my mother and Shea with a few stories from Weeki Wachee—what we saw through the glass bottom of the boat on the river—I go to my room. I climb in bed still wearing my clothes. I dig Emerald's small comb from my pocket and put it to my lips. I breathe in its scent—a mix of her oily hair and shampoo—impossibly sweet and musty at the same time. I run the comb through my own hair and then secure it just above my ear.

I slide through the recent photos on my phone: Clarisse at the Columbia, giving the key lime pie a thumbs-up, me posing with a candy cigar we found inside a candy store, a blurry shot of the yellow-and-red streetcar moving along Eighth Avenue.

I delete each one with a tap of my finger, and just like that, it's as though the entire day never happened.

chapter twenty-two

Shea is eating gummy bears straight from a one-pound bag on her lap. Every five minutes or so, she offers some to me and Clarisse, hoisting the bag behind her and into the backseat. We're on our way to Treasure Island. My mother is driving, and Shea is in the passenger seat, her window down, the collar of her denim vest up.

We'll spend Friday and Saturday night at a hotel called the Thunderbird. Bright and early Saturday morning, the lawyer, Dana Apple, will meet us at her office, and then we'll follow her to my grandmother Ella's house, where I can look around the place and claim the Limoges butter dish.

It was my idea to go to Treasure Island and see Ella's house, and Shea's idea to make an entire weekend of it, turning it into a girls' getaway. We'll head home on Sunday morning. That is the plan.

Plans make you feel as though you're in control. Plans make you feel powerful, a way to organize time, a way to conjure the future into being. Plans are your hopes and dreams written down in a notebook, scrawled on the back of a receipt, typed into the keys of a glowing keyboard. My mother says, if you want to make God laugh, make plans. I say plans are all we have.

Clarisse and I sit side by side in the back of the car, the bare skin of my left leg touching the bare skin of her right leg. We share a pair of earbuds and listen to Pink Floyd, only a thin white wire connecting us, a tendril of sound. George turned us on to Pink Floyd because he's often playing *The Wall* or *The Dark Side of the Moon* in the kitchen when he's cleaning up. George believes that David Gilmour's guitar solo in "Comfortably Numb" is the best guitar solo of all time, and he made us listen to it while he mimicked along on air guitar and pointed out all the best parts.

That first time I heard it, it sounded like birdsong, climbing higher and higher then breaking the air open with sound. I could feel tingling on my bare arms and the back of my neck, as if the music had crystallized the oxygen in the room, and then shattered it, sending small slivers to rain down, landing on my skin like a million little pinpricks. George closed his eyes and swayed back and forth, a gesture of praise, as if he were in church and David Gilmour were God.

I look out the car window at the scenery, which hasn't changed much the entire time we've been traveling—palm trees and exit signs and the occasional road kill, mostly possums and raccoons, creatures that only come out at night, under cover of darkness.

I've always been told to fear raccoons that venture out in the daytime, been warned that, if you see one during the day, it must have rabies, and you should stay far away from it because surely the animal is deranged and will attack you if you get too close. But then I looked it up and found out that's not true at all. There are many reasons why a raccoon might be out and about during the day, especially if it's a nursing mother with babies. The mother raccoon can't go all day without eating. She needs to eat more than usual so she can produce milk. It's amazing what a mother can do, even out in the wild, with no one to help her. She gives birth, she keeps her babies safe, she feeds them, she teaches them how to live. All this happens without human intervention, life going on and on without people in charge.

The Thunderbird is an older hotel, built in the late fifties, the decade when most of the Gulf Coast was developed and little tourist stands started popping up along the water. Shea saw the hotel online and immediately fell in love with it because it's vintage. My mother doesn't like it for that same reason. For someone who loves almost everything else second-hand, my mother likes hotels to be as new as possible. She wanted to stay at the brand-new Holiday Inn we passed on our way into town, the large cursive *H* pulsing with green light on the side of the stucco building. My mother gets paranoid when we travel, and modern architecture calms her down.

The décor of the Thunderbird has an American Southwest vibe to it, its logo a red and green rendering of a thunderbird. The image of the thunderbird has the appearance of an eagle, with its strong profile and large curved beak. In Native American mythology, the thunderbird was believed to control rainfall, its wings so massive that the sheer force of their movement caused thunder to rumble. When the thunderbird blinked, sheets of lightning came down from the sky.

At the hotel check-in counter, Shea gets our room keys, and we load our stuff from the car onto a small brass luggage cart with squeaky wheels. Our room is on the third floor with a view of the Gulf of Mexico from our window. My mother and Shea claim the bed closest to the bathroom, throwing their bags on the scratchy-looking bedspread.

"I hate these ugly things," Shea says, moving all the bags to the floor for a moment so she can rip the bedspread off the bed, roll it up, and stuff it into the small closet. She throws the bags back on the bed and props herself up against the headboard with a pillow. "That's more like it," she says, and then sighs as she makes herself comfortable. "Now I can really take in the view." Shea flashes a smile toward my mother that's more of a smirk, really, and my mother looks like she's blushing as she walks into the bathroom to wash her face, her purple headband in her hand.

Clarisse searches her duffel bag and finds her bathing suit, a red two-piece with little white flowers. "Get your suit," she says to me. "Let's hit the pool before dinner." I look at Shea, and without skipping a beat, she answers the question I'm asking in my head.

"Your mom won't mind," Shea tells me. "Go have fun."

"Take your phone with you!" my mother calls from the bathroom over the sound of running water.

Clarisse and I change into our bathing suits quickly, performing those feats of magic girls learn when forced to change clothes in middle school locker rooms, that time in your life when you are most self-

conscious about your body, which feels stranger to
you with each passing day. If you time it right, you
can get changed without exposing yourself much at
all—maybe a split second flashing of skin here and
there, but that's much better than standing around
naked. Most girls agree on this, but there's always an
exception to that rule. When I was in seventh grade,
it was Brooklyn Marko. She would dress slowly and
leisurely, pulling her T-shirt off over her head in an
exaggerated motion and pushing her panties down to
the floor until they were resting in a pink puddle at
her ankles. I'd watch Brooklyn just long enough, until
I would sense that she was about to feel my gaze, my
eyes on her breasts or the dark clutch of hair between
her legs.

chapter twenty-three

The Thunderbird has a tiki bar on the beach and a swimming pool with a thunderbird depicted in green and red tiles on the bottom. There is a breakfast buffet in the morning, but there is also a Shell station across the street so I bet we will get our breakfast there tomorrow. My mother loves gas station coffee (black), and donuts from a Plexiglas case.

We have the entire hotel pool to ourselves so Clarisse and I take turns doing handstands in the shallow end, counting to see how long each of us can hold the pose. Clarisse can hold her breath longer than I can, which gives her the advantage every time.

Then we swim down to the bottom of the deep end, touching the slimy concrete floor. I open my eyes underwater and see the red and green tiles of the thunderbird, blurry flashes of color. I feel the burn of chlorine in my eyes when I come up for air. Clarisse and I act like little girls, playing and splashing and taunting each other, until a group of three high school boys appear. They are all wearing board shorts and flip-flops, and their bodies are lean and long. They look related, maybe brothers or cousins, each head of hair sandy blond, each face fair skinned and angular.

The boys claim a group of lounge chairs and throw their towels down. They kick off their flip-flops and jump into the shallow end one at a time, each one making a splash that ripples out to the rest of the pool. Clarisse and I swim to the side of the pool and hold on to the edge, our bodies suspended, floating in the deep water.

The boys begin to walk through the shallow end toward us, their smiles so big they are practically giddy, about to burst into laughter at any moment. They stop when the water gets too deep to walk, and then the tallest one motions for us to come over.

Clarisse glances at me and gives me a reassuring look, one that says, *I'm brave enough for both of us.* And I believe her. We swim over to the shallow end and say hello.

The boys are from Massachusetts "but not Boston," they make sure to specify. Two are brothers, and the third is their cousin. They're here with their parents for a family reunion of sorts. It's nothing too official, just a bunch of people from their extended family meeting up on the beach and hanging out. They're early, they say. The rest of their family members aren't arriving until Sunday.

When they ask where we're from, Clarisse tells them we're sisters, and that we live at the hotel. "Our mom works here," she tells them. "So we grew up here, ordering free room service and using the pool whenever we want." I'm certain they're going to see right through this. Clarisse and I don't exactly look alike, and it seems rather far-fetched that the hotel would allow employees and their families to live here. I scan the boys' faces, looking for signs of them calling bullshit, of them telling us we're stupid little girls who are also stupid little liars. All I see is more wide smiling.

"That's really cool," the tallest boy says. "It must be awesome to live in Florida. No winter." He's giving Clarisse the once-over with his laser-beam eye, scanning her body like he's a machine. "How old are you?" he asks.

"I'm nineteen," Clarisse says without blinking. Everyone knows that blinking is a tell, a sign of lying. Other tells are touching your face, looking down, clearing your throat, and taking long pauses. Clarisse knows to avoid them all. "I go to Florida State. She's eighteen," Clarisse says, motioning to me. "She's starting FSU as a freshman in the fall so we'll finally be back together." She drapes one arm over my shoulder, a sign of sisterly love. "How old are you guys?"

They sound off their ages. The brothers are seventeen and fourteen, and the cousin is fourteen too. The seventeen-year-old smiles at Clarisse.

"Do you get a lot of guys hitting on you here?" he asks. "I bet you do." He is cupping water in his hands and then raising them and letting the water fall, making a trickling sound like a leaky faucet.

"It's not so bad," Clarisse says. "When that happens, I just tell them that my mom works in human resources here at the hotel. And she's very good at handling sexual harassment cases. That usually solves the problem."

One fourteen-year-old challenges the other fourteen-year-old to a race to the other side of the pool. They take off with a start, noisily splashing away from us.

"Don't mind them. They're just trying to show off," the older boy says. "They aren't around pretty girls very often." He's looking at me now, eyeing my breasts covered by my purple bathing suit top. My body feels like a silvery fish at the market, shining on a bed of ice as customers walk by and examine me. I stand up a little straighter, pushing my chest out just a little. I almost can't believe that I want him to see me. I'm so used to wanting to be invisible.

An elderly woman in a black bathing suit arrives poolside, her skin sagging and spotted from sun damage. She walks into the pool, the skirt of her bathing suit eventually floating around her like a little black cloud. A few minutes later, two moms arrive with two squealing toddlers—armed with floaties and water wings and foam noodles.

"Let's get out and go down to the beach," the seventeen-year-old boy says.

"Actually, we should probably get going," Clarisse says. "We have to check in with our mom about dinner. But maybe we'll see you later?"

Clarisse taps me on the shoulder, and we walk up the steps and out of the pool. I wrap myself up in my towel, and Clarisse dries her hands on hers and then picks up her phone. I watch the water drip from Clarisse's body while the boy recites his number with the Massachusetts area code, and she taps the digits into her phone.

"I'm Heidi, by the way," she says. "And this is Gretchen." I smile, trying to look nonchalant after hearing my new name. The fourteen-year-olds are racing back to the shallow end now, their lean bodies cutting the water as if it were glass.

The seventeen-year-old smiles with his teeth this time, which are straight and white and perfect. "I'm Oliver," he says. "Nice to meet you."

Inside the hotel elevator, Clarisse and I watch the numbers light up as we are transported to our floor. There is a woman with a baby in one corner and what appears to be a newlywed couple in another.

Clarisse smiles at me and then retrieves her phone from her bag and sends me two texts. *He's hot*, her first message reads, and then she sends a second message that is just a bunch of fire emojis, dollops of identical orange and red digital flames lined up in perfect rows.

I nod silently, smiling at the illuminated screen of my phone. When the stainless steel doors glide open, we step out of the elevator and into possibility.

chapter twenty-four

When we stay in hotels, my mother has a hard time falling asleep in the silence. She needs something on in the background so she likes to keep the television on. Shea can deal with the television, but she can't have anything on with a story or she'll pay too much attention to it and never fall asleep.

After some discussion, they compromise by putting on the Home Shopping Network. It's just past midnight, and the host, a dark-haired woman in a red pantsuit, is announcing the special deal of the day—a delicate diamond and sapphire ring for four easy payments of $71.55. A running tally appears in the bottom left corner of the screen, recording the number of rings sold. It ticks rapidly, dozens of people from all over the country phoning in to buy jewelry at midnight.

My mother and Shea are both turned away from me, the light of the TV screen bouncing off them as they sleep under a white blanket. I can see the shapes of their bodies, mounds of snow glowing in artificial moonlight. Clarisse is already asleep, her hair tangled and still smelling of chlorine. When I came out of the shower, Clarisse was already snuggled in our bed, the blue fuzzy blanket she brought from home pulled up to her chin.

I hate being the last one to fall sleep in any kind of group sleeping situation so that's exactly what always happens to me. Shea would call it a self-fulfilling prophecy, but that's sounds so mystical. It's just that I try too hard to fall asleep first, and then my mind stages a revolt and does the opposite. You know that saying, *The heart wants what it wants*? Well, in this case, the brain wants what it wants, and in this case, my brain doesn't want to fall asleep.

There are too many things to think about. What will I feel when I see the house where my father grew up? What will his bedroom look like? Did Ella keep it in original condition, a shrine to his childhood? Or was it turned into a home office, a den, an exercise room, or a guest bedroom? Will it have a distinct smell? Smell is most closely connected to memory for me. I might smell Ella's house and it will lock into my body somehow. Will I be trapped in the scent of her house, my life reduced to a constant search for the smell?

Like the small bottle of perfume that my mother wears only on special occasions when she has to get dressed up, like weddings or holiday parties. She never wears too much to make it overpowering, just dabs a touch between her breasts before she gets dressed. When I was younger, I would sit on her bed and watch her get ready for these occasions, and I thought she looked so glamorous—in black pantyhose and heels and a bra, but nothing else.

When she opened the perfume bottle, the room took on the scent of musk and amber. As I got older, I stopped watching her get ready because my body started looking more like hers, more like a woman, and the act took on more of a voyeuristic quality. But still, to this day, when I smell a hint of that perfume, those subtle, warm notes, it takes me back to being a little girl and sitting on my mother's bed. You can't control it, the way scent connects to memories, to moments in time. You can't break the association no matter how hard you try.

I look over at Clarisse, damp spots on her pillow from her swimming pool hair, her chest moving gently as she breathes—up, up, up, then down. I sync my breathing with hers, and I close my eyes. I focus on the Home Shopping host's voice as she talks about diamonds—the cut, the color, the clarity—ways to measure what is precious in this world.

chapter twenty-five

In the morning, the four of us walk through the hotel lobby, which smells like burnt coffee. There's a flat television screen on the wall projecting a news program with the sound turned down, the closed captioning crawling across the bottom of the screen in its typewriter font, the black bars seemingly rising from nowhere, just appearing as if from some higher power. It's easy to forget that an actual person is behind those captions, an actual person transcribing all the words. If you watch long enough, you'll see a mistake made here or there, the transcriber backspacing and correcting, a document edited in real time.

There are single people and couples and children sitting around in the lobby, pouring coffee, taking selections from the fruit basket, reading newspapers, waiting for family members to come downstairs. We walk quickly, and Clarisse and I both try to make ourselves smaller, less noticeable, in case the boys from Massachusetts are here. I don't look around at all but instead focus on the thunderbird logo on the glass door ahead of me.

Shea asks my mother, "Why don't we just get our coffee for free here?" and my mother tosses her head back ever so slightly, rolling her eyes just a bit. Nothing too exaggerated, as though she doesn't have the physical energy. "Oh, that's right…you're such a coffee snob. You prefer gas station sludge to anything from a hotel." Shea puts one arm around my mother's shoulders and uses the other to poke her in the ribs a bit, making my mother jump just slightly, an illusion really, as her feet never leave the ground.

Outside, the sun hangs high like a ball of fire in the sky. There are no clouds, nothing but blue on the horizon for as far as the eye can see. It's just a typical day in Florida, the kind of day I'm so used to, although it feels different somehow. The air smells stronger, a more pungent mix of salt and brine. The seagulls cry louder, their shrill *keow keow keow* reverberating across the sky. I'm already on sensory overload when the crosswalk shrieks and the little white walking man lights up, our signal that it's safe to cross.

After coffee and donuts at the Shell station, we

cross back to the Thunderbird and get in the car. Dana Apple's office is about fifteen minutes away so we'll be there soon. There isn't much time to get nervous. My mother calls Dana from her cell phone to confirm that we're on our way. It sounds like a secretary has answered because my mother refers to "Dana," not "you." My mother is wearing a black cotton tank top and black linen shorts with a thin black-and-white-striped scarf draped over her shoulders like a shawl. She is the woman in mourning for this visit. She knows that the details of her appearance could possibly get back to my father. If it does, I hope he is told how beautiful she looks, her hair delicately secured in a knot on top of her head.

Dana's office building is nondescript—just a square, white, one-story building with a red, Spanish-tiled roof. The sign in the parking lot is nondescript too, plain white with blue block letters describing the tenants as LAW OFFICE and DENTIST. The parking lot has two cars in it other than ours, possibly Dana's and her secretary's. "Of course," my mother says, "that's probably her Mercedes." My mother isn't the type to make snide comments about certain professions, but she has been known to conjure a bad attitude in times of stress, a kind of protective coating she wears when needed.

My mother parks, and the four of us get out of the car and make our way to the entrance. The front door of the building is unlocked, and inside the lobby are two interior doors—one marked DANA APPLE and one marked RALPH ROGERS, DMD." There is a large potted plant between the two doors, and I reach out and touch one of the waxy reddish leaves. It's a bromeliad, I think, a staple of indoor tropical plants, with familiar spiky points that almost look like a pineapple plant. They might be related to the pineapple, I can't remember. In the plant world, there are so many connections, so many variations. Plants can be more difficult to decipher than people.

My mother knocks on the door, and we stand and wait. Will Dana think it's strange that it takes four people to claim a butter dish? I didn't think much of my own appearance at the hotel. I just threw on a pair of cutoff jean shorts, a gray T-shirt, and black flip-flops. I don't feel as beautiful as my mother or Clarisse, who is wearing a turquoise tank top and white circle skirt, the kind that fans out when you spin around.

Dana Apple opens the glass door swiftly to greet us. She is taller and older than my mother, probably in her late forties. She has a very short haircut that draws all your attention to her face, her eyes specifically, which are brown behind wire-rimmed glasses. "Ms. Gibson?" Dana asks, probably wondering if it's Shea or my mother she should be addressing.

My mother extends her right hand and says, "Hi. I'm Mira." They shake hands rather stiffly.

"Mira. Nice to meet you," Dana says, making eye contact the way that lawyers are probably trained to do. Their profession is mostly about trust—getting juries and judges and clients to trust them enough to get what they want. "And you are . . ." she says to Shea.

"Oh, I'm sorry," my mother says. "This is my partner, Shea. This is my daughter, Evelyn, and her friend Clarisse." She gestures toward each of us as she makes the introductions, and we each nod when it's our turn.

"Fabulous. Nice to meet you all," Dana says. "Come on in and have a seat." She holds the door open for us while we pass. My cheeks are burning because I know Dana is paying special attention to me, fixing her glassy eyes on me. She doesn't realize that Clarisse is a murderer's daughter too, another spectacle, another freak of nature in the sideshow.

Inside the office, there is a large desk, and Dana walks behind it and sits down. There are two chairs positioned right in front of the desk, and three more lined against one wall. My mother sits in one of the chairs in front of the desk and taps my arm and motions for me to sit in the other so that we're both facing Dana. Shea and Clarisse take two of the chairs along the wall. I cross and uncross my legs a few times, trying to find the most comfortable and flattering pose for Dana. I end up with one of my legs crossed underneath me, sitting on my ankle in a sort of half crisscross applesauce, the way they taught us to sit in kindergarten. It's like the lotus position in yoga and meditation, except you don't have to get your feet to rest on your thighs.

Dana Apple opens a file folder and then makes more eye contact with us, dividing her attention between my face and my mother's. "This is in reference to the execution of the estate of Ella Joyce Hayes," she says in a more official-sounding tone of voice. "Mrs. Hayes has instructed the following items bequeathed to her granddaughter, Evelyn Emerald Gibson: one Limoges butter dish." She breaks character for a moment and adds, "This is all just a formality, as far as the language that is used in the document." She smiles at me, as though to set my mind at ease. As though my mind is in need of easing.

"I have something for you to sign, Ms. Gibson, Mira," Dana says, and then slides a piece of paper across the desk to my mother, who starts rummaging in her purse for a pen until Dana hands her one from her desk drawer.

My mother signs in cursive and then slides the paper back to Dana, who walks over to a tall mahogany cabinet in the corner. She fishes a key from her pants pocket, and unlocks the cabinet. She pulls out a shoe box. "The butter dish is inside," she tells no one in particular, as though she's talking to the air. "It's all wrapped up in bubble wrap so it's secure." She hands me the box. "If you're the type of person who likes popping bubble wrap, then you're in luck, Evelyn."

"Great, so we're all set now?" my mother asks.

"Almost. I understand that Evelyn would also like to see Mrs. Hayes's home?"

"Oh, right," my mother answers. "Well, I just don't want to be a bother, that's all. I mean, I think Evelyn would be fine without seeing it."

"Of course it's no bother at all." Dana smiles at me—a pitiful smile, a smile I've received so many times from people who know about my situation. People who know what my father did and where he is.

We follow Dana's silver Mercedes for about ten minutes until we arrive at a small house on the corner of Gulf Boulevard and Sandpiper Drive. Dana pulls into the sun-bleached driveway, and my mother pulls in behind her. The house is pale pink with mint green shutters, a house that might belong in Candy Land, a home Princess Lolly might call her own. There is a white ceramic birdbath in the front yard. The grass is cut very short, in various shades of yellowish brown, while the neighbors' yards are bright green.

Clarisse squeezes my hand before we get out of the car. Dana unlocks the front door, and we all file into the small foyer.

"The house is going on the market soon, after the estate sale, but the floors haven't been professionally cleaned yet so you can leave your shoes on," Dana tells us. The heels of her black pumps make a click-clacking sound on the terrazzo floor of the hallway, which leads to the living room. There's a circular shag carpet in robin's egg blue at the center of the room. There are two pale yellow chairs, one light blue throw pillow on each. There is an empty birdcage on a large stand in front of the sliding glass door, which leads to the tiny backyard. My mother opens the slider and walks outside, into the sunlight that is streaming between the slats in the vertical blinds. Shea gives Dana a small nod and then follows my mother outside.

I feel myself anchored to one spot, slowly turning in place, taking in the room via a 360-degree panorama. There aren't any photographs on the walls, just several paintings of birds—great blue heron, wood stork, spoonbill, and white ibis. Each painting is large enough to hang alone on each of the four walls. And each painting has a small brass nameplate beneath it, identifying the bird with genus, species, and common name, like you'd see in a museum. Dana clears her throat to remind me that she's still here so I'm not startled when she talks.

"Ella painted them herself," she says, stepping toward me slightly. She's the museum guide coming out of the background to assist me. "Ella was quite an artist, actually."

The birds in the paintings are all wading birds—the kind that eat fish, spending a lot of their time wading in shallow waters, looking for food. They have the most delicate legs, like twigs. Their legs bend backward, like knees in reverse. Ella has captured each bird mid-stride in the water, in various states of balancing on one thin-footed leg. We have wood storks that roam the inlet in Pass-a-Grille. Large and white with dark beaks, they move so gracefully they barely break the water as they stroll the edge.

"And as you may have guessed, Ella was also very much a bird enthusiast," Dana says.

"What will happen to the paintings?" Clarisse asks.

"They will be sold at the estate sale, with the rest of her remaining things."

"Can't Evelyn have them?" Clarisse asks, throwing Dana off her polished guard.

"Well. It's not that simple, actually," Dana begins. "Technically, Evelyn is a next of kin, but because she's a minor, she can only legally receive property that Ella specifically bequeathed to her. Ella had a daughter but she is deceased and she didn't have any children. Ella's son is . . . incarcerated . . . and because the estate is not settled, the executrix must sell property to satisfy the—"

"It's fine," I say, interrupting. I turn to face Clarisse. "I don't want them anyway."

"Well then, feel free to move about the other rooms," Dana says, clearly hoping to lighten the mood.

"How do you know so much about the Hayes family?" Clarisse asks Dana. I walk toward the three bedrooms, each one with the door currently closed. There must have been one for Ella, one for my father, and one for this dead sister. I call to Dana without turning around. "What was Ella's daughter's name?"

"Her name was Ruth," Dana answers. "But everyone called her Ruthie."

I choose the door in the middle first. As I open it, I hear the soft creaking of the hinges, begin to feel the change in temperature—the room gets the most sun exposure this time of day. There is a twin bed against one wall, and the walls are painted peach to match the comforter, which is white with peach flowers. It has slatted windows you crank open and closed with a small silver handle.

I look out through the frosted window glass and see my mother and Shea in the backyard sitting on two redwood chairs with green plastic cushions. Their eyes are closed, their faces angled toward the sun. Shea's left hand hangs from the chair, her fingers grazing the bright grass.

I choose the door on the left next. As I open it and walk inside the room, I hear a snippet of Clarisse grilling Dana in the living room. "Did Ella visit her son often?"

This was surely Ella's room. It's fully furnished and still decorated with what looks like a grandmother's touch. It's strange to think of her as a grandmother though. She never got to meet her only grandchild, after all. But she knew I existed, so isn't that enough? If a grandchild falls in the forest and her grandmother doesn't see her, does she still make a sound?

Ella's room is all shades of blue and green, the bed covered in an afghan with thick stripes of alternating dark blue and light blue. The nightstand is actually a folding tray, the kind that comes in a set and is used for eating in front of the television. On the tray, there's a small silver lamp topped by a pale green lampshade with dark green fringe along the bottom edge. In one corner, there is a light wood chest of drawers and in another, a blue recliner. The floor is the same speckled terrazzo throughout the house, surrounding the bed in a sea of candy-colored confetti.

I quietly open the top dresser drawer, but it's empty. There are no personal effects—no clothing in the closet, no snapshots, no jewelry box—as if the room had been sanitized after Ella's death, staged to look as though no one ever lived here.

My mother and Shea have returned to the living room, saving Dana from Clarisse's interrogation. I hear the low tones of small talk—*nice shoes, oh, you're a preschool teacher?*—that sort of thing.

I choose the door on the right last. A bright sliver of sunlight beams from the bottom of the closed door, and when I open it, I understand why. The room is completely empty, the walls white, the windows bare. This must have been my father's room, any trace of him wiped clean to ward off the evil spirits that may linger.

The sun pours in at an angle, casting my shadow on the floor. My body appears stretched, exaggerated. If I were one of Ella's paintings, the tiny brass nameplate below me would read *Projection of a Girl in an Empty Room.*

chapter twenty-six

When we return to our room at the Thunderbird, I take the shoe box into the bathroom and lock the door. I turn the exhaust fan on so no one can hear the sound of me tearing into the packing tape that seals the box, the rustle of the bubble wrap in my hands as I free the butter dish from its protective cocoon. Someone wrapped the item with extreme care, making me wonder if Ella herself prepared this gift for me, her old hands delicately handling the same materials I'm touching now.

It occurs to me that I didn't even ask Dana how Ella died. Was she active until the end, riding her bicycle every day, or did she lie in a hospital bed for weeks, even months, with a terminal illness? Maybe she had dementia and didn't even know what was happening. Maybe she was prepared for death, getting her affairs in order, visiting her son one last time. Or maybe something stopped her heart unexpectedly, turning her lifeless in an instance. I don't even know whether she was cremated or buried somewhere. All I know is that she's dead, and so is my grandfather, and so is my aunt Ruth. All I know is that my father is the only living member of that family, if you can even call him living.

I unwrap and unwrap until I reach the final layer of plastic bubbles. I can begin to see the dish now through the bubble wrap, the cream porcelain, the octagon shape of the plate, the rounded dome lid. I can begin to see the design painted in the center of the lid, a bird perched on a cherry blossom branch, its feathers long, plumage like a peacock's tail at rest—my view slightly distorted through the air in the bubbles. Finally, the dish is resting on my lap, the packaging scattered all over the hard, white bathroom floor, material a real bird might break apart with her beak, stealing a scrap for her nest.

Light catches the gold accents on the dish, making them shimmer. The drawing is so detailed, that it must have been hand painted. I can see the weight of the brush strokes, some thin, as if the artist's brush barely grazed the porcelain at times. Other strokes are thicker. The bird's tail flows down like a waterfall, feathers that look fuzzy, fluffy as down or the fur of your childhood monster, the one living under your bed. You fear it will grab your ankle if you dare to dangle your bare foot off the side of the bed for too long.

When I was younger, my monster was Freddy Krueger from *A Nightmare on Elm Street*. My mother and Shea had to go somewhere one summer day, somewhere I wasn't allowed to be. So they sent me to a house down the street for the day, where a woman just added me to the crew of children in her charge. There were five of us altogether, two boys, a little girl, and a baby named Jo whose gender wasn't clear to me. Jo had no hair, no obvious markers of girlhood or boyhood. Jo played with blocks and dolls and a little wooden hammer and nail set painted in primary colors. Jo wore white onesies that snapped between Jo's chubby thighs, always playing happily and smiling, not weighed down by the expectations of being a girl or a boy. Just being a child.

Just after lunch that day, the woman, whose name I can't recall now, had an emergency and had to leave for a while. Since I was the oldest, she left me in charge. She said she'd be gone only a short while, and she took Jo with her. I watched from the screen door as she strapped Jo into the baby seat in the back of her Toyota, the other children peeking through the living room window to see what was happening. I think it had something to do with a boyfriend, as there had been an intense phone conversation that suggested something or someone needed to be picked up immediately or else.

After I watched the Toyota pull away down the street, I closed the door and locked it and suggested that we watch a movie. I thought that was the best way to keep everyone from fooling around and hurting themselves or catching something on fire, one of the things I still fear might happen when there are no adults around. I'm certain that fire knows when children are alone and most vulnerable. I'm certain that fire is a villain that wishes to consume us, taking pleasure in eating us like candy, like the old woman in the Hansel and Gretel story. Fire is blind, just like the old woman. That's why it searches and searches, running down hallways and staircases in houses until it finds its prey.

My movie idea would have been a good one except one of the boys found *A Nightmare on Elm Street* on one of the cable channels, and suddenly all the curtains were drawn in the sunken living room and all the children were watching teenagers afraid to go to sleep because Freddy Krueger was killing people in their dreams. It's scary enough to die in a dream, but in these movies, if you die in your dream, you die in reality. We only watched it for about an hour, until the babysitter came home with smiling baby Jo on her hip and a bag of ice cream sandwiches to buy our silence, but I never forgot Freddy, the villain, with his melted skin and bladed glove, five knives instead of five fingers.

Perhaps my father is someone's Freddy Krueger now, the murderer whose face continues to haunt even after death. He's the villain who does things no one can comprehend, although they try and try. They manipulate the puzzle pieces desperately, arranging pieces in every combination, every direction, turn, turn, turning the jigsaw shapes, but the picture will never be complete. There will always be something that doesn't make sense—a bridge that leads nowhere, a missing section of sky.

I turn the dish over, and on the back is a small piece of white tape. It looks like medical tape, the kind you would use to secure gauze on a wound. Someone has written on the tape with a blue ballpoint pen, chubby capital letters that say BIRD-OF-PARADISE.

chapter twenty-seven

We watch the sunset on the beach, Shea and my mother on low-slung beach chairs, each with a frozen rumrunner in hand. My mother's has an orange slice floating in it, pierced with the toothpick end of a cocktail umbrella. The bright turquoise parasol grazes the rim of her glass and must tickle her cheek with every sip she takes.

Clarisse and I are on a beach towel, digging our feet into the sand as far as we can. As we tunnel with our toes, the sand gets colder and colder, wetter and wetter. The deeper you dig, the more water you find in the sand, as if the sea is trying to escape.

There are pockets of people scattered around the beach, everyone facing the horizon. They all look straight ahead, not at each other—strangers in an elevator, waiting for their floor, watching each number as it illuminates, waiting for their destination. We are waiting for the sun to sink below the water, waiting for that moment when it looks as though the Gulf of Mexico is eating the sun. It will last for only a few seconds. You can't blink or turn away or you might miss it. The sun is an orange ball of fire tonight, the sky streaked with pinks and reds. *Nature's light show*, Shea calls it. "Even when I go blind, I'll still love the sunset," she says. "It's not just something you see, it's something you can feel too."

I'm looking straight ahead, not wanting to miss the moment, when I spot the silhouettes of three boys in the distance, kicking water at each other and trying to jump over the tiny breakers that lap at the shore. They are the boys from not-Boston, and I gently nudge Clarisse's elbow with mine to get her attention, motioning toward the boys with my chin, keeping my movements small so as not to alert my mother and Shea.

Yes. Clarisse mouths the word to me.

Then I lean over and whisper in her ear, my hand cupped, a passageway through which only we can communicate—our own private channel, our own frequency. "Keep your eyes on them until my mom and Shea leave," I whisper.

"Okay," Clarisse whispers back, her breath warm on the curve of my outer ear. "But what if your mom and Shea want to stay?"

"They're getting drunk," I say. "They won't last much longer."

The boys run out of the water and toward a group of people who have congregated farther down the beach from us. They have claimed their square of the beach by piercing the sand with tiki torches in four corners. They have blankets and folding chairs and a large red cooler on wheels, and I can hear the adults laughing and talking. Many of the sunset watchers will pack up their things and leave once the big show is over. But the boys from not-Boston and their family don't seem to be going anywhere anytime soon.

The sun inches lower and lower and then finally crosses the line where water meets sky, a disappearing act that makes you think that, if you just kept swimming and swimming toward it, you would eventually be able to lean over the edge of the earth and see the sun falling, falling, falling down the other side. You can't blame early explorers for thinking the world was flat. How was anyone to know they were living on a sphere? There were no clues at first, no curved edges to be seen. We experience everything up close, our collective lens so zoomed in that it's difficult to get perspective. We march along like ants on a melon. We can't realize the magnitude of our surroundings, can't fathom the tiny space we occupy in the context of the larger world.

I stand up and walk over to my mother, resting my hands on her shoulders from behind. I used to sneak up on her this way as a little kid. I'd place my hands on her shoulders and say "Boo!" and she'd practically jump out of whatever chair she was sitting in at the time. This time, I want to relax her, not startle her. She pats one of my hands with one of hers. "Hi, sweetie," she says.

"Hi. Are you having a good time?" I ask.

"Yes, I am," she says, sipping her drink and then tilting her head back to look at me upside down. I can't see her features clearly in the dusky light, but I know her face by memory, know the shape of her eyes and the thin lines that have formed between her eyebrows, parentheses turned away from each other.

"I'm having a good time too," I say. "Thanks for bringing me here. I know you didn't have to."

"You're welcome. And I'm glad," she says, her voice smooth and lower than usual. The rum has relaxed her vocal cords, turning her voice into velvet. Shea stands up and wraps a blue-and-white-striped beach towel around her shoulders. She's a little wobbly on her feet in the cool sand, the towel moving in the gulf breeze like a cape behind her.

"Let's move this party up to the balcony," Shea says as a general announcement. My mother kisses my hand and smiles at me, her upside-down position making it look like a frown on an otherwise happy face.

"Can't we stay down here for a little while?" I ask. "It's our last night. And we've barely had any beach time."

My mother is on her feet now, and she grabs my face, one hand on each of my cheeks. "You can stay for a little bit," she says, and then gives me a kiss on the forehead. "You too, Clarisse!" my mother says, now sounding excited. She walks over to Clarisse, who is still sitting on the beach towel. She grabs both of Clarisse's hands and pulls her up to her feet, almost knocking herself backward in the process. Then my mother kisses Clarisse on the forehead too. "I love you girls," my mother says, as she slings one arm around Clarisse's shoulder and beckons me to join this impromptu group hug with her other hand.

"Okay, okay," Shea says, as my mother laughs. "Let's get you upstairs before you start singing 'The Wind Beneath My Wings.'" Clearly the more sober one, Shea checks the time on her phone and gives us instructions. "Just stay on the beach, okay?" Clarisse and I nod in agreement. "No gallivanting around town."

"Yes, of course," Clarisse says, standing up straight and smiling. We're so close to being free that my insides are crackling with anticipation. Shea and my mother walk arm in arm back to the hotel patio, Shea carrying their shoes in her hand. Clarisse and I stand and watch them become smaller and smaller until we finally see them disappear inside the hotel doors.

"Come on, let's go!" Clarisse says to me, tapping my shoulder and then running toward the water, like we're playing tag and I'm it now. I follow her to the shoreline, where the sand turns harder, packed and wet from the tide washing over it. We wade in to our knees, louder than delicate birds, our legs thicker, making splashing sounds with each step. We stop and stand, staring at the moon in the distance. Its reflection on the water moves in waves—bright ripples of light you can reach into the water and touch. I walk along the shoreline in the direction of the boys from not-Boston and their family, whose chatter and laughter we can hear more clearly as we approach.

Oliver spots us and begins walking toward us. "I thought that was you over there," he says. "Gretchen, right?" The skin on his bare chest is taut from the cooler air, his nipples hardened into small, fleshy beads. I nod and smile, remembering my new name. "And Heidi, right?" he asks Clarisse. "Was that your mom with you?"

"Yeah, our mom and her wife," I answer. "You

should see the pictures from the wedding. They wore these gorgeous vintage dresses, ivory satin and lace. Very old Hollywood."

"Oh, that's awesome," Oliver says. "My cousin Justin and his boyfriend got married like two years ago, but I don't remember what they wore." He grins, looking at me and then Clarisse.

The tide rushes back into the gulf, toward the dark horizon, and we all look down at our feet for a moment, bare and exposed but slowly sinking into soft shoreline sand. I feel the salt sting the open pores of my ankles.

"Wanna come hang out with us for a while?" Oliver asks, his dim outline swaying back and forth slightly, his arms folded across his naked chest. "I promise my family's mostly cool," he says, gesturing back toward his family's plot of sand where they now have a small fire going, shadowy figures gathered around the flames. "My one uncle is kind of a dick, but he's pretty drunk so it's all good."

I take a few steps, getting closer to Oliver. He's so tall that my eyes barely hit his nipples, and so I tilt my head back to look up at his face. "I think we had something else in mind."

Oliver lets out a little *ha*, a quick exhalation.

"Yeah, come with us," Clarisse says.

"Sure, hang on just a sec. Don't move," he says, and then runs toward his family.

My body buzzes with excitement, the rush of electricity you feel when you're about to enter the unknown. I am an explorer in undiscovered territory, so many unknown delights about to reveal themselves to me. I know Clarisse feels it too—that pulse of anticipation like the moment a firework shoots into the sky and you hold your breath because you know that, in a split second, the beauty will unfurl, exploding in a burst of color and light.

As Oliver makes his way back to us, a wide grin on his face, Clarisse clasps my hand in hers, and we start to skip. Our joined arms swing back and forth, and we are two girls creating a breeze with their bodies— a gust, a squall, a gale.

chapter twenty-eight

Clarisse and I skip away from the water, Oliver following closely behind. I can hear his excited breathing, a jagged in and out. I can feel his presence, his energy over my shoulder as we make our way toward a playground. The equipment casts shadows on the sand in the moonlight, swings and slides and a metal cage to climb upon or hang upside down from.

Next to the playground is a small pavilion used as a concession area, its service window closed, a wooden menu board nailed above depicting hot dogs and slices of pepperoni pizza with prices in hand-painted numbers. There are picnic tables and a few trashcans, some seagulls picking around, conditioned to come to this place looking for scraps of food, a chunk of hot dog bun or a stray French fry.

Clarisse climbs to the top of the slide—a bright blue plastic tube that makes her hair stand on end

with static electricity when she emerges from the
mouth at the bottom. She lands on her butt, her body
making a soft thud on the sand. Oliver runs over and
grabs her hands, pulling her to her feet. Then his
hands are on her waist, and he lifts her above his head
for just a moment before putting her feet back on the
ground, a pair of ballet dancers practicing a delicate
lift. Clarisse stands against Oliver's body, looking up at
him as he pulls her even closer, his hands resting low
on her hips.

"Your turn!" she says, breaking free from him.
"Come on, sis," she says to me as she sprints past me,
running back to the top of the slide. I follow her up
the ladder, the bottoms of my sandy feet almost slip-
ping on the metal rungs. Oliver climbs behind me,
breathing heavier than before.

"Let's form a chain," Clarisse says, reaching behind
to grab my feet so that I'm straddling her now. Oliver
sits behind me and does the same, his long legs reaching all the way to Clarisse. I can feel him getting
hard through his shorts, and I can feel myself pulsing
against Clarisse in front of me. Oliver stretches his
arms forward, reaching for Clarisse's breasts. "Uh, uh,
uh," Clarisse warns. "Bad boy."

She lets go of the edges of the tube, and we slide
down to the bottom as one, landing in a pile with

Oliver on his back on the bottom, me on top of him, and Clarisse on top of me. Clarisse jumps up and turns herself around, now straddling my waist so she can see my face and Oliver's. "If you want to touch us," she tells him, "you have to follow our rules."

"Okay," he says, "I'll do anything you want." His words are staccato from the weight of two girls on his rib cage. "Anything."

Next to the pavilion, there's a boardwalk that takes visitors to the parking lot. It's built about two feet off the ground, with wooden posts that disappear into the sand. There is tall beach grass all around, so high you can stand within it and blend right in, perfect camouflage. If you remain still enough and barely breathe, it's like you're not there at all.

I'm the leader. I part the beach grass like I'm parting a beaded curtain. I make a diving motion with my hands, a swimmer separating the water, my body becoming a blade. Oliver and Clarisse walk behind me, navigating around pieces of rock and seashell. When we let go of the grasses, they gently snap back into place, and we are hidden in our own cocoon of sand and wood and grass. Then we duck down and crawl into the space beneath the boardwalk. There is just enough room for our three bodies, as if the space were made just for us.

Oliver lies down on his back between Clarisse and me. He stares up through the slats of the boardwalk, slivers of moonlight making a pattern of light and shadow on his face. Clarisse and I are both propped up on our sides, our elbows sunk into the cool night sand. We face Oliver, but we also face each other. I catch Clarisse's eyes for just a moment. Even in this half dark, they dazzle me.

"So do you like me and my sister?" I ask Oliver.

He grins because of course the answer is so obvious. He says it without words, just a low sound, nearly a grunt. "Mmmm-hmmm."

"Do you want to touch us?"

"Mmmm-hmmm." A little louder now as if the director has appeared from thin air to lead the actors, reminding them of their motivation, of what's at stake. *Try it with more longing this time, more desperate wanting.*

I put one finger up to Oliver's mouth, and say "Shhhhh. We don't want anyone to hear us." I grab his hand, the one closest to me, and slide it under my bathing suit top to feel my bare skin. "Do you want to touch me here?" I ask. Then I guide his hand down between my legs. "Or here?"

"Uh, um, everywhere," he says. I notice his toes are curling and relaxing in rhythm with his breathing.

I let his hand remain between my legs, hoping he can feel me pulsing through my bathing suit bottom.

"Now, do you want my sister to touch you?"

"Oh hell, yes," he says.

"Go ahead, Heidi," I say to Clarisse. "Touch him anywhere you like." I am the director now, placing the characters where I want them within the scene.

Clarisse runs one finger up Oliver's leg, grazing him gently through his board shorts. She pulls her hand away, looking uncertain for a moment. I reach over and place my hand on top of hers, guiding now, our skin joined and melting, blurring where I begin and she ends, as if we truly do come from the same place. Our one hand is not uncertain now, and we slide our fingertips under the waistband of Oliver's shorts. We feel his skin damp, slick with sweat. We slide farther and farther until we reach him. Then Clarisse lets go, and it's just my hand, and I'm not sure what to do exactly, but I have an idea, and the boy's legs squirm in the sand, as I go on and on.

Clarisse lies on her back and wriggles her T-shirt off over her head. She folds it a few times lengthwise, making the thin blue cotton a bit thicker. "Now, let's make this more fun," she says. "Lift your head," she tells Oliver, and she wraps the T-shirt around his eyes, a cotton blindfold that smells like Clarisse. Oliver laughs softly. "There we go," Clarisse says when she's finished securing the T-shirt with a thick knot, and Oliver puts his head back on the sand.

She starts kissing him, and I watch her mouth moving upon his, their lips and tongues moving in rhythm, Clarisse's eyes closed. Can she feel me staring at them? They are so close, their bodies so real—I can smell skin and sweat and salt and sand. I can feel Oliver in my hand, smooth and hard. It feels like an illusion, a figment of my imagination as though I am some kind of inventor, creating this experience, all these feelings. Clarisse opens her eyes to look at me and then pulls away from Oliver.

"Your turn," she says, and the boy turns his eyeless face toward me, his mouth open, his lips plumper than I remember, slightly swollen from Clarisse's kisses. At first, I keep my eyes open and my lips closed, letting him reach for me with his tongue, licking my lips, my chin, searching for my open mouth.

Then Clarisse unties her bathing suit top, and lets the thin straps fall into the sand. She puts Oliver's hand on one of her bare breasts, and I see him squeezing it and rubbing it before I close my eyes, falling into the kissing, into Oliver's mouth that is so warm and wet. I'm losing myself in him, can feel some hidden rhythm unlock inside me, and now I know exactly

what to do, know what will come next. His other
hand is inside my bathing suit bottom now, his fingers
inside me.

As we kiss, I lose all sense of time and being. I
feel as though my body might lift up at any moment
and drift into the sky, a feather on the wind, soft and
weightless as a cloud. I feel a breaking, an overwhelm-
ing urge to cry out. Just as I think I might float away, I
hear Clarisse's soft voice in my ear, bringing me closer
to the ground. "Now, now," she says. "Don't keep him
all to yourself."

I pull away from Oliver's mouth, and he laughs,
saying, "It's okay. I have enough for both of you.
I promise." He takes his hands back—one from
Clarisse's naked breast, one from between my legs. He
unties the drawstring of his shorts, sliding them down
so we can see all of him now. "Who wants to go first
this time?" he asks.

The boy's entire body is muscle—I can sense it
rippling and writhing even though I see him lying
perfectly still—his eyeless face, the blood in his veins
glowing blue-black in the slivers of moonlight, coursing, coursing. It hits me that there is something sacred
about this, about him offering himself, an animal rendering up its soft underbelly to strangers, vulnerable,
only looking for comfort, for pleasure. But to render

can also mean to melt down, as in rendering the fat of an animal killed for its food, for the comfort and pleasure flesh provides when devoured.

Clarisse leans down slowly, putting him in her mouth as he stifles a moan, trying to be quiet. I can hear the water slapping the sand in the distance and an unknown insect chorus singing in broken rhythm. Clarisse's eyes are pinched shut. She's not quite sure of herself, I can tell. In spite of that, she moves like a dancer, her body making time with Oliver's body. I feel wetness between my legs—my insides sticky, a kind of priming. Each cell within me is swelling, swelling. I feel a sudden hot breeze blow through our tiny space, the humidity so high you swear you can reach out and grab the air, feeling it in your hand like a fistful of hair.

I watch Clarisse's mouth on Oliver and enjoy the throbbing sensation building inside me. I drag my fingers across the cool sand, a way to release some of the pressure. I dig in, feeling the coarseness of the sand against my sticky skin. I dig deeper until something stops me—something hard, a jagged piece of rock. I free it from the sand, cupping it in my palm. It's dark and heavy in my hand, the surface bumpy, covered in tiny holes. My toes curl, and I feel a pulsing between my legs.

Oliver's eyes are closed. He runs his hands through

Clarisse's hair. He breathes faster and faster, grabs on to her shoulders, and releases a low moan. I smash the rock against the top of Oliver's head. Bright blood splashes on the sand, a constellation of red appearing before me. The strike makes Oliver shudder, which knocks Clarisse from his body. She hits the back of her head on the boardwalk above us and winces from the pain.

"Evelyn, what the fuck are you doing?" Clarisse hisses and then she looks over and sees the rock in my hand, the blood fanned around Oliver's head like a halo. She starts to cry.

I feel language rise up from somewhere deep within me, knowledge pulled from my very soul. I can see it all clearly now, my focus sharp as the scalpel's edge. There is nothing to block my view of the light of reality, the shining sun of this world I've created. I look into Clarisse's face, as though I'm looking into the infinite, into everything that is at once knowable and unknowable.

"I'm taking the test."

chapter twenty-nine

I examine the top of Oliver's head. I touch him gently, careful not to come in contact with the blood. "He's bleeding, but it doesn't look like much," I tell Clarisse. I hold my hand up to his nose and feel his faint breath, warm on my palm. "He's out cold," I say.

Clarisse watches me, in silence, tears staining her cheeks. She looks at me, then Oliver, then back to me, but she doesn't say a word.

I peek out through the beach grass on one side and then the other. This stretch of the beach is deserted, for now. I see hotels in the distance, some of their rectangular windows lit up, others dark, some tourists awake and watching the water dance under moonlight, some already asleep in anticipation of tomorrow's scene—beach umbrellas snapping open for the day, towels and blankets unfurling themselves in the sun, children running to the shoreline in inflatable arm bands. Water wings we used to call them, a phrase that brings to mind flying fish, those nearly impossible creatures that fly in and out of the water, living in two worlds at once. I see the empty playground—the swings swaying like ghosts in the breeze, the tubular slide twisted like a large varicose vein.

I grab Oliver's feet and drag him until I hit the concrete of the concession stand. This is the easy part. His body glides over the cool sand, making a heavy brushing sound. Now I need Clarisse's help.

"You grab his ankles," I tell her, my voice quiet but firm. She does as she's told. I walk to the other end of Oliver's body and clench my arms tight under his armpits and we lift him up, barely able to keep him from grazing the cement. Our steps are shaky in the beginning but become steadier with adrenaline as we approach the public restroom at the concession stand.

At first, I worry it will be locked after dark. I push the silver plate on the door expecting to be met with resistance, but instead I feel the sweet release of motion and hear the high-pitched squeak of the rusty hinge as the door opens, scraping the cement floor. Now we're inside, the three of us.

I prop Oliver up in a sitting position in the corner of one of the two stalls. He is a life-size doll, a mannequin with bendable limbs, his legs placed in a V to keep him upright, a sturdy base for his limp body. He probably weighs as much as all of me plus half of Clarisse, and we're sweaty and sticky from the exertion of moving him.

There is no electricity inside the beachside restroom, just a skylight to illuminate the space, our slick skin cast in bluish white, like milk. The floor is dirty, scattered with scraps of brown paper towels, a few flattened cigarette butts, an empty soda can that has been crushed by someone's hand.

I kneel down, untie Clarisse's T-shirt from the back of Oliver's head, and instead tie it around his open mouth. I don't want him to scream when I wake him up. Still kneeling, I start patting his cheek with my hand, lightly at first, working up my nerve to slap him hard. The sound of my palm on his cheek makes an echo against the hard walls, punctuated by the drip from the faucet. *Smack, ping, smack, ping.* Everything sounds wet in here, even Clarisse's breathing. Quick and openmouthed, I can feel her working to slow down her heaving lungs until she's in sync with the sound of the water droplets that disappear down the drain.

I whisper-scream into Oliver's ear as loudly as I think I can without anyone outside the room hearing me. "Wake up! Wake up!" I slap his face on both sides now, alternating each time. Ten slaps, fifteen slaps, and his eyelids begin to flutter. He tries to move his mouth for a second but then realizes he's been gagged. His eyelids open, then close, then open again, and each time I can see his eyes are rolled back into his head, the light picking up the whites of his eyes, the absence of iris and pupil.

I grab one of Oliver's hands and make him slap himself with it. His hand is heavy in my hand at first but gets lighter and lighter as he regains consciousness, his muscles slowly taking control. He tries to stand up, but his legs fumble and collapse beneath the weight of his body, a newborn foal trying to walk. He whimpers through the T-shirt, tears pooling at the edges of his eyes—wide eyes, as though his eyelids are suspended from invisible wire or fishing line so fine it looks like nothing at all. I wish I could remember what color his eyes are, but there isn't enough light, and I can't recall what it was like earlier, at sunset, when I looked into his face and I smiled up at him and he smiled down at me, the horizon full of color, streaks of pink and red and orange in the sky.

"What the fuck, Evelyn? Why are you doing this?" Clarisse asks, finally finding a way to make sound. I stand up, turning around to face her. She looks small, a little girl shivering in the night. She hugs her arms to her chest. She doesn't look me in the eye.

I walk toward her slowly, my movements delicate, as if I'm approaching a frightened animal in the wild.

"Evelyn, tell me what the fuck is going on right now," Clarisse says. Her voice is ragged with sobs. She inches away from me until her back is against the wall. She puts her hand on the door handle.

I smile at her but she doesn't smile back. I reach for her, grazing her shoulder with my fingertips. She grips the door handle tighter. "Oh, don't leave now, honey," I say. "You'll miss all the fun." The door scrapes the cement floor as she flings it open and runs out into the darkness.

I add to *The Catalog of Everything I've Done Wrong*: made Clarisse run away from me.

I sit down on top of Oliver, straddling him, my face so close to his our noses are almost touching. I place my hands on his shoulders and I look into his terrified eyes, but I see nothing but myself. He cries a small sniffling cry. "There, there," I say, smoothing his hair with my fingers and then embracing him, my arms around his neck, which is drenched in sweat and streaked with blood.

"This will be easy, if you want it to be," I tell Oliver. "I promise." It feels so natural now, this way of thinking, this way of speaking. It's familiar.

I don't have to consider consequences because

nothing matters anymore, and it feels so right. The world is a black hole. It's been this way all along, but I'm finally realizing it now. Someone once tricked me into thinking that there's both darkness and light in this world, but I can see clearly now, can make out the horizon for what it truly is—pitch black and swallowing me whole. I've been melted and poured into a mold. My father is the maker, and he has cast me in his shape.

I bite Oliver's earlobe, gently at first, tasting the sweat and sand, and then as hard as I can, tasting his blood, warm and metallic. He screams, but it's muffled. "Oh, you have something to say?" I ask. I untie the T-shirt and let it fall away.

Oliver tries to speak, his mouth opening and closing silently like a fish, his shallow breath piercing the air with sound. He tries to keep his eyes open, but it's becoming more difficult. His head falls toward his shoulder; he's losing consciousness again.

Then I feel it inside—the switch flipped, the machinery engaged, the blood coursing and coursing through me like a pulse. I close my eyes.

What comes next is primal. I'm split open and raw. I think for a moment that I should run away and never come back, but then I realize that that's impossible, for I already know my fortune. It's written in stardust, in prison logs, in letters I'll never send, in sediment patterns on the ocean floor, in lines on the warm flesh of my palms.

I open my eyes. Now comes the fire, flames fanned and devouring all the oxygen in the room. It's getting difficult to breathe, but don't worry—it's almost over now. I promise.

chapter thirty

I hold the bathroom door open as I stand in the threshold, watching Oliver's body for signs of movement. He's lying on his back on the filthy floor, his arms and legs splayed. I stare at him until I see the smallest rise of his chest and then release the door, letting the weight of gravity close it.

Gravity has an infinite range—it goes on forever and forever. It cannot be absorbed, transformed, or shielded against. On Earth, gravity gives weight to physical objects and causes the tides. In space, gravitational forces act as a kind of time travel, slowing things down so that, instead of walking on the moon, you're bouncing, taking leaps and bounds with each step.

Water makes you weightless too, but not because of gravity. When your body enters water, the water makes space for you. We don't see it because it can't be perceived with the eyes; it has to be felt with the body. The water accepts your weight, lets you displace it with your own mass. As long as the water weighs more than you do, you float. Your weight presses down into the water, and the water presses back, pushing you up. And because your lungs are full of air, they act like balloons, lifting you to the surface naturally.

I walk into the warm gulf, my body suspended in dark water on this dark night. I propel myself forward with one hand and carry the rock in the other. While still on land, I had wrapped Clarisse's T-shirt tightly around the rock and tied it in the best knot I could manage, stretching the fabric until I was sure it would stay in place.

I swim past the orange-and-white-striped buoys that float in place to warn the tourists. They create a boundary between the safe waters and the open waters. Out here you can't be sure of the depth, which I'm hoping is miles and miles. I drop the rock and let it sink, its weight making it fall hard and fast, although I won't be able to hear it when it finally lands at the bottom of the gulf, fathoms below, the sound muffled by the weight of water.

I float on my back and then paddle quietly toward shore, making my body as silent as possible, leaving nothing in my wake. I stop to rest for a moment, my arms stretched out to my sides, showing my wingspan as if I were a bird, my body making a T shape. From above, it must look like a kind of surrender.

I break my float and tuck myself into a ball, only my head bobbing above the surface of the dark water, disembodied. I look up at the sky, trying to remember that trick to find the little dipper—I know the North Star is a part of it—Polaris it's called, because it's the star closest to the North Pole, used in celestial navigation a long time ago. Can you imagine figuring out where you're going on Earth by looking up at the sky? These days, we don't look up much at all, and if we're trying to find our way, we usually keep our eyes rooted on the ground, scanning for landmarks, for clues of the familiar. I wish I could find Clarisse by looking up into the endless night, wish the sky could somehow point me in her direction—straight toward the girl whose name means shining and bright.

I make it back to the shore and walk out of the water, back to the beach, sand between my toes as I eventually begin to run back to the hotel. I work up speed, now running as fast as I can toward the Thunderbird. I'm pumping my arms, hoping my balled fists can cut through the atmosphere, get me there faster. After a few minutes, I come to a halt, digging my heels into the sand to put on the brakes. The momentum flings me forward, and I land on my elbows and knees in the sand.

I look at the hotels in the distance once more, the small jagged skyline they create, the soft yellow lights in rows and rows of windows stacked up on top of each other. If a building is a body, the windows are the eyes.

"I'm going the wrong way," I say, and I turn and take off running. I can hear blood pumping in my ears. It drowns out the lapping of the breakers against the shoreline. I can feel the cool air turning the skin of my bare arms into gooseflesh. I can taste the sweat on my lip.

Finally, I see the lights of the Thunderbird, blurred at the edges, softened into hundreds of facets. It's as though I'm looking through a kaleidoscope, the prize I won at the Florida State Fair when I was seven. I was sure I could knock all the milk bottles down if I just aimed low enough and hit the right spot, even though Shea said the game was fixed, the bottles rigged with hidden weights so that clearing them all was impossible.

Shea paid two dollars for one baseball—it was firm in my hand, its pieces sewn together with red stitching. I adopted a baseball pitcher's stance, like I'd seen on TV, turning ninety degrees from the pyramid of bottles. The man operating the game smiled big and easy—amused with the little girl and her serious attitude. I wound up for the pitch, raised my leg, placed the ball above my shoulder, and then hurled it in one long motion toward the milk bottles. Shea let out a high-pitched gasping sound when the bottles hit the floor, and I chose my reward—a kaleidoscope made of cardboard and covered in shiny green paper.

I put my eye up to the tiny hole and looked inside. There were mirrors and colors and bits of glitter. I saw a million little diamonds, a million sparks of light. When I held it up toward the sky, it got brighter, shinier. The facets multiplied. My vision expanded. My eyes doubled, tripled, quadrupled, until I lost my vision completely. On the ride home from the fair I tore the kaleidoscope apart. I was desperate to see inside, to find out how it worked, discover the origin of the magic.

But the origin is not a location you can pinpoint, like the place in the ground where a tree sprouts from a seed under the soil or the spot on the treasure map, marked with an X. Walk thirty paces north, then dig. Origin goes deeper than that.

In my dreams, I am a deep blue sea. I dive within myself, hoping to eventually graze my own sea floor, hoping to find something beautiful there, an oyster with divine beauty locked inside. In my dreams, I dive down, down, down, searching and searching, but I always wake up before I can get to the bottom, before I can find out if the pearl is really there.

chapter thirty-one

I wake to the sensation of fingers smoothing hair from my face—my mother's touch, skin I know the feeling of even in the dark. "Time to get up," she says in her soft voice, the one that only wants to love and protect me.

I open my eyes, but the room is dark, the blackout shades still drawn, until Shea pushes them open, morning light streaming into the room as if the sun were hanging just outside our window. "Good morning, starshine!" Shea sings. It's a line from a song in the musical *Hair*, a part of the soundtrack of Shea's childhood. Shea stands at the foot of my bed, hands on hips, a superhero pose, only missing the shiny red cape flowing behind her.

I try to reply, but my lips are dried shut. They feel as though they're made of baked earth, clay fired in a kiln. I finally manage a smile and sit up, rub pieces of sleep from my eyes, and place my bare feet on the scratchy carpet.

As my eyes adjust, I look at the alarm clock on the bedside table, the old-fashioned kind with silver bells on top. I see black numbers and black hands and a white face under glass, but time isn't a concept I can grasp right now. How long ago were we on the beach, my hands running through his hair, his skin wet and warm?

Clarisse's side of the bed is empty. The only evidence of her is the wrinkled sheets, one strand of her hair on the bright white pillowcase, and her green retainer case on the nightstand next to the landline phone, a beige relic that now lives in museums and outdated hotel rooms.

Shea and my mother are packing up the room, overnight bags waiting by the door. Music is playing from the small speaker on the windowsill, the one that goes everywhere with them. Grunge rock guitar tones float high across the room, and drums and bass fill in the lower spaces.

My mother and Shea dance around as they work, Shea twirling my mother like they're in an old movie musical in black-and-white. Shea attempts a dip, lowering my mother until her hair grazes the floor, becoming a shimmery waterfall in the light. They break into laughter at that point, and Shea pulls my mother in for a kiss.

My mother is wearing makeup—black-lined eyes and pink glossy lips—and she looks so pretty I could cry. I hear the shower running in the bathroom and think of Clarisse standing in the tub, water washing over her and down the drain. I haven't seen her since last night when I returned to the room just before midnight and found her sitting in the hallway outside our door, waiting for me. When she saw me, she stood up and knocked and then Shea let us in. Clarisse went straight to the bathroom, and I slipped into bed, falling asleep in what felt like an instant.

Clarisse emerges from the bathroom now in cutoff shorts and a purple T-shirt, her wet hair wrapped in a bleached white towel, a cloud of steam following her over to the little table and two chairs.

Shea loads her arms and shoulders with our bags, and my mother opens the door for her. "I'm going to take this stuff down and get the car cooled off," Shea says. "This train will be leaving in fifteen minutes." She makes a motion with her arm that imitates a train conductor pulling the whistle. This is Shea's role in our family—she keeps the trains running on time; she plans and prepares so that my mother doesn't have to sweat the details of daily living. Shea gives my mother another kiss and walks across the threshold of the room, the door closing with a click.

"Hey," I say to Clarisse as she grabs her retainer case and starts packing her bag.

"Hey," she says back. She looks down at her phone, scrolling through a feed of photos, scenes of what other people are doing with their Sunday mornings. She won't even turn her head toward me, acting as though she will spontaneously ignite if she looks at me. Some people believe that's a real thing—spontaneous human combustion—people bursting into flame from the inside out without warning. It may have happened to a woman in St. Pete in the 1950s. Her name was Mary, and when they found her, all that was left of her was her left foot wearing a black slipper. The rest of her had turned to ash, even though the house showed no fire or smoke damage.

My mother sits down on the bed next to me. I feel her shoulder pressed against mine. I see the sun catching a hint of sparkle in her lip gloss. "I'm glad we came," she says. "This was really good for both of us." She smiles, and I smile back.

We sweep the hotel room one more time, making sure we've left nothing behind. We float down the elevator shaft and into the lobby. We walk through the sliding glass doors and back into the warm sunlight.

We take our places inside the car, and the backseat AC blows cold air on my ankles as we drive away from the Thunderbird.

I can sense a change in movement, a different leaning of the axis, each revolution around the sun slowed down, every moment exploded into small pieces, the pieces breathing and alive, every particle of existence exaggerated. Was it just yesterday that my mother and Shea sat in deck chairs in the same backyard my father played in, his bare child's feet running across the green grass? Was it just yesterday that I unwrapped the delicate butter dish and felt the cool porcelain on my cheek? Did we really see the sunset on the beach last night, pink and red and orange streaking the sky above us? Or was it all a play, a dream, a trick of the imagination and time?

My mother drives down the island's main drag slowly, stopping at every intersection to allow beachgoers to cross the street. They wear brightly colored shirts and shorts, sundresses, and wide-brimmed hats. They carry plastic shovel-and-pail sets for sandcastles and pastel-colored foam noodles for floating.

Shea tunes the radio to the nineties station, Lisa Loeb's voice sweetly reminding I missed you. My mother and Shea reach for each other at the same time, their hands meeting on the center console between them as they clasp fingers and palms. Clarisse is plugged into her headphones, staring out her window so that I can only see the back of her head, the sun catching natural highlights in her hair.

We've traveled a few blocks when I begin to notice them—flashes of red and blue, difficult to make out in the bright white of the sunshine streaming overhead. An ambulance, two state police cars, and a local television news van, all parked in the public parking lot near the causeway.

Shea wonders out loud if it has something to do with spring breakers. *A very drunk girl fell off a hotel balcony last year and nearly died, remember?* But my mother thinks it's too late for spring break, isn't it? *It's the middle of May, vacation season already in full bloom. Maybe it's a tourist, a medical emergency of some sort.*

"I hope everyone's okay," my mother says. She puts her hand to her chest and exhales a small breath, a gesture of remembrance she makes when she sees a car accident or a dead animal. "Sleep well, sweet baby," she'll say when faced with the motionless body of a raccoon on the side of the road, its dark front paws almost clasped together as if in prayer, the fur on its fuzzy tail moving slightly in the wind.

The light turns green, and we drive on.

chapter thirty-two

Instead of working on my English assignment, an essay about *The Crucible*, I'm sitting on my bed, staring at the Limoges butter dish on my dresser. The dish sits next to the nesting dolls my mother found at a yard sale for me. Most people don't know that nesting dolls are made from one block of wood—one origin, one wooden parent for each family of dolls.

The smallest doll is a solid piece of wood that doesn't open. It looks like a tiny bowling pin painted like a girl. Even though there are five dolls altogether, I think of the set as one girl with other girls inside her, one girl with many faces, many bodies. Each doll is painted by hand, her faces so detailed that you can see the individual brush strokes. She has rosy cheeks, perfect little circles of red like a toy soldier. Her hair is tucked into her cape, with just a little tuft of dark curl peeking out, a tendril over one eye.

I try to tune my mind into Clarisse's location, but she feels out of range now. It's been over a week since I've seen her, since we dropped her off at her house on our way back from Treasure Island. I watched her walk to her front door, her flip-flops slapping the soles of her feet with each step. She waved good-bye without turning around, and then she was gone.

I unlock my phone and begin a text to Clarisse. It's midnight, but I'm sure she's still awake. I type and then erase several drafts before finally getting the message right.

Hey. Want to hang out this weekend?

I add a happy emoji to the end of the message, a smiling cat with hearts for eyes, and then hit Send. I open my laptop and go to a study guide page for *The Crucible*. I click on John Proctor's name from the character list and read:

In a sense, *The Crucible* has the structure of a classical tragedy, with John Proctor as the play's tragic hero. Proctor is a good man, but one with a secret, fatal flaw.

I open a new tab, Google "tragic hero," and click on the first result, which explains:

A tragic hero is a literary character who makes an error in judgment that inevitably leads to his/her own destruction.

My phone dings, a text from Clarisse: *Can't this weekend, maybe next? George bought a boat. We're taking it out to Caladesi Island.*

She doesn't invite me to come along, doesn't include a little yacht emoji at the end of her message. I open another tab, Google "Treasure Island Oliver," and then hit Enter. I click the first link, and a video news clip loads on the screen.

It begins with a reporter in a royal blue skirt and blazer, standing in front of a hospital entrance, her blond hair pulled back in a sleek ponytail. Her voice is clear and even. "A Massachusetts teenager was brutally attacked on Treasure Island Beach and is now fighting for his life in a Bay Area hospital. The family has reached out exclusively to Action News to share their story in the hopes that one of our viewers may know something, anything, about what happened to him."

The piece cuts to a man in his mid-fifties wearing round wire-rimmed glasses. A bloated IV bag hangs on a metal pole behind him. "We just don't know why. Why anyone would do this to Oliver," the man says. Oliver resembles him so much I want to look away.

The reporter continues. "Oliver Vernon, from Lowell, Massachusetts, was staying at the Gulf Breeze Resort at Treasure Island Beach with his family when he went for a walk on the beach after sunset. It wasn't until the next morning that his family realized that he hadn't returned to the resort. They contacted hotel security and had just begun searching the beach when the unimaginable happened—a sanitation worker discovered Oliver in restrooms next to the beach access parking lot, suffering from a traumatic brain injury that has left the young man unable to explain what happened to him. Oliver is here at Tampa General, and although authorities are working diligently to find his assailant, there are no leads in the case and little physical evidence. Oliver's father, Tim Vernon, spoke with me in his son's hospital room. Oliver's mother was too distraught to talk on camera."

"The police are doing all that they can," Tim says. The video cuts to a school photo of Oliver, who is handsome and smiling in front of a gray marble background. "But they are basically at a standstill. If someone knows something, anything, we ask that you please call the Treasure Island Police Department. You can remain anonymous. We just want answers." He takes off his glasses for a moment and wipes tears from his eyes.

The reporter stands in front of the hospital entrance again. A phone number appears along the bottom of the screen. "If you have any information about what happened to Oliver Vernon, please call th—" I pause the video before she can finish.

A cold sensation begins in my feet, moving up my body like a current until it reaches the back of my neck.

In *The Catalog of Everything I've Done Wrong*, I add an entry: hurt someone's child.

I minimize the window and open a new blank document to begin writing about John Proctor as the tragic hero. My hands fly across the black keys, filling one, then two, then three pages. I'm inspired, ideas bouncing from my brain to my fingertips like magic. As I write, I imagine a shearing, a sawing of limbs, a taking away. I whittle the character down like soapstone, make him smaller and smaller, until eventually he is nothing at all.

chapter thirty-three

Under the comforter, the little bullet is switched on, trembling in my hand. It's pink and smooth and cool to the touch. It makes a low white-noise sound as it moves. I'm sure Shea would have bought me one if I'd asked, but it was easier to steal it from the novelty store in the mall. I touch myself with the bullet, and it feels even better than using my fingers, just like Clarisse said it would.

Now I'm imagining I'm in Andy's cell, and it's just the two of us. He takes the bullet from my hands, pushes it inside me. The end feels like fireworks—so much bright light, so many bursts of colorful stars. I turn it off, and roll onto my side. I look out the window and into the dry morning.

A text alert chimes on my phone, a new incoming message.

Hey, are you home? It's from Clarisse.

Yeah, I'm home. Why?

Want to go for a ride? I'm actually near your house.

Sure. My hands shake as I type the word, my entire body excited and nervous to see Clarisse. My heart ticks like a windup watch. My mother and Shea have been asking about her so I invented a calamity, a vague "family emergency" Clarisse has been going through during the last weeks, a way to explain her absence to them, her sudden pulling away from my life.

I get dressed and brush my teeth, before going out to the patio to tell Shea where I'm going. She's listening to music through her earbuds, removing one from her left ear to talk to me.

"Where's Mom?" I ask.

"Back in bed. She got up early and went for a run. Then she came home and crashed." Shea takes a sip of her coffee, steam rising from the mug, and then dissipating, dissolving into the air.

"Of course she did." My mother does this every year when the end of school is near—takes up a predawn running ritual. The endeavor usually fizzles out by the Fourth of July, but Shea and I always humor her, pretending we've forgotten her history.

"Have fun and be safe," Shea says, and then I hear Clarisse beep the horn outside, three quick blasts to let me know she's here. "I'm glad things are getting better for Clarisse and her family. I'm sure you two have a lot of catching up to do." Shea blows me a kiss and puts the earbud back in, nodding her head rhythmically to music that only she can hear.

Clarisse is parked in front of my house in George's car, the small blue hatchback we rode in on a day that feels light-years away to me now. She waves at me through the front windshield as I get inside. The interior smells like citrus, an orange air freshener shaped like a tree hanging from the rearview mirror.

"Where do you want to go?" Clarisse asks.

"Um, the causeway is nice. Do you know how to get there?"

"No, but I can punch it in." Clarisse's phone is mounted on the dashboard, clipped to a little stand. She taps in *Courtney Campbell Causeway* and hits *Go*. The causeway is a bridge that crosses Old Tampa Bay, connecting Clearwater and Tampa. On one end of the bridge, there is beach access, and you can park right by the water.

Clarisse and I don't talk much on the way there, the weight of time warm and heavy between us, filled with all the things we haven't said to each other since that night on the beach at Treasure Island. We drive with the windows down, and let our hair dance in the hot summer breeze. We turn the radio up loud enough to drown the sounds of the other cars as we cross the blue bay.

When a women's mechanical voice says we've reached our destination, Clarisse finds a parking spot facing the water. I look into the distance and see men wading in the shallow foam, casting out nets to catch crabs. I see a group of young mothers walking along the shoreline with children of various ages. The women wear bathing suits and wide-brimmed hats to protect their faces from the sun. The children carry plastic pails with shovels to dig in the wet sand.

A pop song is on the radio, synth beating like a heart and a young girl's voice too perfect to be human. Clarisse taps her fingers on the steering wheel in time to the music for a few measures, and then turns the car off. She's wearing sunglasses so I can't see her eyes.

"We need to talk about Oliver," she says. Her voice sounds cooler than I remember.

"What is there to talk about? He's alive. That's all that matters."

"He's a fucking vegetable, Evelyn. You call that alive?" Clarisse asks. She doesn't wait for my answer. "What if he wakes up? Have you even thought about that?" She looks straight ahead, her eyes fixed on the low chop of the water, the small waves glittering in the sunlight.

"He doesn't even know our real names, Clarisse. He has a brain injury. So even if he does wake up, he might not be able to talk, let alone pick us out of a lineup. He probably won't even remember anything anyway. His brain is mush." I reach over, and place one hand on her shoulder, my touch so light on her skin I can barely feel her at first, can only sense the presence of her body near mine.

"You don't get it, do you?" She spits the words at me, pulling her body away from my touch. "You just don't fucking get it." Her voice is louder now, angry. "I came here to tell you that I never want to see you again."

"But he's alive. Oliver's alive. We didn't kill anyone."

"You went inside Emerald's house. You thought about killing her. I know you thought about it."

"No, I didn't think about it. I just wanted to see her. She's my grandmother. You thought I was going to go all that way and not at least see her? I ran out of her house as soon as she realized I wasn't her neighbor."

"You're such a fucking liar. Stay away from me or I'll go to the police." She pounds the steering wheel with her fist. "Fuck, I can't believe I ever bought into your bullshit."

"What bullshit, Clarisse? I didn't do anything to Emerald. And even if I thought about killing her, bad thoughts aren't the same as bad actions, Clarisse, remember? And by the way, if bad thoughts are a crime, then I guess the police will want to know about yours."

"Don't threaten me, you fucking psycho. I don't ever want to see you again. Don't call me. Don't text me. Don't come near me or I'll tell the police everything I know."

"Please, please, Clarisse. I'm sorry. I'm sorry about all of it. But it's all over now. The tests are over now. We passed. We both passed. We're both going to be okay. Everything's going to be okay. Let's just forget this ever happened and start over. Come on, Reesey Cup." I reach for her, but she slaps my hand away.

"I'm not your Reesey Cup, and I don't want to see you ever again. You hear me, Evelyn? Do you understand? If you even try to come near me, I'll go to the police. I'll tell them everything."

I nod my head, yes, I understand. A sick feeling begins inside me, the cells of fear dividing and dividing again, blooming like algae in the sea. Fear churns inside me, a storm at sea. My body becomes a small boat tossed within the relentless waves.

I close my eyes and cover my ears. I just need to block everything out for a bit—Clarisse, the sunlight, the children playing at the edge of the water. I just need to blunt the sharp edge of my senses so I can catch my thoughts, which are barreling through me as fast as a bullet train. I'm still here in the car with Clarisse, but in my mind, I'm in an interrogation room, sitting across the table from a man who demands to know where I was that night in May, demands to know why traces of me were found under Oliver's fingernails, inside his mouth, between his legs.

Clarisse starts the engine and turns the air-conditioning on full blast. "Don't fucking try me, Evelyn," she says. "From now on you're dead to me. And if you don't stay dead, I promise you'll pay for what you did. They'll put you in Raiford with your father, where you belong, you fucking freak."

I look to the horizon, an attempt to steady my churning stomach. My eyes are blurry, my vision watery as if the world were a snow globe turned on its end.

Clarisse drives back to the other side of the bay, over water that glistens in the sunlight. The whole way home I hold my hands against my chest, feeling the beating of my own heart.

When Clarisse pulls up to the curb in front of my house, she keeps the car in drive. She stares straight ahead through the windshield, keeping both of her hands on the steering wheel. I get out of the car without looking at her, and as soon as I close the car door, she drives off. I go inside the house and straight to my room.

Shea hears me, and comes to the threshold. "Back already? I figured you two would be out all day. Perfect beach weather today. There's not a cloud in the sky."

"Oh, well, I'm not feeling so great," I say. "I think I might be catching a cold."

"Sorry, sweetie. Can I get you anything?"

"I'll fight it off. Just going to rest," I tell her.

"Yes, honey, get in bed and take a nap," Shea says. "I can bring you some echinacea tea when you wake up later. It'll help boost your immune system."

"Okay, thanks," I say as Shea closes the door.

I peel off all my clothes, leaving them in a puddle on the floor. I grab a can of duster from my nightstand drawer, and take it to bed with me. The sheets are cold against my bare skin, but eventually, my body adjusts. I enjoy the sensation, how it's slightly uncomfortable at first, almost painful, but then it feels so good, like diving into a cold pool, your lungs contracting hard as you come up for air and gasp, your breath taken away from you for just a second from the temperature change.

I open *The Catalog of Everything I've Done Wrong*, but there are too many entries to add today, and I don't want to think about them, so instead, I put the duster nozzle into my mouth and pull the small trigger.

I inhale and instantly feel lighter, starting to imagine myself floating away. At first I fight the feeling slightly, afraid to let go, but then I inhale again and finally every muscle in my body becomes weightless, and I let the waves wash me away and away until I'm back in Clarisse's closet. We're sitting crisscross, facing each other, our knees touching so that the empty space between our bodies forms a diamond shape.

"Let's play hot hands," Clarisse says. She reaches her hands toward mine, her palms facing up, an animal offering me her soft underbelly. I place my hands on top of hers, feeling the silk of her skin.

"Ready?" Clarisse asks.

"Ready," I answer.

I open my eyes, but I still see Clarisse. She appears

to be standing at the foot of my bed now, getting undressed. She slides into bed with me.

"You're here," I say, and I turn on my side to face
her. "I'm so glad you're here."

Clarisse reaches over, and wraps a strand of my hair
around her finger. "Of course I'm here, Evelyn. Where
else would I be?"

chapter thirty-four

The group at Wavelengths is smaller than usual tonight, but that doesn't bother Greg. In fact, it only serves to bolster his enthusiasm. "Smaller group just means more room for deeper conversation," he says as he removes empty chairs from the circle, and motions for all of us to scoot closer together. We obey, moving in to make a tighter arc. We create a smaller replica of the universe with our atomic bodies.

"Out of sight, out of mind," Greg says in a declarative voice. "We've all heard that before. And it can be true, right? If you don't see something, it can be easy to forget that it exists." Greg scans our faces, searching for the light of recognition, signs that we understand. "If someone you love is away from you, regardless of the reason why, it's only natural that they move into the background, and that might make us feel bad, as though we're forgetting about them, as though we don't care about them. I want you all to know that's completely normal, and it's okay. It doesn't mean that you don't care about them anymore. It doesn't mean that they don't care about you. Let's talk about that tonight, and perhaps some of you will want to share how you deal with those feelings when they arise."

Clarisse isn't here tonight. I keep scanning the room to find her, hoping she's just hiding somewhere, testing me just to see if I'll notice her absence.

Greg sees my searching, and meets my eyes when I finally turn them back to him. "We can have relationships with people who are kept away from us," Greg says. "No matter *why* they're gone. We can carry people with us even though they must stay in one place."

It looks as though I'm here in the room, listening to Greg and the others talk about maintaining relationships, about grounding techniques and coping skills, but in my mind, I'm adding an entry to *The Catalog of Everything I've Done Wrong*: stole county property.

I'm on a street corner at night, not far from Clarisse's house. I'm sitting on her shoulders, and she holds me steady as I work to free a yield sign from its metal frame. She couldn't believe I'd never done it before, assured me that it was easy. "Nothing to it," Clarisse promised.

"What if we get caught?" I'd asked, my hands trembling as I held George's socket wrench and a can of WD-40.

"Ev, it's three o'clock in the morning in Seffner," Clarisse said. "It's the middle of the night in the middle of nowhere. Just trust me." I could feel the warmth of Clarisse's body beneath me, her hands on the tops of my legs as she steadied me.

I sprayed the lubricant on the hex bolts just as Clarisse had told me to do. She'd reviewed the entire process with me while we were still in her bedroom. Jenny and George were sleeping in their rooms on the other end of the house. Clarisse was sure we could sneak out and back in without waking them.

The WD-40 greased the bolts, making them slippery enough so I could pry them off.

"You're almost there," Clarisse said quietly, cheering me on with a whisper in the dark of night. The only other sounds in the air were high-pitched insects mingled with our hushed breathing.

When I eventually freed the red-and-white sign from its post, I tossed it down into the grass, and Clarisse took both my hands in hers. She lowered herself down so that I could slide down her back, my bare feet finally touching the damp grass as I exhaled a sigh of relief.

"What now?" I asked, and Clarisse kissed me on the cheek.

"Now we celebrate," Clarisse answered. She picked up one side of the sign and gestured for me to pick up the other. We walked side by side, back to her house. We slipped in through the patio door, and tip-toed back to her bedroom. After stashing the sign in Clarisse's closet, we took hits from a small glass pipe, and I got higher than I ever had before. I started to feel panicky, my heart racing, agitated. I started crying, and told Clarisse that the weed was too strong. I couldn't breathe. Clarisse took my hand and placed it against her chest. She told me to feel her heartbeat and then focus on slowing my own heartbeat down to match. When that didn't work, she fetched a wet washcloth from her bathroom, putting it over my face until I stopped freaking out, until I started giggling so bad that I had to suck on one end of the washcloth so my laughter wouldn't wake Jenny and George.

After group ends, Greg is standing at the cookie table, sipping coffee from his travel mug, surveying the room the way a proud parent would. I've never approached Greg after group, although he's always told us that he is available to talk before and after each session. I walk up to him and say hello, take a cookie from the plastic tray, oatmeal raisin, and start to eat it.

"Great group tonight, Evelyn. Don't you think?" He looks at me, raising his eyebrows, his way of inviting conversation.

"Yes, good stuff, as usual," I answer. I look down at my feet, and kick at some cookie crumbs on the floor, a little trail of sweetness for the palmetto bugs that are probably hiding in the walls just waiting for the lights to go out, their version of night falling.

"Thanks, Evelyn," Greg says. "I'm really glad that you're here. You are a valuable member of Wavelengths. You can really be a resource for others." He takes another sip of his coffee, and then reaches in his pocket for a tin of peppermints, offering one to me.

"Thanks, Greg," I say, putting a peppermint in my mouth, exhaling icy breath from the cool sensation of the mint. "Hey, I actually wanted to talk to you about something, if that's okay."

"Absolutely," Greg says. "What's up?" He puts the tin back in his pocket, and sets his travel mug on the cookie table, his body language making it clear that he is ready to listen to me.

"You mentioned one night that you do individual counseling too. How does that work, exactly? Is that something I could do?"

"I'm a social worker for Hillsborough County Schools. I move around to the different buildings within the district as needed, but I have an office at Blake High School, near downtown Tampa, and I'm able to see clients there. If you're interested, I can e-mail your mom with the info, and we'll arrange an appointment."

"Yeah, I'd like that," I say.

"Great. Is everything okay?" Greg asks.

"Sure, everything's fine. I guess I just have some things I want to talk about, but not in front of the whole group, you know?"

Greg nods in agreement. "Yes, I know exactly what you mean. That's a great step to take for yourself, Evelyn." He looks serious at first, but then his expression turns softer and a smile begins to spread across his face. "I'm looking forward to starting this part of the journey with you, Evelyn."

"Me too."

In the car on the way home, Shea sings along to Father John Misty, his warm tenor mixing with her alto, sound waves suspended in the air. She drives fast with the windows up and the AC on until we cross over into Pass-a-Grille. Then she drives slower, rolling down the windows so we can feel the salty evening air.

"So what do you have left to do for the semester?" Shea asks. I'll be done with school at the end of the week, the summer stretched out before me like an empty canvas.

"One more trig exam and an essay on *The Crucible*."

"Hey, I read that in my junior year of high school too. It's about the Salem witch trials, but it's an allegory for McCarthyism, right?"

"Yep."

"So what's the topic of your essay?"

"John Proctor as the tragic hero."

"Don't you just love literary analysis, Evelyn? Boiling something down to its absolute essence—it just feels so . . . satisfying."

"Mmm-hmm," I say as Shea pulls into our parking space.

In the living room, my mother is preparing for a summer break painting project. The TV is on and tuned to Animal Planet, a documentary about birds of prey playing in the background while she works. She tears a long strip of blue painter's tape off the roll with her teeth, pressing it into the space between the windowsill and the glass. Then she grabs a wet rag from a bucket and begins wiping the baseboards.

Shea gives my mother a kiss on the cheek. "Stepping out for a smoke, babe," she says.

"I thought you were quitting," I say. I sit down on the couch, grab a pillow, and hug it to my chest.

"Not this week," my mother says and gives Shea the *shame on you* gesture, the one where you point at the person with the index finger of one hand and then use your other index finger to make a rubbing motion, like rubbing two sticks together.

Shea feigns an embarrassed look. Then she laughs and opens the sliding glass door. A whiff of hot night air escapes into the room before she slides it closed. I can smell the honeysuckle that blooms by the patio, a hint of something sweet suddenly in the room.

My mother pauses her work and sits down next to me on the couch. She's wearing her typical cleaning attire and her hair is hidden under a New York Yankees baseball cap. Her eyes look tired but happy. She's breathing deeper than usual, one of her calming techniques. I wasn't born yesterday. I know my mother is about to have a *conversation* with me, that there's something on her mind. It's always a giveaway when Shea abruptly excuses herself.

"What's up?" I ask to speed up the process. She usually benefits from a little nudge.

"Well, I want to check in with you," my mother says. "I feel like I haven't even seen you much since Treasure Island. We really never got a chance to talk about it." On the TV screen, a red-tailed hawk circles a cloudless sky in slow motion while a baritone voice narrates. My mother inches her body a little closer toward mine. "And I thought you might want to talk about it."

The hawk trains its eyes on a field mouse, and dives down, down, down. He pierces the prey with his talons, which are dark and curved and razor sharp. He grazes the ground for a just a split second, and then flies up, up, up into the blue. The narrator explains that the mouse never stood a chance, as though the inevitability makes it easier to handle, a reminder that out there in the wild, it's only about survival.

"Okay, then let's talk. What do you want to know?"

"Well, was it a little intense for you to see Ella's house?" She adjusts her hat by the brim, lifting it up slightly and then pulling it down, nearly covering her eyes.

"A little intense, yeah. But it was fine," I say. The hawk lands on a bare tree branch, ready to enjoy his hard-earned lunch.

"I was on the fence about the whole visit at first, as you could probably tell." My mother laughs softly, a nervous little laugh. "But in the end, I'm very happy that we went. It gave me a sense of closure, and I hope that it did the same for you."

Closure. Greg talks about that at Wavelengths from time to time. The families of my father's victims are seeking it, and they may feel it when he's executed—when they hear his final words, when they watch him take his final breath.

"It did feel like an ending," I tell my mother. I say it because that's what she wants to hear. I say it because it's true.

"Oh, that's good to hear," she says. "And there's something else I want to talk to you about." She wraps the cleaning rag around her finger, and then lets go to watch it unfurl. "Do you remember going to the psychic when you were little? Miss B? She worked out of a little house?"

"I remember."

"Do you know why I took you there?"

"I don't." I hug my pillow tighter while my brain swims in a current of my mother's thoughts. Sometimes I'm convinced that the blood running through our veins has the power to connect, the power to form an invisible river between my mother and me, and we are the only ones who can feel it.

"I used to be afraid of a lot of things, Evelyn. Worried about things I couldn't control. Your father was one of them." She stands up and walks over to her bucket of warm wash water to hand me a rag. I get up, and now we're both wiping down walls, getting them ready for tomorrow's paint. "I used to worry about you too,

Evelyn. I used to worry about your future. When you were little, you would have these moments when you would, I don't know, just zone out. It's like you would disappear behind your own eyes. I felt like you were disconnecting or something. I don't know, it's hard to explain, really, but I just thought, if I could find out about your future, I could stop worrying. If I could just know that you were going to be okay."

She dips her rag into the soapy water, twisting it to wring out the excess water. I repeat her movements. "It wasn't the most appropriate thing for a parent to do. I mean, you were very young. It was my issue, Evelyn, not yours, and I'm sorry I took you there."

I can barely see her eyes under her cap, but I know that tears have formed, small dewdrops at each outer corner.

"Mom, it's fine. Really."

"Oh, Ev, thank you." She puts her arm around me for a moment, gives me a sideways hug, and then continues her work.

"I have something I want to talk about too."

"Oh yeah?"

"Greg is going to e-mail you about me starting individual counseling with him. It was my idea. I asked him about it tonight. I'm actually looking forward to it."

"Oh, honey, that's so great." She leans over again and kisses me on the cheek this time.

"I'm okay, Mom. Really. You don't have to worry about me anymore. I've got it from here."

I see the concern melt from her face as she transforms into something I've never seen before—optimistic.

I add another entry to *The Catalog of Everything I've Done Wrong*: gave my mother hope.

We continue working side by side, washing down the wall before its fresh coat of paint, before the new color covers all traces of what used to be.

chapter thirty-five

I wake before my alarm goes off, my thoughts hazy, my brain still swimming in a dream about Andy. It's so vivid that I try to convince myself that it wasn't a dream at all but a memory. I try to convince myself that it really happened, that it really *is* happening. I close my eyes and repeat it like a mantra, *It's real, it's real, it's real.* I tell myself that Andy is next to me in this bed, tell myself that his body is synced with mine. I focus on my lungs expanding and contracting until I swear I can hear him breathing too. I focus until I feel his mouth on mine, until I feel his fingers running along my skin.

I don't need to look at his picture to conjure him. He's etched in my mind, my heart, maybe even my soul, although I'm not sure if I believe in souls. I'm not sure what I believe in anymore.

A knock on my bedroom door interrupts me,

forcing me to give up the dream and open my eyes. I hear my mother's voice from the other side. "Can I come in?"

"Sure," I say. She sits on the edge of my bed. She's wearing black linen shorts and a gray tank top, her hair pulled back in a low ponytail.

"Get dressed! I thought we'd go to the Sea Horse for breakfast before your appointment with Greg."

I pull my comforter over my head. "I'm not in the mood for tourists today, Mom."

"Come on, Ev, please. It'll be fun. We haven't been there in forever. Pecan pancakes. Grits with extra butter." She peels the comforter from my face and flashes a hopeful smile. "Please," she says again, her palms pressed together as if in prayer. "Pretty please."

"Well, okay," I say. "But only because you said *pretty please.*"

My mother orders her favorite dish at the Sea Horse—biscuits smothered in sausage gravy and topped with two eggs—"the hangover cure," it's called on the menu. I drown my pecan pancakes in real maple syrup before I devour them. I salt my buttered grits generously before they disappear.

We get our coffee refills to go and drive to Tampa for my session with Greg. My mother drops me off at Blake High School, telling me she'll pick me up in about an hour. She'll go check out nearby Riverwalk while she waits for me, a palm-lined scenic trail that snakes along the Hillsborough River.

Inside the school, I walk down an empty blue hallway. There's something eerie about a school during summer vacation, all the energy drained from it, abandoned by the students and teachers. Although it's quiet now, there are signs of previous life. A banner hangs in the stairwell, wishing students a safe and happy summer. Trophies and plaques shine from within their cases, symbols of achievement, artifacts of the past.

I enter the main office and sign in at the reception area, where a secretary clicks her fingertips on a computer keyboard. She directs me to a door labeled GUIDANCE, and after I pass through it, I walk down a short corridor of speckled floor. I find his office door, a plastic nameplate attached to the glass: GREGORY COTTOM, LCSW-C. I sit down on a worn blue office chair and wait, wiping the sweat from my palms on my jeans.

Greg will help me. He will find something in his therapist's binder that will fix me. He will reach into his messenger bag of tricks, pull out something to seal my dark center, and fashion a tourniquet, twisting and twisting until the center stops leaking, until the darkness is flushed from my bloodstream. Greg will have a hundred ways to fix me, I'm sure of it. I fill my brain with possibilities but wring them out like water.

Greg opens his office door. "Hi, Evelyn. Come on in," he says, smiling. I walk in and sit down on a dark red office chair with hard plastic armrests.

The room is decorated like a kindergarten classroom instead of a high school social worker's office. There's a bulletin board behind him edged with a bright yellow scalloped border. There are brilliant blue cut-out letters on the board spelling out the word FEELINGS. There are small clouds cut out of construction paper, each cloud wearing the name of a different emotion. *Fear* floats next to *anger*, which floats next to *disappointment*. I want to make every cloud of emotion disappear, forcing them back into vapor.

"How is summer treating you so far, Evelyn?" Greg asks. He straightens the row of knickknacks on his desk: an owl made of green glass, a cat figurine, and three monkeys fashioned out of shells, typical touristy trinkets you can find at any of the shops along the beaches. The monkeys are striking the poses of *see no evil, hear no evil, speak no evil.*

"Pretty good so far," I say.

"Oh yeah? Just pretty good? What have you been up to?"

"Well, I'm going to take an acting class at Suncoast."

The AC rumbles on, sending a hiss of refrigerated air out through the ceiling vent, rustling the clouds of emotions on the wall. The edge of *anger* lifts slightly as though it's trying to rise up and escape into the atmosphere.

"Wow, that's wonderful, Evelyn. I'm glad you're having new experiences. Good for the brain, you know—all those neurons firing."

"Yeah, it's nice to have something else to focus on for once."

"What do you mean? What are you usually focused on?" Greg's voice hangs in the air. He raises his eyebrows slightly, waiting for me to answer. I breathe in, wondering how to say it. I breathe out, realizing there's only one way to say it.

"Death." There's no turning back now. "I'm usually focused on death. I mean, well, I think about death a lot. And I'm afraid I think about it too much."

Greg makes a quick note on a yellow legal pad in front of him.

"Well, it's completely natural to think about death, Evelyn. We all do it from time to time. That's a part of what makes us human—our awareness of death and our own mortality." He sounds relaxed, nonchalant, as if he's not worried about me at all. As if he thinks he knows how to deal with someone like me.

"Yeah, well, is it normal to think about death even when you don't want to? Even when you're trying to think of other things? It's like it's stuck in my subconscious or something." Behind Greg is a small, square window that overlooks the courtyard. I can see the sky is turning, shades of light blue getting darker, the signs of a thunderstorm brewing. They happen so regularly in the summer afternoons here that you can set your watch by them.

"It's not a good idea to get caught up in what's normal or not normal. In fact, I avoid using those words at all. There is no such thing as normal when it comes to the human psyche. Nothing is black or white. There are so many shades of gray, Evelyn. There are so many ways of being, so many ways of reacting to experience." He makes another note on his legal pad before taking a sip from a stainless steel water bottle on his desk.

"But shouldn't there be a limit to how much someone thinks about death? I mean, at what point does it become unhealthy? At what point is it bad for you?"

"Well, Evelyn, there is no clinical answer for that. I want you to consider that maybe you're being a little hard on yourself. Certainly, under your circumstances, I think it's understandable that you might think about death a little more than the average person." He makes another note on his legal pad. His pen sounds sharp against the paper.

I grab a tissue from the box on the corner of his desk and twist it around my index finger, something to keep my hands busy. "My circumstances," I say. "So it's always going to be about my father, isn't it?"

"Well, facts are facts, Evelyn. We can't change your situation. We can't change what happened, can't change the fact that your father did what he did. But I wouldn't say it's *always* about him. You can't trace every problem you have back to just one source. It's more complex than that."

"I don't know. Sometimes I think it's pretty simple, really. I just need to get rid of these thoughts."

"I don't think it's a matter of getting rid of the thoughts about death, Evelyn. I think instead we should be exploring the meaning behind the thoughts together. Can you give me an example? When you say you can't stop thinking about death, that's rather abstract. Tell me in a more concrete way."

"I don't know if I can," I say.

"Why?"

"I'm afraid you won't understand. You'll think I'm crazy or something."

Greg laughs softly through his nose. "Evelyn," he says, "we don't use that C word in my line of work.

Okay?" He looks me squarely in the eyes. "I'm not going to pass any judgment. I'm not going to think any less of you. Just tell me about the thoughts. I can help you if I know what we're dealing with here."

I hear a hissing sound in my brain like static, a TV tuned to a channel with no signal. "I just want it all to stop," I say. I put my head in my hands. "I want it to be over." I'm sobbing, losing control. Greg stands up and walks around his desk toward me. He lowers himself to my eye level, crouching next to my chair.

"Evelyn, it's okay," Greg says. "You are processing a lot of emotions. Talking about it will help. I'm here to listen and to guide you. Maybe you'd like to start seeing me for more one-on-one sessions. Together, we will come up with a plan to help you work through these thoughts and feelings. You aren't alone in this, Evelyn."

Greg looks at me with such kindness in his eyes. He means well, but he is wrong. I *am* alone in this, and that's how it has to be because who wants to stand with the girl at the edge, staring down into the nothingness below? Who wants to be there to see the moment she lets go? Clarisse was the only one, and I fucked up, and I lost her. Greg doesn't know how to fix things. I don't know why I let myself believe he did. There's only one person who can help me. He's the one I need to see.

"Thank you, Greg."

"No thanks needed, Evelyn. It's what I do. I'm really happy you've taken this step. I have a good feeling about your future."

"Me too," I say.

Outside, the thunderstorm begins. Rain pelts the window. I stare at the three monkeys on Greg's desk.

It seems possible to speak no evil. You have a choice in that matter. You control what you say, mostly, unless you count strange phenomena like automatic speech or speaking in tongues or talking in your sleep. But even then, you could argue that the subconscious is in control in those cases, and the subconscious is still you after all—your brain in distilled form, boiled down to its essence.

It seems possible to hear no evil, mostly. You can plug your ears as soon as you hear evil announce itself. But see no evil, that's the tricky one. Sure, you can cover your eyes once evil approaches, but evil doesn't always looks like evil until it's too late so how are you to know when you see it? There's rarely a warning until evil is already pressed so close to your face that you have to look.

chapter thirty-six

S ummer feels brand new, as though June, July, and August can burn away the mistakes of the other seasons. As though we'll all emerge differently in the fall.

I'm taking an acting class at Suncoast Theater Company. My mother thought I should do "something creative" this summer, and cyberschool will allow me to use it as an elective art credit. Suncoast holds classes at their theater in downtown St. Pete, not far from the Dalí and the Old Curiosity Shop, which is a Starbucks now.

Corey Bradford is our instructor for acting. We meet weekly in a small performance space with an elevated stage and folding chairs for seating, very DIY. There isn't much room between the stage and the seats, making the experience feel more personal than a traditional theater, the performers close enough to the audience that you can see their facial expressions.

During our first class, Corey sits on the steps leading up to the stage while we sit in the first few rows. He's young, still in his twenties, with the chiseled features of a cartoon prince and a deep voice that drenches his words in masculinity. He worked on a cruise ship right after college, providing entertainment while fighting seasickness and, after a few years, realized his calling for teaching and his desire to remain on dry land.

Some of the kids in this class know each other, self-proclaimed theater geeks who have been attending summer classes at Suncoast together since elementary school. Girls outnumber boys in the class two to one, probably because many teenage boys think that self-expression through drama—portraying emotions, playing make believe—is a silly endeavor.

After Corey is done with introductions, he gives each of us a questionnaire on a clipboard, a "self-inventory," he calls it, a list of questions about ourselves meant to make us ponder who we might be as artists. He encourages us to walk around the theater and explore while we formulate our answers.

"Movement is essential to thinking," he tells us.

I walk along the rows of chairs, chewing the end of my pen as I think about how to answer the first question: "Which actor inspires you the most and why?"

The walls inside the theater are cinderblock, painted dark green. I can see tiny cracks, clusters of spider veins, if I look closely enough. The other kids are milling around, mostly whispering and socializing instead of working on their assignments. I stand still for a moment and then start to write, until I feel someone behind me, hovering over my shoulder.

"Emma Watson," he says, reading from my paper. "Nice. Are you a Potterhead?" I turn around. The student has straight, dirty blond hair that grazes his shoulders and a little goatee on his chin. He's wearing skinny jeans and a black T-shirt that says NIRVANA.

For a second, I think he's said *pothead*, and I worry there is something about my appearance that might be giving me away. Then I realize he's talking about fans of the *Harry Potter* movies.

"No," I say. "I mean, I have seen all the movies, but I'm not fanatic about them. I was actually thinking of her performance in *Beauty and the Beast*."

"I'm Dylan," he says, extending his hand to shake mine.

"I'm Evelyn."

"Nice to meet you, Evelyn."

"Same," I say and walk away. I turn my energy up, trying to boost the signal, and see if I can get him to follow me.

"Hey, wait," he calls. I turn around to face him. He tucks his pencil behind his ear. He's cute. Maybe he could be good for something. "I've seen your answer. Don't you want to see mine? That's how this works, you know."

I look into his eyes, and I can see that he's attracted to me. The eyes are the windows to the soul, after all. I imagine what his body would feel like against mine. I imagine how the skin on his neck would taste on my tongue.

"Wow, you give it away that easily, huh?" I say. I twirl a strand of hair around my finger.

"We're still talking about our answers on the questionnaire, right?" He's trying not to smile, trying to keep some of his cards to himself, but I can read his poker face. I know what he's thinking.

"I don't know, Dylan. You tell me." I turn around, walking away. I feel him watching me. I focus on my body's movements, feel my hips sway with each step. I tune into the sound of my shoes on the hard floor beneath me.

Later in the hour, Corey is explaining directions for our first exercise. We will each pull a note card from a bowl, and that note card will have a simple declarative sentence written on it. We must say the sentence conveying various emotions—fear, excitement, love, anger—which Corey will call out to us once we are on the stage, the stage lights blinding us so that we can't see our audience.

"The trick is to forget that the audience is even there," Corey says, jumping down from the edge of the stage but landing like a gymnast, soft and graceful. "The audience matters, yes, but once you get into that flow, the world must fall away. All your focus, all your attention must be trained on the craft."

He takes his place in the aisle of the dimly lit theater. His footsteps echo, the sound following his body until he stops and turns around. "Volunteers to go first?" he asks, his voice reverberating in the silence as Dylan raises his hand. "Dylan, awesome. Show us what you got."

Dylan walks by me on his way to the stage. "This one's for you, Evelyn," he tells me. He hands me his note card and then climbs onto the stage as if he's lifting himself out of a swimming pool and onto dry land. I can't take my eyes off him as he moves, his body long and lean, built for motion, so effortless. I look down at Dylan's note card, creased in my hand, and read the small blocky letters Corey has written. *I will if you will.*

At the end of class, Corey passes out scripts of *Our Town* by Thornton Wilder, the first play we'll be studying in class.

"*Our Town* is a metadrama," Corey says. "Make sure you read up on that term while doing your background research on the play for next week. I also want you to research the year Wilder wrote the play— 1938. In drama, it's very important to understand what was happening in a historical context when a play was written. It can help us get to know the characters and where they're coming from."

I'm sitting in the front row, packing up my bag, when Dylan sits down next to me.

"Tom Hanks." He looks straight ahead, but I can tell that he's watching me from the corner of his eye.

"Excuse me?"

"From the questionnaire. An actor that inspires me. My answer was Tom Hanks. Now we're even."

"Are we now?" I ask.

"Sure, until you feel like showing me something else." He stands up and slings his backpack over one shoulder. He's completely still for a moment, practically begging me to respond.

"Unlock your phone," I tell him. I extend my empty hand, and he does as I say, placing his phone into my palm. I add a new contact for myself, tap my phone number into the blank fields, and hit Save. "You can text me if you have questions about *Our Town*. Or anything else." I hand the phone back to him, making sure that our fingers touch during the exchange. I consider winking but then wonder, would that be going too far?

He looks down at the phone's screen for a moment before sliding it back into his pocket. "I will definitely have questions," he says.

"Good," I say. "I will definitely have answers."

chapter thirty-seven

I have a few hours before Shea picks me up so I go down the street to the Starbucks to start my research for class. I sit in a corner on a comfy chair and balance my laptop on my lap.

Online, I learn that *metadrama* is a term used to describe a play that has elements of awareness of an audience, like a character giving an aside to the audience or other instances of breaking the fourth wall. In theater, the fourth wall is that invisible barrier between performer and audience member which usually remains intact, but not in *Our Town* as I find out that there is a main character called the Stage Manager, who is fully aware of the audience.

I research the plot summary and read a little about Thornton Wilder's background. He was rather bored with theater when he wrote *Our Town*, which is why he wanted to do something so different, to shake things up. The play begins in 1901 and covers a period of ten years. I try a few different search terms and read about American life during that time period, which isn't very interesting so my mind starts to wander back to Clarisse. If only I could know where she is right now, what she's doing. Is she thinking of me? Will she ever think of me again?

I go to Instagram to find Clarisse's page. She's deleted me as a friend, making her account private. I can see her profile photo but nothing else. It's a picture of her sleeping at her desk at school, her head resting on her arms, which are folded in front of her on the beige Formica. I wasn't going to contact her; I know better than that. I just wanted to see a real picture of her, something other than the phantom memories that run through my mind while I'm trying to fall asleep.

I pull up Andy's blog. There's a new entry for this week.

LETTERS FROM THE DEATH HOUSE

Dear Sis,

I don't know how much longer I can hang on. Every day I stay in this place, the outside world gets further away. This prison might as well be floating around on

*a different planet right now, that's how disconnected
I feel from everyone and everything. It's been such a
long time since I held someone's hand or gave someone a hug, I think I'm forgetting what touch feels like.
Sometimes I wonder if my life before Raiford was just
a dream. Sorry, I know I'm rambling. My thoughts
are running around in circles in my head and it's getting harder to catch them.*

*You'll probably say I should talk to someone about
how I'm feeling and all this depressing stuff. We have
shrinks and counselors here, but I don't think they
know what to say, really. What could anyone say to
someone like me right now?*

*I'm so alone, and I know that you're out there, sis,
so don't let that get you down because you mean a lot
to me. But really, I'm alone in here. This might be my
last letter. I don't know what else to say, so I'll just
say goodbye.*

Love you sis,
Andy

An idea enters my mind, and although I try to get
rid of it, it just won't leave. Some ideas are sticky like
that. They attach to you and won't let go, like sucker-
fish against the glass of the aquarium.

Now I'm on a travel site, looking up hotels near Raiford. There actually aren't any hotels in Raiford proper because there's not much of anything in that town, really, except the prison, some bail bondsmen, a few check-cashing places, and a row of housing for the warden and correctional officers. There's the Motel 6 in Starke. There's the Budget Inn in Lawtey. The Motel 6 looks clean enough. The picture shows a double bed draped in a maroon-and-gold-striped bedspread, the cheap scratchy kind. I could stay there, just a place to sleep between visits with him. Sure, I'll have to settle for seeing him behind glass, a telephone line stretched between us, but at least I will be able to lay my eyes on him. At least I'll be able to see him in the flesh. But would he even want to see me? I decide it doesn't matter. Once he sees how far I've come, he'll understand.

Even though I don't really want to, I hover the mouse pointer over the icon for my saved bookmarks, the archive of my father. Even though I don't really want to, I click the icon and a list of entries appears—web pages, videos, court documents, newspaper articles. I click one at random, and a video begins to load on my laptop screen. I fish my earbuds from my bag and plug them in so I can hear. I start the video. For the first time, I don't do anything to stop it. I simply let it play.

A reporter stands in front of the St. Johns County Courthouse, north of downtown St. Augustine, just off US Route 1, the longest north-south road in the United States. Her name is Melinda Sherrill. She wears a crisp white blouse and a navy blue skirt. I watch and listen as she reports on the day's proceedings, talking directly to the camera, her perfect white teeth contrasted with deep red lipstick. Her voice is clear and steady, without an accent or dialect of any kind. She speaks in the bland Midwestern English that is standard for newscasters, that overenunciated style that extinguishes any traces of the person's background, with no clues of origin to distract the audience from the message.

Melinda is sharing details from the first day of jury selection for my father's trial. It's the local news at noon, the Florida sun straight up in the sky, high noon as the cowboys called it, although the correct term is *solar noon*. It's easy to forget that we can understand our surroundings just by looking at the sun, which is also a star. It's easy to forget the names of celestial bodies that guided our ancestors, easy to forget that we can track the passage of time by looking up.

Melinda says that jury selection is expected to take several weeks because the prosecution is seeking the death penalty. Melinda reminds us that the stakes are always higher with capital cases. In order to obtain a capital conviction, a conviction that will lead to a death sentence, the jury must be unanimous in their decision. If just one jury member disagrees, it will mean the difference between life and death for my father.

At the time of jury selection, it's already 2004, four years after the murders. Melinda Sherrill has to provide a brief recap of my father's crime for the viewers. She has to put what he did into context, letting the audience find where it fits into history. Perhaps some non-local people have forgotten about the case, the entire incident blending into the background of the collective psyche along with all of the other heinous crimes we learn about and then eventually forget. The body can contain only so much sadness, after all, so much grief, so much fear and anxiety, until it inevitably spills out, some of the trauma getting lost, leaving the radar. That story of the factory worker who went on a shooting rampage can't stay with you for eternity—there isn't enough room to store all of that pain. You have to take it in small doses, liquid drops of pain on your television screen at night, on your radio in the morning, on the newsstand any day of the week.

Melinda Sherrill doesn't show teeth when she smiles but still manages to have a pleasant look on her face, a vital skill for a newscaster—to cover serious stories without looking too dire, without allowing the terror to show itself through your skin. She assures the audience she will cover the entirety of my father's trial and sentencing for First Coast News, Channel 12, the local news affiliate based in Jacksonville, because they want to keep you informed. She repeats that they are your first choice in local news that affects *you*.

The video fades out to black, and I click on another link from the bookmarks. This time, it's an interview with a young man who was working at a kiosk selling personalized license plates at the time of the shooting. The young man is identified only as Rick, his name appearing in white letters at the bottom of the screen with the words *mall employee* next to his name. Rick appears eager to share his experience with the invisible reporter. He looks directly at the person asking questions, just off screen.

Rick is good-looking with prominent cheekbones and a small nose. He wears a cowrie shell necklace and reminds me of the type of guy you might encounter hanging out on the pier at Clearwater Beach near dusk. He might be strumming "Blister in the Sun" on an acoustic guitar or playing a game of Frisbee with friends. Rick says he'll never forget what he was doing when the shooting began. He was helping a customer

flip through a binder of sample plates when he heard
the first shot fired in the nearby jewelry store and heard
a mix of voices screaming and glass breaking.

"It took everyone a while to realize what was going
on," Rick says, his voice sounding concerned as he
walks us through the trauma of realizing that people
were being murdered at his place of employment.

The voice off camera asks Rick about the aftermath
of the murders, wanting to know how it felt to return
to work knowing that mall employees and customers
were brutally gunned down just yards away from his
kiosk. Rick looks down for a moment, and then back
into the red eye of the camera. "It was tough, for sure,"
he says. "I knew the employees who were killed, a
woman and a man. I would see them together in the
food court sometimes." The voice asks Rick if he's
afraid to come to work at the mall now. "No, I won't
let it scare me," he assures the audience. "If anything,
it makes me feel grateful for every day I have, you
know? It makes me realize how precious life really is."

When senseless violence happens, the people left
behind want to believe that they were saved for a
reason, that they were spared to fulfill some divine
purpose, as though some higher power believed that
they should be saved without telling them why.

I click on the next video, this time a reenactment of

the shooting itself, where computerized figures stand in for people, including my father, his figure in red to denote that he has blood on his hands.

I click again, and a St. Johns County sheriff's deputy appears on the screen, dressed in dark green and gold, a pointed metallic star catching the sunlight as he walks toward a podium topped with multiple microphones and clears his voice to speak at a press conference to describe to the public in detail about law enforcement's response to my father's crime— the shooting rampage, the casualties at the mall, the southbound car chase, the failed attempts at hostage negotiation, and the discovery that the victim inside the car was shot to death in the head.

If you let your imagination run, which is always dangerous, you can imagine the scene in that car, picture my father with one hand on the wheel and one hand on the gun pointed at his wife's head. You can continue this scene in your mind, dreaming up a hundred different scenarios, so many possibilities for dialogue, so many various ways she could have been pleading for her life, begging her husband to spare her.

Sometimes I imagine them talking about my mother and me, for how did we factor into my father's decision? How did we make it better or worse?

Perhaps she promised him that she didn't mind, that he could have his child with this other woman and she'd still take him back, wouldn't leave him again no matter what. But maybe that wasn't enough for him, maybe he wanted more, needed more, his wants and needs devouring her and eleven other people when all was said and done. I pause the sheriff's deputy, and he freezes midsentence, almost looks like he's about to sneeze.

In the Starbucks, an old man blows on his coffee and takes a slow sip. He sits alone, a newspaper unfolded on the table. He pulls a pair of glasses from his pocket, adjusts his gaze, and begins to read. He's missing that look of loneliness I see on other old people, the one that makes me sad, makes me have to turn away. He looks up from the paper and clutches his arm, just above his shoulder. I can't stop it. I just have to watch. Remind myself it isn't real. He gasps for air, sweats, and flails. He falls to the ground, trembling in a seizure. His coffee shines in a puddle next to him on the floor.

Three women sit on the comfortable sofas, having an animated conversation, talking with their hands and laughing. They're dressed in exercise clothes with yoga mats at their feet, apparently fresh from class. They have identical ponytails, identical manicured nails. The tallest woman draws a small gun from her purse, a silver revolver with a black handle. She lifts it to her temple and pulls the trigger. She slumps down in her chair. Blood runs down her neck like rivulets and pools in the sharp edges of her collarbone. Her eyes turn empty and white.

A little girl feeds a black-and-white cookie to a baby, maybe her little sister, as their mother takes a video with her phone. The baby reaches for the sweetness with chubby fingers. She licks her lips as her mother laughs, watching through the screen. The baby's eyes get wide. She opens her mouth but doesn't make a sound. She kicks her legs. Her lips turn blue. Her sister hides her face with her hands and begins to sob.

A young man and woman appear to be on a date, barely touching knees under the table. He pulls a switchblade from his shoe and stabs her in the throat. Her dress seeps red, turning damp and dark, the color of a dozen roses.

I open a new tab, type *Florida death row inmates*, and hit Enter. I scroll through a list, sorted by incarceration date. I find his name. The blue DC number next to it is a hyperlink. Click on it. Wait for the page to load. Tell yourself you're about to see a man who looks nothing like you, a man who is not your father, who could never be your father in a million years.

A picture of Michael Joshua Hayes appears on the screen. Look into his eyes. There. Right there. You have his eyes, silly girl. Of course you do.

chapter thirty-eight

Orcas are nicknamed killer whales, but most people don't realize that they are actually more closely related to dolphins than whales. In kingdom Animalia, all creatures are classified. There is a hierarchy: life, domain, kingdom, phylum, class, order, family, genus, species. Every creature fits in somewhere. An orca's genus name is *Orcinus,* meaning "belonging to Orcus" or "of the kingdom of the dead." In Roman mythology, Orcus was a god of the underworld, punisher of broken oaths.

Dylan and I are on our first date at Ocean Wild, an aquatic zoo and amusement park in Lakeland, walking through an exhibit all about orcas. Once we started texting, it didn't take him long to ask me out.

I scroll through a touch screen display depicting orcas in the open seas, jumping and arching and splashing down. It's called porpoising, that rising above then submerging, that delicate dance between water and air.

It's meant to be educational, a way for you to gain an appreciation for the animals before you enter the arena and watch them perform tricks for the promise of dead fish, the audience providing oohs and ahhs in unison as the orca jumps out of the giant swimming pool, diving back in with a splash. The exhibit itself is designed to make you feel as though you're under-water, your path lined with footlights that glow deep blue, and sound effects pumped in overhead, the lull of rushing water.

We walk toward a television screen, stopping for a moment to watch a brief explanation of the various parts of an orca. We learn that, while many perceive those white circles of skin on either side of an orca's head as its eyes, the animal's eyes are actually just below the white. The white circles are called eye patches. The eyes are nestled in the orca's slick black skin, so small and beady compared to their giant bod-ies. But what fascinate me most are their tongues. An orca's tongue looks like a separate animal. Thick and muscular, it looks powerful enough to strangle you.

When we walk out of the dark blue of the exhibit and into the bright white of the open-air stadium, it takes a few seconds for our eyes to adjust. We find seats on the bleachers, up toward the top. Upbeat music begins to play. The orca trainers emerge from backstage and wave to the crowd, mostly parents with young children. Some of them hug plush killer whales, others eat neon pink cotton candy out of sticky plastic bags.

Dylan is staring at me. I can feel his eyes fixed in my direction.

"What?" I ask.

"I just can't believe you're really here with me," he says.

"Pinch yourself," I say. "Maybe you're dreaming."

Dylan laughs and puts his arm around me.

The lead trainer is a blond woman with short hair. She wears a black-and-white wetsuit designed to make her look like a tiny killer whale. She perches on the animal's nose, and then lifts off at the precise moment that the orca becomes a rocket and the woman becomes part ballerina, part diver. She goes down, down, down to the bottom of the deep blue sea, and although it's a concrete pool and not the ocean itself, I imagine her touching the floor and feeling the dark earth underneath before coming up for air.

"You've just got this mysterious vibe," Dylan says. "Makes me want to know everything about you. Like what's your middle name?"

"My middle name is Emerald."

"Evelyn Emerald Gibson. Wait, so your initials are EEG?"

"Yes, just like the abbreviation for electroencephalogram."

"That's some kind of heart test, right?" he asks.

"Brain test, actually. It measures electrical activity in the brain."

"Oh, so you can read minds then?"

"Why, of course I can. I'm reading your mind right now."

"Can you tell me what I'm thinking?" he asks, but before I can answer, he's kissing me, and his hand is on my knee. I put my hand over his, sliding it under my dress.

"Is there somewhere we can go?" I ask him.

"But the show's not over yet," he says.

"Ah, but maybe it's just getting started."

Dylan has his own car, a red Volkswagen coupe with deeply tinted windows, a sunroof, and seats that recline all the way back. We leave Ocean Wild and drive to Plant City, through the backwoods of Hillsborough County, where farmers grow strawberries and raise cows, where the air smells faintly like hay and manure and honeysuckle, the breeze blowing warm and fragrant with life. We take side roads and back roads and dirt roads, keeping the windows rolled all the way down, letting warm air whip our hair. Dylan reaches over and touches my knee, one hand on the steering wheel and one hand on me.

Dylan says he grew up out here. His grandfather had a strawberry farm, and Dylan's family lived in a little ranch house on the property until the bank took it all in 2008. We drive past a small gravel lane barely visible through the high grasses, and Dylan takes his hand from my knee, to motion in the direction of his old home.

"Down there, that's where we used to live." He puts his hand back on my bare knee, and begins sliding his palm toward my thigh, his fingertips eventually grazing that spot between my legs, making me warm and wet.

He pulls off the main road, and now we're driving through a field, dry grasses crinkling under the tires. He puts the car in Park and unbuckles my seat belt. I crawl into the backseat. Dylan follows, sitting down next to me. I sit on top of him, straddling him, and we start to kiss. His mouth tastes like peppermint, his hands warm and buzzing all over me now.

I can feel him through his jeans, hard and pressing against me, tiny pulses coming from him, the rhythm matching my breathing as we kiss deeper and deeper and I lose myself in the scent of his hair, bright tropical notes of coconut and mango.

I whisper into his ear. "I'm a virgin, you know. I hope that's okay." I pull away from him and look into his eyes, marvel at how the light catches the colors, exposes every swirl of blue, each fleck of gold.

"Yeah, of course," he says, grinning wide. "Are you sure you want me to be your first?"

"I'm sure. Are you sure you want to be my first?"

He laughs, and kisses me some more. I can feel him getting harder. I reach for his belt buckle, but he stops me, lifting me from his lap. "Hang on," he says and gets out of the car.

I hear the trunk pop open, and then hear him rummaging through it. Minutes later, he comes around to the passenger side door, and opens it for me. He has a blanket over his shoulder, a bright blue beach blanket. He takes my hand and leads me farther out in the field. There's an old barn in the distance, and we're walking toward it. "It's been abandoned since I was a kid," Dylan tells me, pulling me closer to him, his arm around my waist as we walk through the knee-high grass that tickles my legs.

Inside the barn, Dylan spreads the blanket out over the dirt floor. He takes his shirt off, lifts my dress over my head, and unhooks my bra. His hands are so sure, so steady, on my goose-bumped skin. I know that he's done this before, that I'm not the only girl he's brought here, but it doesn't matter. I focus on the streaks of sun that stream in through holes in the worn walls, and the patches of light that illuminate our bodies.

Dylan takes both of my hands in his, kisses my palms, and then lays me down on the blanket on my back. I look up at him, certain that he can see the stars that are surely in my eyes, certain that he can feel the heat I'm generating. I'm drawn to him, my body rushing along a current only I can see and feel.

Dylan drops to his hands and knees now, and leans over me. He kisses my neck, and I become a raw nerve of sensation, high on anticipation. He retrieves a condom from his pocket, tearing the wrapper with his teeth. He unbuckles his belt, and I close my eyes. I feel him inside now, and my entire body heats up like it's about to be set on fire. I keep my eyes closed and let it burn.

My body takes over, automatic movements I don't have to think about. My desire is leading me now. I just have to feel. Dylan's breath is warm against my neck. With his voice low, he moans softly. I'm close to letting go, my body about to untether itself from this earth.

"You feel so good," Dylan says in my ear. His hair tickles my neck, and I open my eyes. But I don't see Dylan's face—I see Oliver's. He's foaming at the mouth. His eyes roll back into his head. I pinch my eyes shut and reach for Dylan's shoulders. I dig my nails into his skin, a reminder of what's real.

"You feel so good," he says again and again, and I feel it too, a stirring from deep within me, a pulsing that radiates from inside out. I bite my lip until it's over, until Dylan's body collapses against mine and I open my eyes again.

We get dressed, and then Dylan wraps his arms around me, pulling me close.

"I don't want you to get the wrong idea," he says. "This isn't just about sex for me. I mean, I really like you." He smiles at me, and I smile back.

"Good," I say. "Because I really like you too."

We walk back to the car, and Dylan opens my door for me. I lean my cheek against the window as he drives me home. When we reach the Bayway, near the tip of Cats Point, I see a lone fisherman packing up his equipment for the day—long, dark fishing rods, and a net with a silvery pole and green mesh in which to scoop snook, pike, or grouper, the catch of the day.

In *The Catalog of Everything I've Done Wrong*, I add: fucked Dylan on the first date.

I close my eyes, and the sticky idea arrives again. It clings to me although I've tried to shake it away. In the beginning, it took shape slowly, but now it's gaining speed, picking up mass and momentum like a snowball rolling down the slope of a hill.

I need to see him. It's the only way. I need to go. I need to see him. I thought there were other answers, but I know better now. I need to see him. It's the only way.

chapter thirty-nine

On my laptop screen, Melinda Sherrill is wearing all black today, reporting for First Coast News. It's the day of my father's sentencing so I can't help but interpret her clothing choice as symbolic, given the fact that she usually wears bright colors, cheerful reds and blues and yellows. I know from reading the newspaper coverage from that time period that my father's death sentence was practically a slam dunk, the district attorney confident that jurors would do *the right thing*—the moral thing, the only just thing—and sentence my father to death.

The video quality is a bit fuzzy, Melinda's facial features slightly dulled at the edges. The sun is shining so brightly in the video that I can practically feel the warmth emanating through the screen. As Melinda speaks, she is flanked by two palm trees, sago palms I believe, their trunks shorter and thicker than most

others. The pink archway of the St. Johns County
Courthouse entrance is visible in the background over
her shoulder.

Melinda talks more slowly than I've heard her
in other clips. "Without question, the most heart-
breaking moments today were the impact statements
read by family members of the slain victims. There
was barely a dry eye in the courtroom as Helen
Raul's husband spoke through tears, reading a prepared statement about how the killer's actions left
him without his wife of twenty-eight years and his
children and grandchildren without the mother and
grandmother they so dearly loved. He told the
packed courtroom how Helen would dress up as
Mrs. Santa Claus and visit children at the library over
the holidays, a time of year that always brought her
immense joy. But this Christmas, the red dress will
go unused in the closet, her husband revealing that
he still hasn't had the heart to go through her belong-
ings yet, even though it's been nearly six years since
the tragedy."

Melinda's eyes look tired in this segment, and I
can see that she carries the sadness and horror from
the day with her. I can see that she will carry what
my father did with her forever. She may need to call
upon it someday, may need a reminder that there are

people like my father in the world, people who are sent to deliver pain and heartache, people capable of turning others' worlds upside down, people who are the right hand of chaos.

I want to jump inside the video and ask Melinda why she never interviewed me, why my words are absent from her reporting, why I wasn't mentioned in the list of Michael Joshua Hayes's victims. It's a pointless question though, really, for I understand that nobody wants to hear from the murderer's family unless they have some morbid fascination, unless they believe killers to be some kind of celebrity. Melinda's audience only wants to hear about revenge and the stories of the people left behind.

The video turns to black. My reflection blinks back at me through the dark mirror of my laptop screen. I open a blank Word document, staring at the flashing cursor until it hits me like a wave, a curl of water that rolls from my brain to my fingertips, a current that taps out letters, spelling all the words I need to say. I write and write, filling page after page until my mother knocks on my bedroom door.

"You ready? It's almost time to go!" She practically sings the words, her voice alive with energy. We have tickets for Death Cab for Cutie at the Sun Dome in Tampa tonight, one of my mother's favorite bands.

She's never seen them live before and can barely contain her excitement.

I save the document, but I don't give it a name. By default, the program names the document after the first words I've typed across the top of the page in capital letters—THE CATALOG OF EVERYTHING I'VE DONE WRONG. I exit the program, close my laptop so it goes to sleep, and then slide it under my bed.

"I'm ready now," I call to my mother.

At the concert, I stand between Shea and my mother, who rests her head on my shoulder as we listen to Ben Gibbard's earnest baritone on "I Will Follow You into the Dark." It's an older Death Cab song from their album *Plans*, which came out when I was five years old. She played that album on heavy rotation that year, in the car and around the house. I remember it beaming through the speaker in the bathroom, my mother's voice echoing as she sang along in the shower, music mixed with the drone of the water as it rained down.

Five-year-old me took the song literally—the dark was simply what happened when you turned out the lights. Following someone there just meant walking behind them. The older me now knows more about following. The older me knows more about darkness.

My mother and Shea hold hands behind my back. I feel the warmth of their interlocking fingers against me. I breathe in deeply and let my lungs expand with the air of their love, letting it wash over me like a breaker that slams against the shore, transforming into seafoam, dazzling bright white in the sunlight.

Back in my bedroom, after I've kissed my mother and Shea good night, I pull my laptop from under the bed and turn it on. I enter my password and then open my list of saved bookmarks. There's one link I haven't clicked yet, one door I've haven't walked through. It's a documentary about the death penalty, but one that doesn't take the typical perspective on capital punishment. The typical point of view is usually that of the victims' families, the people who've had a loved one ripped away from them by the condemned murderer. This is what the popcorn-crunching crowd is interested in—they want to see the misery on their faces, feel the pain and rage as they speak of their unspeakable loss, of lives cut short, birthdays that will now pass without celebration, a little boy who will never know his mother.

Everyone loves a good revenge story. They take comfort in knowing that someone will pay dearly for evil deeds—an eye for an eye, a tooth for a tooth, the punishment fits the crime. They feel better knowing the roles will be reversed, the murderer put to death, the monster given a taste of his own medicine, the bitter pill pushed down his throat until he chokes and dies. They take comfort in this and call it justice, secure in their power to decide another's fate. But this documentary is different. It attempts to humanize death row inmates, to bring about an argument against the death penalty and show that there is more to a person than just one evil action.

I let the video play and then click the progress bar at the bottom, sliding the little white circle to the right until I find the scene I'm looking for—Ella Hayes, my grandmother, the woman who painted birds and collected porcelain. She was alive then, mourning her son's fate for the camera. As Ella talks about my father, the film cuts from her face to some home movie footage the family provided. Grainy without any sound, it's the kind of movie you have to project onto a white screen, the machinery warm and making a whirring sound as the tape glides through the apparatus. The home movie shows my father, no older than six or seven, in shorts and tall white tube socks, a red backpack square on his back. The Florida sun shines relentlessly as he walks up the bleached steps of an elementary school that looks scrubbed clean and brand new.

"Oh, my Michael, well, he was always smiling, always laughing," Ella's voice says. "He was just such an easygoing child. And he really loved school, he just adored it. Everything about it. He would barely sleep the night before the first day of school, he'd be so excited."

My father stops at the top of the stairs and turns around to face the camera, which now zooms in closer on his face. My father waves vigorously, smiling to show missing teeth. He waves and waves, his movements appearing sped up, that slightly exaggerated quality that old motion pictures have. He blows a kiss to the person behind the camera. "He loved that song 'You Are My Sunshine,'" Ella's voice says. "He always wanted me to sing it to him before bed." My father opens the heavy glass door of the school entrance and disappears into the building.

I click to stop the video.

I pull up Andy's blog and wait for it to load. The screen turns bright white, and an error message at the top tells me this site can't be found. I type the URL into the address bar again and hit Enter. It must be a mistake. I must have tapped the wrong keys. Same blank white page. Same message. I type it again and again, but I keep getting the same result. Can't connect to the server. Check your network connection. Error. I try to tune into Andy's frequency, try to conjure him in his small cell at Raiford, but I can't find him. I slam my laptop closed and start pacing the room.

I find the can of duster I stashed in the closet and take a few long hits of the freezing cold air. The Limoges butter dish catches my eye. I walk over to it, trace the smooth enamel with my finger, and then pick it up. I grab a dirty towel from my hamper to wrap the butter dish inside. I go into the bathroom, turn the shower on full blast, and lock the door. I swing the towel against edge of the bathroom sink, once, twice, three times, until the porcelain inside is smashed to pieces.

The steam from the running shower fogs the mirror, making the me feel faint. I turn the shower off and lie on my back against the cool tile of the bathroom floor until I'm steady again. Then I walk back to my bed, sit down, and open my laptop. I read *The Catalog of Everything I've Done Wrong* again. It's all here, everything in order, everything in its place. I add one more entry: destroyed something beautiful.

I inhale and exhale and inhale again. I feel every hair growing on my head and every cell pulsing beneath my skin. My body is alive and new. I soar high into the sky—up, up, up, until I can't get any higher. I swim through constellations shaped like mythical creatures. I leave only clouds in my wake. I look down at the earth, and it all makes sense.

chapter forty

The windows in Tampa General Hospital don't open, sealed shut for the sake of safety and sanitation. When you look out, you must invent the breeze, conjure the smell of trees and lakes and flowers. You know these things exist out there, somewhere beyond the glass, but it's easy to lose your bearings when you spend too much time in a hospital, which is why so many people fear them. Too much time in such an unnatural place and your understanding of the natural world may begin to slip away. To remind yourself, you have to summon the spirit of the natural world, like girls at a slumber party hoping to contact the dead, their fingers barely touching the planchette of the Ouija board, their hearts and minds open to speaking to the beyond, the unknown. *Are you there, spirit? Answer yes or no.*

Standing at the threshold of the room, I can barely

see him among all the flower arrangements, and the Mylar balloons grazing the ceiling, but then his face comes into focus. It takes a few moments, but I finally find him. I walk toward the foot of his bed, listening to the beeps of the monitor, watching his heart make peaks and valleys on a screen. He looks smaller than I remember, his hands resting on the tops of his thighs as if someone has arranged them carefully, told him to stay perfectly still, told him not to move a muscle. His hair looks soft to the touch, freshly washed. His head is propped up with large white pillows, and his eyes are closed.

The television on the wall is tuned to a game show with the sound off. There are two chairs for visitors between the bed and the large window. The vertical window blinds are pushed to one side, sunlight illuminating the checkered blue and green floor tiles.

Strands of plastic tubing run from machines to his arm and his chest, pumping liquid into him, removing toxins, an intricate network devised to keep a body alive. He breathes on his own, his chest rising and falling, keeping rhythm with a silent song that only he can hear. There are cuffs attached to his calves, applying pressure to his legs for circulation, preventing clots that can form from immobilization.

"His name is Oliver," a woman voice says behind me,

and I turn to face her. She's wearing a lanyard around her neck, a laminated card suspended from it with the word VOLUNTEER printed in large blue block letters.

"Hi, I'm Jordan," she says. She shakes my hand and seems pleased to meet me. She's in her early twenties, maybe a college student. She has a small metal cart on wheels with her—two shelves of board games, cross-word puzzle books, playing cards, a small portable CD player and stack of CDs.

"Hi. My name's Dorothy," I say.

"Oliver loves being read to," Jordan says, searching her cart for something. "Ah, here it is. I marked the page where we left off last week." She hands me a book, a paperback copy of *Charlotte's Web*. The cover is weathered, a million tiny creases in the soft spine.

"Does he have family?" I ask. "I mean does he get many visitors?"

"Oh, his family isn't from around here. They live somewhere in New England. Massachusetts, I think? His mother used to be here round the clock. She prac-tically lived in that chair for the first month," Jordan says, motioning to the recliner in the corner, a wide chair made of mauve vinyl with wooden armrests. "The plan is to transfer him up to Mass General as soon as they can. They have an intensive neuro rehab center there that might be able to treat him, once the brain swelling goes down. The doctors say he's still just too fragile for transport right now."

Jordan looks at Oliver with pitiful eyes, the way you might look at a dead baby bunny on the side of the road. She exhales lightly, but loud enough to convey her sadness. "So the family is back up north now, and they said they will travel down when they can. They just left last weekend, I think. Really nice people. I don't judge them for needing a break, you know. It's super hard on families. I'm sure you understand."

I shake my head in acknowledgment. "I can't even imagine."

"I know," Jordan says. She lowers her voice to a whisper. "Oliver has a really sad story too, but most patients do, as I'm sure you know if you've been around the block, so to speak."

"I know what you mean. So many sad stories," I agree. "But I didn't know that we could volunteer with patients in comas. I mean, I guess I thought someone like him would be in intensive care or something."

Jordan looks behind her as if to see if anyone is within earshot. "Oh, he's not actually in a coma," she says. "The doctors call it unresponsive wakefulness syndrome. He was attacked on the beach—some kind of blunt force trauma. It was a whole big deal. I saw it on the news, but I don't remember all the details."

Jordan looks out the large window, appears temporarily lost in thought for a moment before turning her attention back to me. "Well, Dorothy, have a great day!" she says to me, and I nod and smile in return.

Jordan pushes her little cart out of the room and down the sterile hallway, the slight squeak of the wheels echoing, bouncing off the hard walls, the sound getting smaller and smaller as she gets farther away.

I put *Charlotte's Web* under my arm and slide my phone from my pocket. I type *unresponsive wakefulness syndrome* into the search bar. The results appear on the screen, small blue words glowing on an ultra white background. I turn the brightness down, scrolling through scholarly articles and academic journal abstracts until I find something in *The Washington Post*, the story of a young American woman who was studying abroad and returned to the United States in a state of unresponsive wakefulness. In the article, a doctor explains the condition and speculates on the young woman's future.

Unresponsive Wakefulness Syndrome is a result of a traumatic brain injury that causes the brain to halt the ability to create thoughts and experience sensation. Patients in this state are awake but show no signs of awareness. They may be able to open their eyes, display basic reflexes to actions, and wake up or fall asleep at various intervals.

Oliver inhales and exhales evenly, the air escaping from his lungs with a faint hiss each time. His breaths are metered, as if he is measuring the right amount of air in every one, his body creating portions so that he gets just the right amount of oxygen. We learned in biology that breathing is an involuntary function. You don't have to think about it. Somehow your body just knows what to do to keep you alive.

Patients may be able to swallow, grunt, or smile without external stimulus, but their communication and cognitive mechanism is very limited and they are unable to obey verbal commands. While each case varies depending on the origin and extent of the brain injury, most patients with UWS do not appear to understand language.

Oliver's eyelids begin to flutter, but his eyes remain closed. I place one hand on his forehead. His skin still feels so alive, so warm to the touch. I trace the arch of his eyebrow with my fingernail, delicately at first, and then pressing harder. The pain doesn't register. He doesn't move, doesn't make a sound, no expression on his face, no acknowledgment of sensation, as if all of his nerve endings are locked in deep sleep.

Recovering from Unresponsive Wakefulness Syndrome is not uncommon, especially in younger patients. Each case is unique depending on the nature of the injury to the brain, but there are many cases of patients regaining full consciousness after months, or even years, with proper neurological treatment.

On the TV screen, a game show contestant spins a wheel, and the colorful spaces blur and blend as the contestant claps silently. The host smiles, his makeup creasing at the corners of his mouth. I put my phone away. I find the dog-eared corner, open the book, and read aloud.

On the page, dawn breaks at Zuckerman's farm. Lurvy brings Wilbur his breakfast, a pail of pig slop to fatten him up. But there's something different about the spiderweb this morning, and when Lurvy sees it, he drops his bucket, and rubs his eyes. Two words are woven into the sticky fibers of the web—Charlotte's first message, still wet with dew, still glistening in the early morning light. Charlotte hopes these two words will put a plan in motion to save Wilbur's life.

At the end of the scene, I mark my place, fold the yellowed page, and close the book. I place it to rest on the bedside table, another story for another day.

Oliver opens his eyes and appears to be looking toward the ceiling, as if he can see his own reflection in one of the silver balloons suspended above. I turn the volume up on the television, making the game show noises louder, the buzzers and the audience cheering. A contestant wins a pair of watches, a trip to Aruba, a stainless steel refrigerator. I wave one hand in front of Oliver's eyes, but my movement doesn't register.

I wish I could say I felt a trip wire activated, a tether snapped inside me, but there is no breakdown, or breakthrough, nothing that propels me over the edge. At least not that I'll remember. What I'll remember is the way my hands looked. How I clutched the pillow, my knuckles stretched, fingers splayed against the bleached white pillowcase. What I'll remember is how I pushed down so lightly at first and then harder and harder until I didn't have to push anymore. What I'll remember is the taste of his skin as I leaned over and kissed his ear.

A warm sensation washes over me, the exhilaration of crossing the finish line, that threshold you've held in your imagination mile after mile, certain you would reach it if you just kept running.

I take the stairs instead of the elevator, two at a time, my body bounding down toward the ground, toward the daylight that is out there, waiting for me. In the lobby, the floors shine with the polish of a new day, and the sliding glass doors open like magic as they sense my body breaking the threshold. I step into bright white, my eyes adjusting to the sunlight. I walk the bleached sidewalk until I see Dylan's car parked along the street, glossy as a candied apple.

"Well, well, well, aren't you a sexy little candy striper?" Dylan says as I get in. "So where to?"

"Are you up for a little road trip?" I ask.

"You know I'm up for anything with you," he answers. He reaches over and gently tucks a stray hair behind my ear. "What do you have in mind? Disney World? I'll hold your hand in the Haunted Mansion, I promise."

"Actually, I've always wanted to go to Kingsley Lake. Have you ever heard of it?" I call up an aerial view on my phone and show the image to Dylan— a near-perfect circle of blue water surrounded by a dense forest of trees, a full moon shining against a green sky. "It's the oldest lake in Florida, and it's got clear water, so you can see all the way to the bottom.

It's in the middle of nowhere, but you wouldn't mind going nowhere with me, right?"

Dylan doesn't answer with words, just leans over and kisses me softly on the mouth, and this time it feels even better than it has before, even better than I ever imagined it could.

I type an address into the GPS, the Motel 6 in Starke, six miles west of Kingsley Lake. Dylan puts the Volkswagen in gear, and we head north on Bayshore Boulevard, a scenic route that snakes along the edge of Hillsborough Bay.

The water is opaque, dark denim stretched as far as I can see. I turn the radio up, making it loud enough to drown out the sound of my wildly beating heart.

chapter forty-one

I slip from the hotel bed where Dylan is still sleeping, his toes peeking out from the polyester comforter. He'll wake up later, stretching his arms out to reach for me. His eyes will search the room, and he'll find the note I've left for him, stuck to the mirror on a pink Post-It.

D—

Had to see the lake one more time.

Love, Evelyn

I gather yesterday's clothes from the floor and get dressed without turning on the light. According to the Florida Department of Corrections website, the prison opens for visitors at 8:00 a.m. so I need to get going. I slide my feet into sandals, grab Dylan's keys, and walk out the door. Outside the air is sticky, the sun slung low in the sky. I rummage through my bag for mouthwash, take a swig, swish, and spit the green remains onto the concrete of the Motel 6 parking lot.

I punch my destination into the GPS, selecting a route full of back roads—fourteen miles from Starke to Raiford, northwest County Road 229 most of the way.

The road is narrow without a shoulder—just two lanes carved through a forest of slash pines and palmettos. I think about meeting him for the first time, imagine the sensation of my eyes finally meeting his. My chest feels tight, as if the blood is being squeezed from my heart.

I grip the steering wheel tighter, press my foot heavier on the gas. I imagine the first words he might say to me. I've had so long to think about it, to conjure up every possible scenario.

I already know what I'll say to him. I've been practicing.

Last night, as we walked barefoot along the edge of Kingsley Lake, I caught a glimpse of something dark, and was sure it was the long body of an alligator gliding across the surface of the water. I grabbed Dylan's hand and ran from the water and then buried my head in his chest until he assured me it was nothing, probably just a shadow.

"They'll only hurt you if you hurt them," he said as he rubbed my back.

There aren't many houses along this road, just a pair of mailboxes here and there, a few small signs of life. The houses are set back along dirt roads, trees obscuring them from the main drag mostly, but in one spot, there is a clearing, and I can see a white mobile home with red trim around the windows and a rotting wooden deck. There's a doghouse in the yard but no dog. A little girl's bicycle, but no little girl.

When the GPS tells me to turn onto FL-16, I've almost reached my destination. I see an American flag waving high and a Florida state flag waving a bit lower, the red bars striking against the white. Then finally, a sign, smaller than I'd imagined, the signal I've arrived. FLORIDA STATE PRISON: UNION CORRECTIONAL INSTITUTION. I know he's inside, somewhere within this maze of low buildings that looks more like a school campus than a prison.

For the first time, he and I are in the same place. We are two people living on the same coordinates, breathing the same atmosphere. I lean my face out the window and inhale as deeply as I can.

I see an observation tower in the distance, the kind you see in prisons in the movies or on TV, where a guard can watch the inmates while they exercise in the yard. The yard is surrounded by tall metal fencing, barbed wire coiled at the top just in case anyone tries to escape. The idea seems ridiculous at first— why would anyone risk scaling a fence and getting stabbed by barbed wire just to emerge on the other side, bloody and bawling, into the clutches of an armed guard or the jaws of a police dog? But then I remember—when you have nothing to lose, what's one more risk, one more crime, one more chance at freedom? Perhaps your own two legs can take you farther than you thought.

I park the car and walk to the entrance, where a guard asks me to state my business. "Visiting an inmate," I say, and my voice sounds younger than I want it to. I want to sound brave and mature, not like a scared child who's never stepped foot inside a prison, who's never even seen a gun up close like the one that's snug in its holster on the guard's belt.

He motions toward a cluster of people waiting to see a woman behind a glass window. "You'll head over there and wait in line. She'll give you paperwork and get you through to processing." I start to walk away, but he puts his hand up to stop me. "Hang on," he says. "Folks, just a reminder," he says. I look behind me and see about a dozen people lined up and waiting. The guard addresses us as a group, using a voice that's louder than before. "Each visitor is only allowed fifty dollars in cash on them and one car key. Anything else should be secured in your vehicle at this time. You will be subject to pat-down searches and metal detection. No exceptions." He says it all without smiling and finally puts his hand down so I can go.

When it's my turn at the glass window, the woman hands me a form to complete and asks for my ID. I re-trieve it from my pocket, sliding it through the small opening to her. I try to steady my hand as I fill out the paperwork, but the woman can see my shaking. She examines my ID and then makes eye contact with me for just a second.

I hand the paperwork back to her. She signs it and then pushes a stamper onto a soft black ink pad, mak-ing a dark mark at the bottom of the page. She clicks her mouse a few times, and then a small printer spits out a yellow visitor sticker with my name on it. She hands it to me along with my ID.

"Attach this badge to your person, above the waist, please." I peel the sticker from its backing, pressing it onto my shirt just above my heart. "Walk through that blue door on the right for search procedures," she says. "Don't worry, one of the female guards will search you." I nod that I understand, and she flashes a closemouthed smile as if to say she's sorry in advance for all of this trouble.

Through the blue door, I enter a large room where a woman counts and records the cash I have on hand, catalogs the jewelry I'm wearing, records the color and style of my shoes. She writes it all down on a yellow legal pad attached to a clipboard. She dons blue rubber gloves and searches through my hair. She asks me to move my bra around, to see if anything is hiding there. She motions for me to stand with my feet hip-width apart and my arms extended. I turn my body into a star while she runs her hands over me and pats my pockets. She grabs a security wand and waves it all around me, scanning my skin for hidden metal objects. She asks me to open my mouth, shining a small flashlight inside.

Once I'm cleared, I walk through green double doors and step onto the cracked concrete of a fenced-in walkway. The chain link creates a tunnel between buildings, ensuring that visitors stay on the approved path and don't make a break for it or try to access a restricted area. Before my body can adjust to the humidity, I walk through another set of double doors, back into the chill of the air-conditioned building.

I am met by three armed guards and a metal detector.

"Right hand," one of them says to me, and I offer it to him. My fingers flutter as he stamps FDC onto my skin in fat blocky letters. Another guard motions for me to walk through the metal detector, and I do. The machine doesn't make a sound, and I let out a breath I didn't realize I was holding in.

"Clear," the third guard says in an urgent tone, like a doctor on TV about to shock a cardiac patient with paddles, asking everyone to take their hands off the body so they don't feel the jolt. "Booth seventeen. Through that metal door."

I walk through, find my numbered spot, and sit down. I lean one elbow on the stainless steel counter in front of me, my bare skin temporarily shocked by the cold surface. Everything is shiny and metal here—the counter, the stool I'm sitting on, the walls of the privacy booth. The glass in front of me is bulletproof, cross-hatched with thin wire. I stare at my feet and start counting the specks of blue and green on the tile floor. A woman cries softly somewhere. I can't see her, can only hear her muffled sobs, as if she's covering her face with a handkerchief or her shirtsleeve.

Across the glass from me, the seat on the other side is empty. I hear an analog clock ticking loudly on the wall behind me and feel the presence of the armed prison guard breathing as we wait.

Will I recognize him when he's finally in front of me, his face in flesh and bone instead of pixels through a computer screen? I silently ask the universe for a signal, some way to know it's really him.

Then, as if by magic, he appears on the other side, wearing a white jumpsuit with short sleeves and a pointed collar, yellowed buttons fastened all the way to the top. He moves more slowly than I thought he would and sits down gently. His lips curl into a half smile. I feel a flutter in my chest and then tears welling up, as if someone has found my lost pet and I just have to prove I'm the owner by making the dog answer to its name when I call.

I study the patches of dark hair on his forearm, the patterns they make against his pale skin. He reaches for the telephone on his side—an identical smooth black handset on my side that looks heavy but feels light in my hand when I pick it up. I mirror his movements and bring the receiver to my lips.

Enough standing at the edge, peering down into

the darkness below. It's time to jump. My body breaks the water like a coin dropped into a fountain. I dive down, down, down, until I reach the bottom. I find the words, gather them in my arms, and come up for air at last.

"Hi, Dad."

Dear Reader,

In the spring of 2010, when I first conceived of the themes in *Girl at the Edge*, an orca named Tilikum was in the news for fatally injuring a trainer at Sea World in Orlando. After the killing, Tilikum was separated from the other orcas and confined to a small isolation tank, the equivalent of a human forced to remain in a bathtub indefinitely. His story would eventually be detailed in the 2013 documentary *Blackfish*.

I started to research Tilikum and found that he had a daughter named Katina. I began to imagine a memoir written from Katina's point of view, in which she attempts to make sense of her father's violent act and subsequent isolation, which in my mind was reminiscent of solitary confinement in prison.

I'd read *The Call of the Wild* by Jack London in seventh grade, and it was one of my favorite childhood books. I revisited London's work and other books written from the perspective of animals— *Watership Down* by Richard Adams and *The White Bone* by Barbara Gowdy. Ultimately, I felt that taking on the point of view of an animal was too daunting of a task for me as a first-time novelist, and so the animals became people, and I wrote the first chapter of *Girl at the Edge*, narrated by Evelyn, the daughter of a murderer on death row, grappling with her own identity and trying to figure out how to navigate the legacy her father has left through his violent act.

Whether human or animal, I think we're all at the mercy of both nature and nurture. My hope is that Evelyn's story inspires you to consider your own feelings about this complex topic and to explore how it affects us all.

Karen Dietrich

READING GROUP GUIDE

QUESTIONS AND ANSWERS WITH KAREN DIETRICH

Q: What is your answer on the question of nature vs. nurture?

A: My thoughts are complex, but I think the main issue for me is this: our nature inevitably becomes a part of our nurture. When you grow up knowing a lot about the sins and flaws of your family, it has a dark impact. I wrote about Evelyn as a way to continue working through my own personal experiences of growing up in the shadow of trauma. In my case, it wasn't a violent act but instead family dysfunction. I grew up being told that my maternal lineage was troubled, to put it mildly. For me, these facts loomed large in my psyche as a child as I worried that I was "doomed" to be a flawed person, to follow in the footsteps of my mother's dysfunctional family. I often wondered how I could escape this fate, and while my real-life circumstances weren't as dire as Evelyn's, many of the anxieties she wrestles with are close to my own.

Q: You have also written a coming-of-age memoir. What do you have in common with Evelyn?

A: We are both quiet and observant. We are both prone to obsession and can easily become infatuated with certain ideas, objects, and people.

Q: When you sat down to write this novel, did you have a plot in mind or do you prefer to go wherever an idea takes you?

A: When I began writing, I only had the general premise in mind and the notion of Evelyn devising a test to see if she's capable of murder. The rest happened as I wrote through multiple drafts. I like the feeling of making choices as a writer while my characters are also making choices within the story. We're all just making it up as we go.

Q: What part of writing do you most enjoy, and what part fills you with angst and dread?

A: I most enjoy drafting, because it's a process of discovery. I love immersing myself in the imaginary world I've created, exploring any idea that excites me. I get addicted to the feeling of infinite possibility that comes with facing a blank page and flashing cursor. Editing is the part I dread the most, because it forces me out of that space and into my logical and analytical side, which is important, but just not quite as fun.

Q: What did you edit *out* of this book?

A: In a very early version of this book, Evelyn's grandmother, Emerald, was actually a character present in Evelyn's life. Mira was more of a detached mother and Emerald did a lot of the raising of Evelyn. When my agent suggested taking Emerald out as a main character, I decided to make her estranged from Mira and Evelyn, which made Emerald a perfect target for Evelyn's test.

Q: How has your master's degree in poetry affected the writing of this book?

A: I wrote very short poems in graduate school, challenging myself to remove any unnecessary words.

When you write with that type of economy in mind, you get very serious about word choice—not just any word will do, so you choose words that can do a lot of heavy lifting, so to speak. I kept that idea close to me while writing *Girl at the Edge*. I wanted to avoid extra words.

Q: You're in an indie rock band with your family members. How does your interest in music influence your writing?

A: I've always had a deeply personal connection to music. Some of my most vivid early memories are coming home from kindergarten and watching MTV while my father slept on the couch. When I'm going through something difficult, I find the lyrics and melodies of favorite songs can talk me down from the ledge. Music is oxygen for me—a necessary ingredient of life—and so it affects everything I make.

Q: When you were growing up, what were your favorite books? Can you see how they have influenced your writing?

A: I had a few favorite young adult books growing up—*Tiger Eyes* by Judy Blume, *The Outsiders* by S. E.

Hinton, *Mrs. Frisby and the Rats of NIMH* by Robert C. O'Brien, and the Ramona Quimby books by Beverly Cleary. I also read a lot of favorite adult books as a child: *The Member of the Wedding* by Carson McCullers, *The Naked Face* by Sidney Sheldon, *Rosemary's Baby* by Ira Levin, *In Cold Blood* by Truman Capote, *Carrie* and *Pet Sematary* by Stephen King. When I remember these books, I don't recall the stories in detail, but rather the emotions these writers made me feel while reading. These books influenced me because they made me want to replicate that—to make the readers feel something.

Q: Name a book not your own that you wish everyone would read.

A: I wish everyone would read *Fahrenheit 451* by Ray Bradbury. If you last read it in high school, read it again. I think Bradbury mastered the art of the short novel with this book. You'll be hard-pressed to find a passage that doesn't feel urgent and necessary.

Q: What are you writing next?

A: I'm working on a novel about a woman who moves to Florida to escape the increasingly grim circumstances of her life in rural Pennsylvania. She soon discovers that although you can run from trouble, trouble will always find you. It's a thriller, but I can't reveal much more than that. I'm making it up as I go.

DISCUSSION QUESTIONS

1. A critical question in *Girl at the Edge* is which influences a person more, nature or nurture? What is the answer in Evelyn's case?

2. Does Evelyn's age make you view her differently? Do you think we assume that children are innocent and/or not capable of bad deeds?

3. How trustworthy is Evelyn as a narrator? Were there moments where you doubted her reliability and why?

4. During that night on the beach with Oliver, how much of the events do you think Evelyn and

Clarisse planned or discussed beforehand? And
which girl do you see as the leader of the events?

5. How do you interpret Evelyn's sexuality? Do you
   think she is truly in love with Clarisse? Is she truly
   attracted to Oliver?

6. What was Evelyn's motive for visiting Oliver in the
   hospital? Do you think her actions were premeditated?

7. Is Mira a good mother? Why or why not? How
   would you have handled Evelyn if she were your
   daughter?

8. Do you agree with the items on Evelyn's *Catalog of
   Everything I've Done Wrong*? What would you add
   to or subtract from that list?

9. Do you feel that Evelyn's relationship with Greg
   and the Wavelengths support group was helpful to
   her? Do you think Evelyn will ever tell Greg or the
   group about her visions?

10. How do you explain Evelyn's obsession with Andy?

11. When you found out whom Evelyn was visiting at Raiford, were you surprised? Were you expecting her to visit Andy?

12. How do you think Evelyn felt when she saw her father for the first time?

13. Did Evelyn's story change or reinforce your opinions on the death penalty?

14. If Evelyn had never been told the truth about her father, do you think her life would have turned out differently? What kind of woman do you think she'd grow up to be?

15. What you do think happens to Evelyn after the story ends?

acknowledgments

Thanks to Alice Martell, who guided me through many drafts of this novel over the years and who always said she was in it for the long haul. I'm grateful to work with such a smart and generous agent.

Thanks to Beth deGuzman at Grand Central, who saw something in my work and took a chance on it.

Thanks to Alex Logan, my gifted editor, who challenged me to make this book better every step of the way. Thank you for the razor-sharp editorial insights and for all the cat photos.

Thanks to Paula McLain, brilliant friend and writer. You are always there to answer my SOS, responding with kindness and love and stellar advice.

Thanks to the entire Dietrich family, the most encouraging and loving brood around.

Extra-special thanks to Jill Dietrich and Bob

Dietrich—this book wouldn't exist without your generous support of my writing over the years.

Thanks to the women who always deliver when I need a laugh, a pep talk, or an impromptu therapy session—Brenda Rodgers, Melissa Bisesi, Jenna McGuiggan, Mary Furlo, and Michelle Keenan.

Thanks to the Wesleyan Writers Conference for granting me a scholarship to attend, and to Alex Chee, who read some early pages of this novel there and offered perceptive feedback.

Thanks to the musical artists I've mentioned throughout this novel. Your music inspires me to keep creating.

Thanks to Robert Dietrich, my thoughtful son, and RJ Dietrich, my extraordinary husband, for collaborating with me on art and music and life, and for all the walks around Fifth Ward. I love you both so much.

about the author

Karen Dietrich is a writer of fiction, poetry, and memoir. She earned an MFA in poetry from New England College. She also writes music and plays drums in Essential Machine, a band she formed with her husband. Karen was born and raised in southwestern Pennsylvania and currently lives outside Pittsburgh with her husband and son.

Learn more at:
KarenDietrich.net
Twitter @KarenDietrich

YOUR
BOOK
CLUB
RESOURCE

VISIT
GCPClubCar.com
to sign up for the **GCP Club Car** newsletter,
featuring exclusive promotions, info on other
Club Car titles, and more.

 @grandcentralpub

 @grandcentralpub

 @grandcentralpub